KU-297-130

NOT IF I SEE YOU FIRST

NOT IF I SEE YOU FIRST

eric lindstrom

HarperCollins *Children's Books*

First published in Great Britain by HarperCollins *Children's Books* in 2016
HarperCollins *Children's Books* is a division of HarperCollins *Publishers* Ltd,
HarperCollins *Publishers*
1 London Bridge Street
London SE1 9GF
www.harpercollins.co.uk

1

Not If I See You First
Text copyright © Eric Lindstrom, 2016
All rights reserved
HB ISBN : 978-0-00-814630-6
TPB ISBN : 978-0-00-814634-4

Eric Lindstrom asserts the moral right to be identified
as the author of this work.

Printed and bound in England by Clays Ltd, St Ives plc.

Conditions of Sale
This book is sold subject to the condition that it shall not, by way of trade
or otherwise, be lent, re-sold, hired out or otherwise circulated without the
publisher's prior written consent in any form of binding or cover other than
that in which it is published and without a similar condition including this
condition being imposed on the subsequent purchaser.

MIX
Paper from
responsible sources
FSC˚ C007454

FSC™ is a non-profit international organisation established to promote
the responsible management of the world's forests. Products carrying the
FSC label are independently certified to assure consumers that they come
from forests that are managed to meet the social, economic and
ecological needs of present and future generations,
and other controlled sources.

Find out more about HarperCollins and the environment at
www.harpercollins.co.uk/green

For all who love,

Especially,

Shannon,
You got me started

Rachel,
You made me finish

Susan,
You keep me going

Be fearless

Prologue

My alarm buzzes and I slap it off and tap the speech button at the same time. Stephen Hawking says, "Five-fifty-five AM." Just double-checking, like always.

I crank open the window and stick out my hand. Cool, misty, but not too humid. Probably overcast. I pull on clothes—sports bra, sleeveless shirt, shorts, track shoes—without bothering to check anything, since all my running clothes are black.

Except my scarves. I finger through them, checking the plastic tags, gauging my mood. I feel strangely unsettled, so I pick one that might help: the yellow cotton with embroidered happy faces. I tie it around my head like a blindfold, settling a smile on each of my closed eyelids.

The rising sun is warm on my cheeks; the sky must be clear, at least at the horizon. I lock the front door and slip the cold key into my sock. Where the path turns to sidewalk, I turn right and start to jog.

The three blocks to the field are programmed into my feet, my legs, my equilibrium. After seven years of this I know every bump, every crack, every exposed root in the sidewalk. I don't need to see where I'm running; I can feel it.

"Parker, *STOP!*"

I stumble to a halt, waving my arms like at the edge of a cliff. And if a backhoe came yesterday, there very well could be.

"I'm so sorry, Parker!" It's Mrs. Reiche's suffering-suburban-housewife voice calling from her porch. Now she's trotting down the driveway, keys jangling. "Len's brother came last night..."

I try not to imagine running into the side of his van. I walk forward, hands out, until I touch cold, dew-covered metal. "You don't have to move it." I trace my fingers along the slick car body as I walk around.

"Of course I'll move it. It'll be gone when you get back."

I find the sidewalk again and continue as the van growls behind me. I wait at the corner until Mrs. Reiche shuts it off to listen for traffic. I hear nothing but chattering birds, so I step into the intersection.

When I touch the chain link fence of Gunther Field I turn right. Fourteen steps to the gap and a left turn through it, one hand slightly forward in case today is the first time in years I misjudged the distance. I pass straight through, like always.

The field is over a hundred yards across. If any new obstacles have shown up since yesterday chances are low I'll find them with a single walk-through, but as crazy as it is to run here at all it's even crazier without walking it first.

I reach the far fence at one hundred and forty-two steps. Pretty typical and all clear. After a few more minutes of stretching, I'm ready to run. Seventy-five strides at a fair pace, a couple dozen walking steps to touch the far fence, and back again.

After five turns, it's time to sprint.

Sixty strides gets me within two dozen walking steps of the far side. Then sidestep a bit to line up again because of drift. The still air is warmer than yesterday but feels cool as I fly through it. The worst heat of summer is weeks away.

Ten sprints and I'm done. After crossing the

street I jog to cool down, but I slow to a walk near the Reiches' driveway. I heard the car move but once a problem occurs to you it takes a while to forget it. On the other side where the driveway slopes up to become sidewalk again, I speed up.

The instant I open the front door I know something's wrong. I don't smell any breakfast. Even cereal days include toast. In the kitchen I hear only the normal sounds of a sleeping house: refrigerator humming, clock ticking over the stove, my breathing, and when I stop that to listen more closely, my heartbeat.

I head for the stairs and stumble on something in the hall. I squat and find my dad lying on the floor, wearing flannel pajama bottoms and a T-shirt.

"Dad? Dad! Are you okay?"

"Parker," he says, his voice oddly flat. Not strained or injured.

"Did you fall? What happened?"

"Listen," he says, still sounding nothing like he should if he were really lying at the base of the stairs. "Everyone has secrets, Parker. Everyone *is* a secret."

That's when I wake up, like always, but it's exactly

what really happened last June third, the week after school let out and two weeks after my sixteenth birthday.

Well, except for two things. One, I really did almost run into the Reiches' van, but that was a different day a couple weeks later. And two, my dad wasn't lying at the bottom of the stairs. I found him still in bed, and he'd been dead for hours.

Chapter 1

Marissa is sobbing. Again.

"And then he...he...he didn't..." Her deep voice almost sounds like grunting.

Pathetic. And she's smart, too, except about Owen.

"Can't you guys talk to him?"

I don't reply and neither does Sarah. We offer good advice—for free even—but never get involved. We've told Marissa this countless times; it would waste oxygen to say it again. We just have to wait for her to dry out. There's nothing to do till the bell rings anyway.

Last school year this scene repeated itself every few weeks. Marissa rarely speaks to me otherwise. I can't clearly remember what she sounds like without wailing, snuffling, gasping, coughing on tears and snot, and really needing to blow her nose.

It's a common belief that losing your sight

heightens your other senses, and it's true, but not by magnifying them. It just gets rid of the overwhelming distraction of seeing everything all the time. On the other hand, my experience of sitting with Marissa consisted almost entirely of hearing everything her mouth and nose were capable of in sticky detail. That's what unrequited love sounds like to me. Disgusting.

"Parker? Can't you do something?"

"I am. I'm telling you to find someone else." I pause, per the usual script, so she can interrupt.

"Nooooo!"

I'm the reigning queen of not giving a shit what other people think, but Marissa's indifference to a Junior Quad full of people—on the first day of school no less—seeing her imitate a shrieking mucus factory...it humbles even me.

"Marissa, listen, soul mates don't exist. But if they did, they would be two people who *want each other.* You want Owen, but Owen wants Jasmine, so that means Owen is *not* your soul mate. You're just his stalker."

"Wait...Jasmine?" I enjoy a moment of peace as

the surprise of this information, which we told her last spring, quiets her for a moment. "Isn't she...?"

"Yes, Jasmine likes girls, but she hasn't found one in particular yet, so Owen stupidly thinks he has a chance. That makes him following her around only slightly more pointless and sad than you following him around. In fact—"

Sarah clicks her tongue and I know what it means but at some speeds I have too much momentum to stop or even slow down.

"—the only thing you and Owen have in common is being in love with someone who doesn't love you back, someone you don't even know. Have you ever even looked up words like *love* or *soul mate* or even *relationship* in a dictionary?"

The silence that follows is the perfect example of the thing I hate most about being blind: not seeing how people react to what I say.

"But..." Marissa sniffs productively. "If we spent some time togeth—"

Saved by the bell. Her and me both. But mostly her.

*

"Well, if it isn't PG-13 and her All-Seeing-Eye-Dog." The familiar screech is to my left and accompanied by a locker door clattering open.

"Please tell me her locker isn't right over there," I say to Sarah in a stage whisper. "I found out over the summer I'm allergic to PVP. Now I have to carry an EpiPen in my bag."

"Oh," Faith says in her snippy voice. "I'm PVP? That's...People...People..."

"Polyvinylpyrrolidone. Used in hair spray, hair gel, glue sticks, and plywood."

"Well, I think PVP means People...who are...*Very Popular*."

I laugh, breaking character. "Fay-Fay! Did you just think that up?"

"Of course I did! I'm not as dumb as you look."

The odor of kiwi-strawberry tells me what's about to happen and I brace myself. I'd call it a bear hug except Faith is too skinny to do anything bearish. I hold on a bit too long and then let go.

"Do you really have an EpiPen?" she asks.

"God, Fay," Sarah says. "Do you even know what that is?"

"My nephew's allergic to peanuts. And do you know you're a pretentious, condescending bitch?"

"Yes, I doooof!" The brush of air and Sarah's answer tells me Faith gave her a hug, too.

"Can you believe all these strangers?" Faith says, making no attempt to whisper. "This place is a zoo."

"At least it's them invading us," Sarah says, "and not the other way around."

All true. The town of Coastview can't support two high schools anymore, so Jefferson closed and everyone came here to Adams. The halls are so jammed with people who don't know The Rules, and not just the freshmen, that I had to hold on to Sarah's arm to get through the chaos to my locker. Breaking in this many newbies will be messy, but at least I don't have to learn the layout of an entirely different school.

"Oh, hey, here comes another one," Faith says, closer and softer, this time remembering Rule Number Two, and she hugs me again. "I'm sorry I was stuck in Vermont all summer. You know I'd have come if I could, don't you?"

"I'm fine," I say quickly, hoping that will end the subject.

"Did I see you guys talking to Marissa this morning? Was she crying?"

"New year, same bullshit," Sarah says.

"Please tell me it's over a new guy. Really? No…"

I imagine various facial expressions and nods and eyebrow waggling filling in the gaps.

"That's what you spent the morning talking about? Pretty selfish of her…Wait." I can hear that Faith has turned to face me. "Does she even know? Didn't you tell her?"

"Right," I say. "Oh, Marissa, while you spent the summer crying over some complete stranger, my dad died and my aunt's family moved here because my house's better than theirs."

"So…" Faith says. "That's something you just thought, or you actually said that?"

"Jesus, Fay. I'm honest but I'm not mean."

"Some exceptions apply," Sarah says.

"I have to go." I unfold my cane. "With all these noobs in the way, it's going to take a while to get to Trig."

"Haven't they assigned her a new buddy?" Faith asks Sarah as I tap down the hall. "Who is it? Didn't

Petra move to Colorado or somewhere?"

I'm grateful they can talk about my buddy without sounding awkward. It can't be one of them—Faith is too busy socially (translation: *popular*) and Sarah doesn't qualify because she's not taking enough of my honors and AP classes. But there's a girl from Jefferson who's in all my classes, and she was willing, so the choice pretty much made itself.

*

As soon as I settle into my usual seat for every class—in the back right corner and reserved for me with a name card—it starts.

"So you're blind, huh?"

I cock my head toward the unfamiliar male voice, coming from the seat directly in front of me. Low-pitched, a bit thick around the vowels. The voice of a jock, but I just keep that as a working hypothesis awaiting more evidence.

"Are you sure you're in the right class?" I say. "Calculus for Geniuses is down the hall. This is just Trig."

"I guess you're in Kensington's class? Isn't it kinda early for this?"

I don't know what this means, or who Kensington is. A teacher from Jefferson, maybe.

"Hey, douchebag," says a male voice to the left of Douchebag. "She's really blind."

Interesting. The second voice is softer, and calm in a way you don't often hear insulting big heavy jock voices. It's familiar but I can't place it.

"No, Ms. Kensington does this thing where you need to pretend—"

"I know, and she doesn't hand out canes. Besides, it's first period on the first day."

"But if she's really blind then why would she wear a blindfo—"

"Trust me, dude; just shut up." Harsh words but said with a friendly voice.

For my scarf today I chose white silk with thick black Xs on each eye. It was that or my hachimaki with *Divine Wind* written in kanji, but I didn't want to confuse the noobs with a mixed message. Either way, I know I made a mistake leaving my vest at home.

I usually wear a frayed army jacket, arms torn off, covered with buttons that friends bought or made over the years. Slogans like *Yes, I'm blind, get over it!* and *Blind, not deaf, not stupid!* and my personal favorite, *Parker Grant doesn't need eyes to see through you!* Aunt Celia talked me out of it this morning, saying it would overwhelm all the people from Jefferson who don't know me. She's wrong, it turns out. They need to be overwhelmed.

I hear shuffling and the creak of wood and steel as someone sits down hard to my left.

"Hi, Parker." It's Molly. "Sorry I'm late. I needed to stop by the office."

"If the bell hasn't rung, you're not late." I try to sound casual but actually let her know that being my buddy just means helping with certain things in classes, not life in general.

"Hey, so your name's Parker—" Douchebag says.

"Awww," I interrupt him with my sweet voice. "You figured that out because you just heard someone say it. And I know your name for the very same reason. *Douchebag* isn't very nice, though, so I'll just call you D.B."

"I'm—"

"Shhh..." I shake my head. "Don't ruin it."

The silence that follows is the perfect example of

the thing I love most about being blind: not seeing how people react to what I say.

"I—" D.B. says, and the bell rings.

*

"The stairs down to the parking lot are ahead," Molly says.

I sigh inwardly. Actually, I'm tired; maybe I sighed outwardly, I'm not sure.

Classes let out a while ago but Molly and I worked out a schedule to do our homework in the library after school for a couple hours and afterwards I call Aunt Celia to pick me up. Molly's mom is a teacher who also came over from Jefferson—she teaches both French and Italian—and they carpool.

"Good," I say. "Those stairs have been there at least two years now. I bet it'd be really hard to get rid of them with the entire parking lot being five feet lower than all the classrooms."

Silence.

I consider reminding her of Rule Number Four, understanding that it hasn't been long since I gave her the list, but it's been a tiring first day and I don't have the energy.

I don't need a chaperone anywhere on school grounds. I know exactly where the handicapped parking space is and two years of Dad parking there trained the unhandicapped people to stay the hell out of it. Molly insisted she was walking with me just because, but I knew better. The combination of blind people, stairs, and cars terrifies the sighted, but it's actually pretty safe. Cars are only dangerous when they're moving, and they only move in certain ways and places, and they make noise you can hear, even hybrids. Stairs are like bite-sized paths that your feet can feel the size and shape of all the time.

"You know, Parker..." Molly blurts out with some energy, maybe impatience, but then doesn't continue. She sighs.

"What?"

"Never mind."

I want to let it drop, too. I haven't spent enough time with Molly to know if I'm going to like her or just tolerate her—the amount of energy I'm going to put into this depends a lot on which it's going to be— but either way we're going to be with each other more than with anyone else, all day, every day, all year.

"You can't take it back," I say, just as a fact, not an accusation. "I know there's something in there now. Spit it out before it gets infected."

I can hear her breathing. Thinking breaths. I calculate whether to prod her more or wait her out.

"It's just..." she finally says. "I know we only just met..."

Another breath.

"Do you want me to help you?" I ask. "Or let you flounder around some more?"

Molly blows air out her nose. I can't tell if it's the laughing kind or the eye-rolling kind.

"Yeah, sure, help me out." I hear a little of both. A good sign.

Embedded in the concrete path under my sneakers is the bumpy metal plaque describing the founding of John Quincy Adams High School in 1979. I know exactly where I am.

"Here." I hand her my cane. "Fold this up for me?"

She takes it. "Why?"

I turn and walk briskly toward the stairs, arms swinging, counting in my head...*six...five...four...three...*

"Parker!" Molly scurries after me.

...two...one...step down...

I march down the stairs, counting them, hitting them hard and confident, legs straight like a soldier, each time sliding my foot back to knock my heel against the prior step.

At the bottom I keep marching and counting silently till I reach the curb, where I know Aunt Celia's car will park. I stop and spin around.

"Cane, please?"

It touches my hand. She didn't collapse it like I asked. I do and slide it into my bag.

"Maybe you're thinking I'm a stereotypical blind girl who's out to prove she doesn't need anyone's charity. But instead of being nice to people who are just trying to help her, she's a bitter and resentful bitch because she's missing out on something wonderful that she thinks everyone else takes for granted."

Now I'm starting to wonder if Molly is just a loud breather, though I didn't notice it in the library and it was pretty quiet in there.

"Am I warm?" I ask.

"Not very. But not everyone has to be."

It takes me a moment to get it—which isn't like me at all—and now it's too late to laugh.

I smile. "Touché."

Aunt Celia's car pulls up and stops.

"I suppose you can tell if that's your aunt's car, just by the sound?"

"Pretty much, yeah."

"My dog can do that, too."

I turn my head to face her, something I don't often bother doing.

"I'm starting to like you, Molly Ray. But believe me, it's a mixed blessing."

"Oh, don't worry. I believe it."

The car door *thunk*s open. Aunt Celia calls out, too loudly, "Parker, it's me, hop in!"

I sigh, definitely outwardly.

Chapter 2

Hey, Dad.

School was okay. Better than it could have been. Even though half the people didn't know the other half, everyone knew enough people so it wasn't too awkward. It'll take time to get all the noobs up to speed on The Rules, but I have plenty of help.

Some people I don't know very well were helping me with the noobs. Maybe just to be nice, or maybe it makes them feel important telling other people what to do. Or maybe they were protecting me like I'm the school mascot. That would really suck. I'm nobody's poster child.

The ride home was quiet, just how I like it now. I don't know what cars are like when I'm not in them but I get the idea people talk at me more because they think I'm bored sitting there without any scenery. My view never changes, but other than different people and cars on the street every day, I don't think their view changes much either.

I told Aunt Celia a couple months ago she didn't need

to entertain me while driving; now she doesn't talk in the car at all. She's black or white about everything. I said it nicely—I wasn't telling her to shut up or anything—but she clammed up anyway. Maybe her feelings got hurt but it's not my fault if people don't like the truth.

"Hi, Big P," my cousin Petey calls down from the landing.

"Hey, Little P. How was school?"

He trots down and sits on the third-from-the-bottom step next to me.

"Boring."

"You're too young to be bored at school. You're not supposed to get bored until the *fourth* grade."

"I was bored in the second grade, too," he says proudly.

"So was I," I whisper.

"Why are you sitting here?" he whispers back, probably just because I whispered first.

This truth I don't want to tell, not to Petey anyway. It's a tough enough situation as it is, my house filled with relatives—who I used to only cross paths with every couple years—now sleeping in my dead dad's room and home office. I don't want to tell him how I miss talking with Dad on the ride home from school, or how we wouldn't be done when we got home so we'd sit at the kitchen table and talk some more, drinking iced tea, until he finally had to get back to work. I don't want to tell Petey how I didn't think about this until I climbed into Aunt Celia's car today, when the silence—which I created and now can't break—sucked all the air out of the car until I thought I'd pass out. How I want to sit at the kitchen table and talk to Dad now, but if I do everyone will think it's weird, me sitting alone in the kitchen doing nothing. I don't care if people think I'm weird, but they would bug me with questions.

Like Petey's doing now, because sitting on the stairs doing nothing is weirder than sitting at the kitchen table. But I don't want to tell him that instead of sitting in my room having a one-sided conversation with my dad where no one can see, I want to do it in a place where I feel him: in the kitchen, in his office (off-limits, since it's my cousin Sheila's room now), or at the base of the stairs, where I never sat with him in life but sometimes do in my dreams.

"I'm just resting. It's been a long day."

"Wanna play Go Fish?"

Not particularly. But I can't do what I really want to do either. "Sure thing, Little P. How about Sheila?"

"Her door's closed."

We both know what this means. Do Not Disturb.

"All right, you get the cards, I'll pour the drinks. Last one done has to deal."

He pounds up the stairs. I sit a moment longer. Aunt Celia makes Petey pick up his room every night before bed but he just throws everything on shelves and never puts anything in the same place twice. He has a few decks of cards but only one braille set he got from me, so it'll take him a few minutes to find it.

I don't know if they're going to let me just sit quietly to talk to you every day, Dad, but I'm sure as hell going to try. I might need to go into my room and close the door like Sheila, because you're right, everyone has secrets, and that includes me.

*

Dinner is pork chops—too dry like always—mashed potatoes, applesauce, and canned peas. All of Aunt Celia's meals are cartoons, like something you might get if you were a captive in an alien zoo and they fed you what they thought people ate by watching TV.

I didn't offer to help because Aunt Celia always says no thank you. Which would be fine except she only says it to me. She tries to be nice about it with different reasons, sometimes hinting that she's cutting me a break since I'm "having such a hard time." It's really because the best way to help is chopping and she can't stand seeing a blind girl holding a knife. Whatever. Everything we're eating tonight is stuff I can prepare in my sleep. I'm glad to have less work if that's what makes her happy.

"Parker, did you and Sheila see each other much at school today?" Uncle Sam asks.

"Dad!" Petey says, mortified. "Not cool."

"What?"

I know what my junior protector means. "It's okay, Little P. The word *see* can mean a lot of things, like bumping into someone, or dating them, or understanding them. So no, I didn't *see* Sheila today. Maybe she did *see* me, though, if you *see* what I mean."

Petey laughs. No one else does.

"We don't have any of the same classes," Sheila says in her why-do-we-have-to-talk-about-this voice. "And our lockers are nowhere near each other."

Uncle Sam doesn't point out the small size of the school or the possibility of sitting together at lunch or ask how she knows where my locker is if she didn't see me. I'm glad. He usually knows when to stop.

"How's Molly working out?" he asks.

"It always takes a while to break in a new buddy, but she seems promising. She has a lot of Rules to learn."

Sheila snorts. Well, a burst of expelled air, definitely the eye-rolling kind. I let it go.

"Little P has a good story to tell," I say.

"Yeah—" he begins, but Aunt Celia interrupts.

"Please don't call him that, Parker. I've asked you before."

"He likes it, don't you, Little P?"

"It was my idea! Right, Big P?"

"He won't like it later, and by then it'll be stuck."

"The day he asks me to stop calling him Little P, I will, that's a promise. I only call him that at home so if anyone else hears it, it won't be from me."

"It's just...it just doesn't sound...It's not appropriate."

"Your concerns have been heard," I say lightly. "Go on, Little P, tell your story."

I expect a pause for everyone to have an eyebrow conversation about my defiance but Petey can't hold back and jumps right in describing how a fishbowl in his class got knocked over. The fact he's excited doesn't necessarily mean the fish survived—it could have gone the other way and he'd have told the story in pretty much the same tone.

While Petey describes the drama of saving the tetras in chaotic detail, I map out my pork chop with short stabs of my fork and dull knife and then saw the meat away from the bone. I'd caused a minor uproar when they first moved in because after I cut my food I don't switch my fork to my right hand for each bite. This is a concept that (1) had never occurred to me, (2) is common etiquette supposedly, at least among people who still obsess about things like this, and (3) is something I find utterly bizarre. Even stranger was how Aunt Celia not only disapproved of this, and my dad for letting me do it, but also had some half-baked notion of stopping it. Uncle Sam saved us from the most ridiculous argument imaginable by saying the way I eat is how they eat "across the pond." While this didn't make it optimal to Aunt Celia, it somehow made it legitimate enough for her to let it go and save face. It was my first glimpse of what it would be like living with Aunt Celia under my roof.

*

I'm on my bed with my laptop, reading with the help of Stephen Hawking's voice. I rarely read actual printed books and only occasionally use a braille terminal. A lot of the time I listen to audiobooks or browse the web with text-to-speech software, and what better way to learn stuff than hearing it from the smartest guy in the world?

I'm on my nightly Wikipedia crawl, enjoying the irony of reading about cuckoo birds. They lay their eggs in other birds' nests and then those birds raise the cuckoo chicks as their own, like nothing odd is happening. In my house it's the other way around.

My phone rings with Sarah's ringtone: *quack quack quack...*

I disconnect my earbuds from the computer and plug them into my phone. "Hey."

"Hey," she says. "Any fires tonight?"

"Nope. Just a few sparks when Aunt Celia told me again to stop calling Petey *Little P.*"

"It's a terrible nickname."

"Not appropriate, she said."

"You know that's Celia-speak for she thinks it's perverted, and it is. He'll hate it later when he figures it out."

"Jesus, Sarah, he's eight. And if you think *Little P* means his dick, then *Big P*—wait, never mind. Should have thought that through."

She chuckles and it warms me. Sarah hardly ever laughs.

"Sheila still not talking to you?"

"No change there. None expected."

"My theory's holding; I figured she'd steer clear."

"I'm not the best one to show her around anyway. I can't point out much and I doubt she's interested in how many paces it is from the cafeteria to the nearest bathroom."

"True. How's Molly?"

"Not sure yet. I'm hopeful. Probably won't be a disaster. Ask again later."

"Sure thing, Magic 8 Ball."

"Okay, tell me what you know."

It begins, our nightly recitation of what was observed

and inferred throughout the day. My list is always much shorter than Sarah's of course, since she's the eyes of this operation and I'm the mouth, but no one can deny that when I shoot it off, it's very well informed.

We used to be systematic, working through the day class by class, hallway by hallway; now we jump around without missing anything. She describes what people and things look like and I list times and places and describe voices and sometimes sounds and odors so she can zero in on who I'm talking about to get a visual and other info later. I tell her about D.B. from Trig because I suspect he'll be a pain and I might need more tools to deal with him. I mention the calm voice that shut down D.B.'s heavy jock voice and how it sounded familiar yet still not anyone I knew, like how listening to someone with an accent sounds like the other person you know with that accent even though they have different voices.

During a pause where I expect Sarah to jump in, she doesn't. I let the silence go to see how long it lasts. After a few more seconds I know something's up.

"What?"

"I'm waiting for you to tell me about it."

"About what?"

"You really don't know?"

"Know what?"

"That voice? You don't know who it was?"

"Do you? You weren't even there."

"Kay was. She said she was ready to hold up her math book like a shield but you were smooth as glass."

"Kay said that? *Smooth as glass?*"

"Of course not—it was *Kay*. She had verbal diarrhea for five minutes. Do you want to hear all that instead of my perfect three-word summary?"

"Jesus, Sarah—"

"It was Scott."

"Scott? *Scott?* It didn't sound..."

The floor vanishes. My stomach twists and I'm falling and I slap both hands on the bed and push my spine into the headboard.

"His voice changed," she says. "Last time you heard him was in the eighth grade. He was only thirteen."

We'd talked about how we'd know some of the immigrants from Jefferson—quirks of geography had us going to the same elementary and middle schools but different high schools. Some of them had been on my shit list before but my list is so long I wasn't worried about a few old names reactivating. Somehow all this didn't include realizing Scott Kilpatrick would be one of them.

"Parker?"

I grab my phone. "Gotta go."

"Wait! Don't hang—"

I hang up and yank the cord to pull the buds out of my ears, too fast and at a bad angle and it hurts.

Scott Kilpatrick. Biggest asshole on the planet. Absolute top of my shit list. Exclamation points. ALL CAPS.

Quack quack quack—

I switch off the ringer. My throat is closing, aching like I have a cold, and my face is getting hot.

Scott Kilpatrick. Breaker of Rule Number One. Forever subject to Rule Number Infinity.

Bzzz bzzz bzzz...

I bury the phone under my pillow.

Scott Kilpatrick. Parker Enemy Number One.

Chapter 3

The Rules:

Rule # 1: Don't deceive me. Ever. Especially using my blindness. Especially in public.

Rule # 2: Don't touch me without asking or warning me. I can't see it coming, I will always be surprised, and I will probably hurt you.

Rule # 3: Don't touch my cane or any of my stuff. I need everything to be exactly where I left it. Obviously.

Rule # 4: Don't help me unless I ask. Otherwise you're just getting in my way or bothering me.

Rule # 5: Don't talk extra loud to me. I'm not deaf. You'd be surprised how often this happens. And if you're not surprised, you ought to be.

Rule # 6: Don't talk to people I'm with like they're my handlers. And yes, this also happens all the time.

Rule # 7: Don't speak for me, either. Not to anyone, not even your own friends or your kids. Remember, you're not my handler.

Rule # 8: Don't treat me like I'm stupid or a child. *Blind* doesn't mean brain damaged, so don't speak slowly or use small words. Do I really have to explain this?

Rule # 9: Don't enter or leave my area without saying so. Otherwise I won't even know if you're there. It's just common courtesy.

Rule # 10: Don't make sounds to help or guide me. It's just silly and rude, and believe me, you'll be the one who looks stupid and ends up embarrassed, not me.

Rule # 11: Don't be weird. Seriously, other than having my eyes closed all the time, I'm just like you only smarter.

Rule # INFINITY: There are NO second chances. Violate my trust and I'll never trust you again. Betrayal is unforgivable.

Chapter 4

Despite lying awake for most of the night after Sarah dropped the Scott bomb on me, I jumped out of bed when my alarm buzzed, still not sleepy. Now, finally, halfway through my seventeenth sprint, I flop onto the dewy grass of Gunther Field, exhausted. I should cool down with a jog, or at least a brisk walk home, but I can't force myself up. The knife in my ribs telling me I pushed too hard is nothing compared to the ache ping-ponging between my chest and my stomach, the ache that was there before I started running, the ache I was trying to drive away.

A charley horse stirs in my left calf—clearly my body will not be ignored. I sit up and pull on my toes with one hand and massage the unhappy muscle with the other. Not enough oxygen, not enough water, not enough time, not enough space.

I manage to avoid a major spasm and stand up.

I don't know how far I am from the fence; I don't normally stop mid-sprint. After a few dozen steps I slow down and hold out a hand until I touch it.

Damn it, I don't know which side of the gap I'm on. I choose left and walk along, dragging my fingers along the chain link, *bump bump bump bump bump.* After a dozen steps I think I probably went the wrong way. I don't like this—I don't usually get disoriented here. I turn and walk back. Fifteen steps later I find the gap. I had just missed it.

I wipe my face with the bottom of my shirt—both are damp but the shirt less so and it helps. The air is cool but I'm burning up. I try deep breaths to calm my heart, my lungs, my stomach. It starts to work. I feel control returning.

He knew who I was but didn't say anything to me directly. Did he realize I didn't recognize his voice? Or did he just know I wouldn't talk to him, smooth as glass?

I should like that, being smooth as glass, shouldn't I? Unaffected, unconcerned. That's exactly what I want to be. Why should I suddenly hate it that some people might think that about me? Why should I care what anyone thinks anyway?

I don't. I was just caught off-guard, that's all. And only Sarah knows it. Not that I'd care if anyone else did, because I wouldn't. I don't.

*

I sit down in the cafeteria with Molly, who also brings her lunch, and start eating. Thinly sliced turkey, Swiss, light mayo and mustard, like always. Sarah will show up in a few minutes after filing through the hot-lunch line with Rick Gartner, her Sort Of Boyfriend. I told Molly last period she was welcome to join us—I don't know what she did yesterday, since I spent that lunch period working out logistics with audio textbooks at the office. I warned her that a lot of people call us the Table of Misfit Toys but not in the ironic complimentary way. She said she wasn't worried about labels. I said that was both wise and foolish. She agreed.

"What do you mean, Rick is sort of Sarah's boyfriend?" Molly asks. "Is he or isn't he?"

"Do they seem like boyfriend-girlfriend to you?"

"I met them yesterday for all of five minutes."

"If I hadn't told you, would you have worked it out?"

"I don't know. Maybe."

"There you go. You can call him Sarah's Maybe Boyfriend. I know they're sometimes more than friends so I call him her Sort Of Boyfriend."

"They break up and get back together a lot?"

"Not exactly. So much for not worrying about labels."

"It's not the same thing. I'm not worried, just catching up. Here they come."

"Parker. Molly." Rick clatters his tray and silverware onto the table. Sarah does the same only quietly.

"Hey, Rick," I say. "Have a good summer?"

"Not really. Hung out with losers mostly."

"Me too."

Molly must look bewildered because Sarah says, "We all spent the summer together."

"Is that all you're eating?" Rick asks.

"It is," Molly says. "It's not much or I'd offer you some. Do you like coleslaw?"

"He likes being an asshole," Sarah says, and almost sounds like she means it. "Eat your lasagna."

"I was going to offer her some," Rick says. "Not that I'd be doing you any favors, unless you like cardboard soaked in tomato sauce."

"Thanks anyway," Molly says.

"I haven't seen Sheila yet," Rick says, taking one of his classic conversational left turns.

"I haven't seen her either," I say.

"Hilarious. How about some new jokes this year?"

I smile. "It wasn't a joke. You need some examples? *This* is a joke." I grab a button on my vest, I think the one that says: *Have I seen you here before? NO!*

"You've truly opened my eyes, Parker." Rick chuckles. "Now that I know what jokes are, will sitcoms make me laugh, 'cause, man, they just put me to sleep."

"No promises. And no, I haven't bumped into Sheila here. Only at my house. Don't know why you care, though...she's got a boyfriend...you've sort of got a girlfriend..."

"It's just weird. I know you guys are, well...whatever. It's just that you're the only one she knows here."

"It's complicated," Sarah says.

"You mean it's a girl thing?"

"Rick," I say with my tolerant voice. "We let you sit here because you're sort of Sarah's boyfriend, not because you're one of the girls. If you don't understand, just accept the confusion. Or embrace it."

"Confusion requires giving a shit. Making nice with your stuck-up bitch cousin isn't high on my list—it isn't even on my list at all. I get it that she's in a new school and that sucks for her but it sure as hell wasn't your fault. She needs a sense of proportion or at least some fucking compassion."

I smile. "I don't care what you say, Sarah; this guy's A-Okay." I hold out a fist and feel a knuckle-bump. "Maybe he can be my Sort Of Boyfriend, too. Or all of ours."

"I'm still window shopping," Molly says. "No offense."

"None taken," Rick says. "I knew it already when you turned down my ketchup-covered cardboard. Which I need to wash down. Anybody want a drink?"

"My usual—a can of C-6?" I say.

No one else speaks and he leaves. I say, "I'm pretty sure I haven't been complaining about Sheila. Not around Rick anyway."

No replies.

"Sarah?"

"I didn't tell him much. Just what you'd expect about moving to a new town in the middle of high school."

I shrug. "There's nothing else to tell. We also don't get along generally but I don't get along with lots of people."

"Because they don't follow The Rules?" Molly asks.

"Because they're mindless overly complicated drones who don't say what they mean and get bent out of shape when I do. *And* they don't follow The Rules. Which shouldn't even be called Parker's Rules anyway. It's just a lot of common sense that common people commonly lack."

Rick sits back down. "Here." He brushes my fingers with a cold can.

"Thanks." I pull the tab with my palm over the top to block the light burst of foam and then take a sip. Mmmm...pure C-6 goodness. Cold Carbonated Caffeinated Caramel Colored Cane sugar. Completely delicious.

"I just saw Sheila," Rick says. "Near the cashier talking to the Dynamic Trio—well, Faith and Lila anyway, I didn't see Kennedy. She didn't go sit with them."

"It might take longer," Sarah says, "with all the clique-clash-chaos."

When someone new comes to school, they get tested, cataloged, processed, and absorbed pretty quickly, often into the same group they just left. With whole schools combining, however, it's way more complicated. Every king-of-the-hill from Jefferson brought a whole entourage and we have no idea what will happen with the school clique-scape. Sarah and I think Sheila will become part of the Cream, topped by the Dynamic Trio—Faith, Lila, and Kennedy—but we don't know whether it'll be the Jefferson Cream or the Adams Cream, if they remain separate, which seems unlikely, or if they combine, which seems even more unlikely.

"We'll see," I say. "At least we've resolved Rick's confusion."

"Nope, still confused. Trying to embrace it."

"Any one of the Dynamic Trio has more in common with Sheila in a random lunch-line encounter than I do after a whole summer with her. I couldn't discuss designer jeans if you put a gun to my head. I don't think it matters, though."

"Still confused."

"I don't think Sheila will become a long-term member of the Dynamic Trio because under all that lip gloss and style and bitchy backstabbing, Faith's a dark horse. She has hidden depth."

"Still confused."

"Well, go back to embracing it then. But if Sheila joins up and they become the Dynamic Quado or whatever, eventually she'll say the wrong thing about me and when she does, Faith will burn her to the ground and salt the earth where she stood."

*

Quack quack quack. I answer my phone.

"Hey."

"Hey. It's been exactly twenty-four hours. You ready to talk now?"

"Wow. How about a kiss first? And how was your afternoon, Sarah?"

"It kind of crawled by if you really want to know. So how about it?"

"You didn't *give* me twenty-four hours. We just didn't have any time alone."

"Doesn't matter. It's been twenty-four hours. We're

alone now. What happened?"

"Nothing."

"Nothing. Nothing at all."

"That's right, nothing happened. I didn't talk to him and he didn't talk to me. I'm not sure he was even there. I never heard his voice today."

"That's..."

"Impressive, I know."

"I was going to say a familiar song."

"I have an advantage over you full-featured models: if you don't make accidental eye contact, it's not awkward."

"What the hell do you know about accidental eye contact?"

"What you've told me many times. And don't forget I had seven years of twenty-twenty before the accident. I had plenty of awkward eye contact in the second grade. Remember Patel?"

"We're not going to talk about him. We're talking about—"

"Nothing happened. Nothing's going to happen."

"He'll be in your Trig class every morning from now till June. You're just going to pretend he isn't?"

"That isn't as hard as it sounds—"

"It's not hard, it's crazy. He's going to come talk to you eventually. Then what? Give him an Amish shunning?"

"It worked at Marsh."

"For a couple of months till we graduated. You think it'll work for the next nine months?"

"I..."

"Two years?"

And just like that, I'm not having fun anymore. I wasn't actually having fun before, but I wasn't having a serious conversation either.

"There are no guarantees in life," Sarah says. "But I *guarantee* he's going to talk to you. He's going to apologize—"

"He already tried—"

"He'll try again. He'll say he's sorry—"

"I don't want him to—"

"That won't stop him. He'll find you alone and talk to you and if you think it won't happen you'll get caught by surprise and not know what to do—"

"I'll know what to do."

"What? Ignore him for days and weeks and

months? That's fine for thirteen-year-olds but we're not kids anymore. He's going to say he was just a kid himself and it was just a stupid thing and he's sorry and he wants you to forgive him—"

"I can't."

"I know you can't—"

"But you think I should."

"I didn't say that—"

"Jesus, Sarah, you're on his side! You think I'm making a big deal over—"

"No, Parker, listen to me. I'm on your side—"

"Then why are you badgering me?" My voice quavers. This disgusts me and I harden it. "You weren't there. It was unforgivable."

"I know it was. Un-for-givable. I just want you to be ready."

"If he tries any of that I'm-sorry-for-what-my-thirteen-year-old-self-did bullshit, I know *exactly* what I'll say. I'll say fuck you Scott Kilpatrick and your sad little story about being a stupid kid. When people do dumbass things everyone has to live with the consequences so get back to living with yours and I'll live with mine and don't ever talk to me again or

you'll just embarrass yourself because I won't answer.
There, how's that?"

"That'll do, P. That'll do."

Chapter 5

"I swear to God, Rick, you better not be blowing on your food."

Every Friday is Bar-B-Que Day and I hate it. Rick knows the smell of Boston baked beans and scorched corn turns my stomach and he likes to blow the smell toward me.

"It's hot," he says with his smiling voice.

"For two years now," Sarah says, "the food here's never been hot."

"Even the hot salsa yesterday wasn't hot," Molly says. "The mild salsa was probably just chunky ketchup."

"Yuck," I say. "That'll teach you not to forget your lunch."

"Excuse me," says a voice I don't know. Sounds like a male teacher standing over us.

No one says anything. I can't even tell if he's talking to us. I sip my C-6.

"I'm Coach Underhill. Can I talk to you a moment, Parker?"

I choke a bit and cough into the crook of my arm. "Me? I already fulfilled my P.E. requirements. Ask Coach Rivers—she'll tell you."

"It's not that. I saw you running this morning."

The hair on the back of my neck stands up.

"Running?" Molly says.

"Early this morning. I—"

"Way-way-wait a minute! Can we talk outside?" I stumble to stand up, grabbing my cane.

"Sure, of course. Sorry to interrupt."

I lead him out into the hallway, moving slowly through the crowd. "Can you find a place where no one can hear us?"

A door squeaks open to my right. "This room's empty."

Once inside, the door clicks shut.

"We're alone? You're sure?"

"Yes. Are you afraid of something? Or someone?"

Fear, no. Dread, yes. The thought of this P.E. teacher standing at the fence watching me run this morning is bad enough, and if word got out...

"Who told you?"

"No one. I live nearby, on Manzanita. Have you been running there for long?"

"Years. Please don't...wait, have you told anyone?"

"No, but—"

"Please don't!" Dread leapfrogs right over fear and lands square on near panic. Running in Gunther Field is a major ingredient in my sanity soup. If people find out and come to gawk, or worse, come in so I can't even be sure the field's empty...I'd have no way of knowing they were there. Like this morning. I'd have to stop.

"Is someone bothering you?"

"It's just...private. And I'm not blind to the fact that it's a freak show. I don't want an audience. Please don't tell anyone."

"Okay, I won't."

"Why didn't you say anything this morning?"

"You'd have had no reason to believe I'm a teacher instead of some random stranger talking to you with no one else around. I didn't want you to feel unsafe."

"I can handle strangers—I do it all the time. But I can't see you so if you don't say anything, I don't know you're there and it's like spying on me."

AKA Rule Number Nine.

"Isn't that true of anyone walking by?"

"It's different with people I know, or who know me."

"I see," he says, but I don't think he does.

"It's okay, you didn't know. Just don't tell anyone. Not even all my friends know."

"It's not a freak show. The only way anyone could tell you can't see is that big blindfold flying out behind you like a banner. It's quite a sight."

"Exactly."

"You're a very confident runner. Have you ever had a guide dog?"

"Nope. Never needed one, not for what I do mostly. Maybe later when I graduate high school and need to get around in more strange and busy places on my own."

"Do you mind if I ask who taught you how to run?"

I'm feeling better knowing the cat's still in the bag, but this irks me.

"Why would someone need to teach me how to run?"

"Well there's running and there's running. You look like you've had training."

"Oh. My dad used to run. He taught me some things. How to breathe and stuff."

"Have you ever thought about trying out for track?"

I laugh. "No. You understand why I run at six in the morning in Gunther Field, right? It's big, it's empty, it's *square*. No lanes to stay in? No people around?"

"Plenty of runners have some degree of visual impairment. If you don't mind me asking, how much can you see?"

"Um...I can't see anything."

"I understand, but I mean, you still see some light, right, but just can't focus?"

I don't like talking about this but decide to cut him some slack.

"Nope. All black. A car wreck tore my optic nerves. My eyes are fine, only...lights out."

"I'm sorry. I shouldn't have assumed—"

"It's all right, most blind people can see a little. You were just betting the odds."

"No, I mean, I thought you had light sensitivity

issues because…why else would you wear blindfolds?"

I laugh. "These are just clothes. Like wearing a hat. A fashion statement no one can copy because if they did, they wouldn't be able to see."

He doesn't laugh, which is sad, but then I hear a smile in his voice when he says, "I was just curious. Actually, in Paralympics all visually impaired runners wear blacked-out goggles so those who can see a little don't have an advantage."

"That's…terrible." I laugh.

"Anyway, they all have guide runners. If you wanted to run track, we could work something out."

"No thanks," I say, and to give it some finality I reach for the door but I find only air. I step toward it slowly, waving my arm.

"There's nothing to be afraid of."

I snort and my hand finds the doorknob. "Did I look afraid?"

"Not when you were running. You did a minute ago when you thought people might watch you do it."

Ah, well, that's something else entirely.

*

Molly sits with me on the stairs waiting for Aunt

58

Celia. It's routine now for her to walk with me to the parking lot to hang out till my ride comes.

We're not talking. I think about this, like always. We've either run out of things to say after only a week, or she's in a mood I haven't been able to detect, or she's working out how to ask an awkward question, or she's—

"Do you know Scott Kilpatrick?"

Damn.

"I used to," I say lightly. "At Marsh Middle School. Why?"

"You know he sits in front of me in Trig?"

"Yeah, I heard his voice. Do you like him or something?"

"I don't know him well enough."

"Plenty of people don't let that get in the way of a good crush," I say.

"He looks at you sometimes."

I stiffen. I don't want to have this conversation, yet I also don't want to draw attention to this.

"I'm sure people look at me all the time. The Resident Hallway Obstacle. The Bull in the China Shop."

"And your blindfolds do draw the eye."

I'm wearing tie-dye today. I sense an opportunity. I grab the tail and hold it up.

"You like this one? I made it myself. What's it look like?"

"You don't know? I mean, no one's ever told you?"

"Tie-dye is hard to describe. It's like a Rorschach test. What's it look like to you?"

"Mostly blues and greens and some aqua. Blotches of red, streaks of maroon, some purple. Parallel stripes, vertical but probably just how you folded it. Looks almost like you rolled up a hippie version of an American flag. What does that say about me?"

"Practical, objective, nothing fancy. Faith says things like burgundy and fuchsia instead of maroon. Some people say it's swirly or project a lot of dreamy feelings into it."

"How do you know that's what you're wearing?"

"It's tagged, see?" I show her the tag at the end. "I make these plastic braille doodads and sew them in. Most everything I wear is tagged."

"That's cool. But that's not why Scott looks at you."

Damn.

My throat tightens. I'm getting warm again. I think Molly and I are becoming friends, maybe good friends, so she'll find out eventually. If that's true, I don't want to spend ten times more effort now avoiding what's inevitable.

"We were best friends since fourth grade. Then toward the end of the eighth grade we...started kissing. That's all. It didn't last long. We broke up and then went to different high schools."

"Must've been some really bad kissing."

I snort. "It sure wasn't. But it...I mean he..."

I take a deep breath.

"We'd only been together a couple weeks. Then at lunch one day we went into an empty classroom we would go to, you know...then I heard snickering."

My breathing speeds up. I can't explain this without feeling it all over again, like it's happening right now. The suffocating panic of trusting someone so completely, drinking them in, and having it suddenly turn to burning hot poison. I deepen my breaths to slow them down.

"There was someone else in the room," Molly says.

"Seven someones. At first it scared the shit out of

me and I jumped and Scott and I bumped teeth and everyone in the room started laughing. Then they were all talking at once. I don't remember what they said, mostly congratulating Scott and jeering about how I'd been scammed. I pushed Scott hard and he knocked over a bunch of stuff, and I was halfway down the hall before he caught up with me, saying he was sorry, that he told them because they didn't believe we were a couple, and other bullshit I don't remember anymore. I ducked into a bathroom and waited there till class started. Then I went to the office and called home and my dad came and picked me up."

Silence.

"Scott kept calling me...I didn't answer and deleted all his messages without even listening. He kept trying to say he was sorry in school but I wouldn't talk to him and my friends helped keep him away, especially Sarah and Faith. Then he came to the door and Dad sent him away—chewed him out, too—I didn't hear what they said. After that he stopped calling or trying to talk to me. When we were in the same room at school I just pretended he wasn't there. Then we graduated and went to different high schools and that's really all there is to it. Ancient history."

There. All the gory details, nothing hidden, casually delivered. Done. We can move on.

"I don't know what to say," Molly says softly. "That's awful."

The unexpected tenderness makes my heart pound.

"No big deal—just kid stuff," I say and immediately wish I hadn't. I don't want this to turn into a big thing so I'm trying to toss it off lightly but not dishonestly. Saying it's no big deal isn't honest. It *was* a big deal. Still is.

"Are you kidding? It's a nightmare. It's horrible. You say Scott was your best friend before that?"

"For years. *Actually* four years: one, two, three, *four*."

I'm getting dizzy. If she shrugged off this story like a trivial childhood drama I'd be fine, but hearing her voice, agreeing that it means a lot more than it sounds...

"I can't imagine it. If it was me, I'd have killed him. I want to kill him now."

My chest tightens some more. I can't talk about this much longer. I didn't want to kill him when it happened; I wanted to kill myself. I saw a side of the world I knew existed but thought I could protect myself from, and in that moment I saw that I never could. There's no absolute safety to be found anywhere. Not the kind I want anyway.

"So, yeah." I sigh. "I knew Scott Kilpatrick. Or I thought I did. Then I found out I really didn't."

Because no one can know anybody, really. Not completely.

Molly shifts and jostles me a little. I feel her hand on my shoulder. I get it that she nudged me first so her hand wouldn't be a surprise, to touch me without startling me and also without having to awkwardly ask permission. I'm so grateful for her understanding Rule Number Two this well after only a week, I wonder if I can keep it together.

I don't have to wonder for long. Aunt Celia arrives and saves me. The irony almost makes me laugh. Almost.

*

Hey, Dad.

Pretty typical week. Good things happened, bad things happened, like always. I'm sorry we don't talk after school anymore; it's too hard to get time to just sit alone. Petey thinks I'm bored or at least not busy. From now on I think I can only talk to you right before bed.

I'm also sorry I'm talking to you like you're actually listening. I know the universe doesn't really work that way. If it did, if you were really watching, you wouldn't need me to explain all these things. Still, this is how my brain wants to do it.

Now I wish I knew what you said to Scott that day you sent him away. Whatever it was, it worked. I don't think I ever told you how grateful I was for that. If he'd kept after me like we were in some pathetic romantic comedy, I think I might have unraveled.

Except I did unravel. I know that. Mostly on the inside. Maybe you did, too. I could hear it in your voice, how after that you knew you couldn't always protect me. I tried to get you to believe that it wasn't your job. I don't think I tried hard enough.

I cross my room and take the plastic pill bottle out of my scarf drawer, like every night. It's the bottle of

Xanax that was sitting empty on Dad's nightstand the morning I found him. The bottle I didn't know existed until that moment but had been hiding in plain sight for a while. The bottle the insurance company used to deny paying out his life insurance that would have kept the house in my name instead of Aunt Celia's. The bottle I wanted back so much I punched the police detective over and over again until he promised to give it back once the case closed, which happened only a week later. The bottle Aunt Celia claimed proved what she'd always believed, that Dad was the weak one even though it was her own sister who drank too much wine that night and drove the two of us into that bridge support, killing her and making sure her screaming face would be the last thing I ever saw. And most important, it's the bottle that taught me everyone has secrets. *Everyone.* No matter how much you love them and think you know them and think they love you back.

I open the bottle, take out a gold star, lick it, and press it firmly on the poster board hanging on the back of my door. A clean white rectangle filling up with stars that, when anyone asks me about it, I just say is tactile art, my Star Chart. Every night I get to add a gold star if I earn it. Tonight's makes eighty-one gold stars. Eighty-one consecutive days without crying.

I know it was an accident. Oxycodone for your back, then some more when it didn't work along with some ibuprofen for swelling, plus some Xanax, and then a couple beers that made you forget you already took them and you took more, and extra Xanax because you were having a bad week, all adding up to stop your breathing sometime between one and three in the morning. I know you wouldn't have left me here alone on purpose, no matter what the cops or the insurance people or my closest relatives say. I know it.

But I also know you kept your feelings inside, and they were bad enough to need all those pills. I don't think it would have changed what happened, because I'm sure it was an accident, but maybe if I'd known I could've helped. Maybe you wouldn't have needed the pills in the first place. Maybe.

I take off my scarf and tuck it and the pill bottle in the drawer and slide it closed. I brush the light switch to make sure it's down—sometimes people don't turn it off when they leave because it's too weird for them to turn off the light when someone's in the room—but it's down so I know the room looks the same to everyone else now as it does to me. Or maybe not. I dimly remember how the moon and stars and streetlights keep everything from being as completely dark as it looks to me now.

I crawl into bed.

Good night, Dad.

Chapter 6

Petey has an endless fascination with anime, which isn't great for me. I'm told the appeal is mostly visual and all I get is hearing bad actors reading badly translated dialog of badly written Japanese scripts. But it's Sunday morning so I'm wearing my hachimaki while he wears his karate gi and the new purple belt he earned yesterday.

Someone walks into the living room and flops down hard on the leather easy chair. It's Sheila; she's the only one who would throw herself down nearby without saying anything. Now she's texting. I sit with my head back on the sofa, not really listening to the show. I'm not even sure what it is anymore but it doesn't matter because I can tell by the sudden crazy electric guitar and synth explosion that it's the closing credits.

Aunt Celia calls from the entryway, "You girls ready?"

"Going somewhere?" Petey asks, sounding hopeful.

Even Sheila can tell he's angling to come along and she says in her bored voice, "The mall. Shopping. Clothes. You'd hate it. Then we'd all hate it."

"You're coming anyway," Aunt Celia says. "Dad took his car in for an oil change."

Petey groans.

"It'll be fun," I say. "I need new running shoes. You can help me get them."

"But I don't want to stand around for hours while Sheila tries on a million pants."

"Nobody does, sweetie," Aunt Celia says, walking into the room. "That's why we're dropping her off. We'll come home after we buy Parker shoes."

"Shotgun!" Petey shouts as we leave the house.

"Uh-uh, in the back," Aunt Celia says. Dictators don't follow rules they don't like. "I'm up front with Sheila."

"But if—" Petey says.

"It's a *provisional* license," Sheila says. "I can't drive with anyone in the car unless Mom's there sitting next to me. Get used to it."

In the back with Petey, I hold out my hand and

whisper, "One, two, three, four..."

He grabs my hand in the proper grip and whispers back, "I declare a thumb war."

*

In the Ridgeway Mall parking lot, we meander around. I can't tell if it's crowded or she's just trying to save walking five extra feet.

Aunt Celia says, "I thought you were meeting your friend at the food court? That's way at the other end."

"Yep," she says. I have no idea who this new friend is.

Sheila parks and almost before the engine is completely off, she's gone.

"Can I go to the video game store?" Petey asks.

"We're not buying any video games today."

"Just to look?"

Petey likes helping me but shopping is apparently a step too far, even for him.

"We need to help Parker get shoes, then we're going straight home."

"I don't need help, actually," I say. Not to stir up trouble; it's just true. "We're coming up on the door where the pet shop is, right? Once we're inside, I'll meet you back here in half an hour."

"Great!" Petey says.

"No, no. Of course we'll help you, Parker."

"Thanks, but there's really nothing for you guys to do. I know where I'm going and what I'm buying, and I have my credit card. I'll text you if anything changes. If I get back to the pet shop before you guys, I'll play with the puppies till you show up."

"I don't think that's a good idea."

That's where it tips. I confess that suggesting the pet shop was a dig—the only thing more exhausting than Petey trying to get a video game is Petey trying to get a puppy—but the rest was an honest attempt to give her a chance. She blew it.

"I can't buy shoes on my own for half an hour but Sheila can wander around all day?"

"It's not the same, Parker," she says in her world-weary voice.

"It's exactly the same."

"I'm sorry, but it isn't. You don't want to talk about it—"

"No, I absolutely want to talk about it. Why, exactly, do you need to be with me?"

"Well, it's just easier when we—"

"I don't need easier."

"How are you going to pick what you want?"

"I already know what I want. I tell them, they get it, I give them my credit card, it's done."

"What if they overcharge you? Shouldn't you pay in cash?"

"No. They scan the box and it goes straight to the credit card. If you pay cash, the register can say sixty bucks but the guy tells you a hundred; then he puts the extra forty in his pocket and you're screwed with no proof of anything. With the credit card I check online when I get home and see if it cost what the guy said, then I only pay if it's right."

Silence.

Aunt Celia's only been living with me three months and there are lots of things we haven't run into yet. I didn't figure today was the day to have a showdown over shopping alone, but I also didn't figure on Petey pushing for the video game store, which he has every right to.

"I only want to help," she says.

She sounds like she means it. Like I'm hurting her feelings. But if someone's feelings get hurt when they insist on giving me something I don't want, I don't see how that's my fault. It doesn't get us anywhere, though.

"Tell you what. Follow me if you want and you'll see I'm fine. It won't be any fun for Petey but it wasn't going to be anyway."

"You want us to follow you?" she asks. "Like ten steps back?"

"No, but I can't stop you either. Do what you want. Just don't interfere unless I'm doing something life-threatening. Either way, I'll meet you back here in a half hour or I'll text you."

Sigh. "Fine."

I cane my way over to the wall. In all the arguing I almost lost track of where it should be, but the sound of puppies to my left orients me. I know there are no benches or other protrusions along this wing of the mall so I cane along it easily, tapping hard enough for people who aren't looking to hear me coming.

There are seven stores along this wing. My cane hits the side wall, and then not when I pass a store entrance, and then wall again. After seven gaps, I know I'm in the center hub.

This is the first time I expect Aunt Celia might intervene because I'm heading straight for the fountain. On purpose, but she doesn't know that. It's only shin high and she probably thinks I'll plow into it. My cane strikes the rim and I stop. No one says anything.

Except a little boy nearby whispers loudly, "Mom! Mom! Look!"

Who knows what that's about. Maybe me or maybe a turd floating in the fountain. Now comes the tricky part: orienting to the shoe store from here.

"She's pretending she's blind!" the boy says in a whisper loud enough to echo.

It's always a question whether or not to ignore these things. I can tell he isn't far away, so I lean toward him a bit.

"I'm not pretending," I say in a loud whisper. "I'm really blind. And *not* deaf."

He gasps and I hear scrambling. Maybe he's hiding behind his mom.

"Then why're you wearing a blindfold?" he asks.

"Come on, Donnie," says a young woman. "Don't bother her."

"I wear it because it's pretty. And because Japanese pilots in World War Two wore them when they crashed into things on purpose. Sometimes I crash into things, too, though not on purpose."

I realize this might be offensive, even if they aren't Japanese. Too late now.

"Kamikaze!" he shouts, followed by plane noises, bullet noises, and an explosion noise, all of which probably adds several ounces of spit to the air.

With that taken care of, time for the tricky part. The wing of the mall with the shoe place, Running Rampant, is opposite the fountain, which is round. It works best if I tap my way around by sidestepping, always trying to face the same way without pivoting, or else it's hard to keep track of my direction. As I do it, the airplane noises diminish. When I think I'm there, it's time to see if I got it right.

I walk far enough forward to know I'm generally in the main wing, and then I start trending toward the right where I know the store is. I manage not to bump into anyone, like people who are probably just facing away, gawking at the window displays or whatever, and don't hear my taps.

When I reach the doorway I pass through and walk straight until I tap a barrier that should be a shoe display. I reach out and touch canvas and shoelaces. Success. Now it's a waiting game, and usually a short one.

"May I help you?"

It's a guy's voice. Maybe my age. I don't recognize it.

"That depends. Do you work here?"

He chuckles. "Yeah, I'm an employee. Want to touch my name tag?"

"Not until we know each other better. Unless it's in braille."

"It's not. It says Jason. Are you looking for someone?"

"Nope." I lift my right leg a bit and turn my foot to the side. "Can I get a new pair of these in an eight?"

"Hmmm...I don't think we carry those anymore."

"The closest thing is fine. I'm not that picky."

"In black?"

"Definitely. I am picky about that. No stripes or colors or any wacky stuff. If I run at night I want to get hit by a car because they can't see me."

"You might as well run at night since you don't

need any light. I'll be right back."

He leaves. No reaction to me running at night, or running at all; he even made a crack about it. I could like this guy. Except I don't know if he's seventeen or twenty-seven and that's a tough thing to ask, even for me.

I say "No thank you, I'm being helped" to three different people before Jason returns.

"There's an empty bench about three steps to your right," he says.

While I tap over and sweep my hand, he keeps talking. "I don't know if you care about brands—"

"I don't." I find the bench and sit down.

"Okay. They discontinued the shoes you're wearing and replaced them with these, which are close but they put in more arch support and some B.S. spring-foam technology in the heel that doesn't help but doesn't hurt either. Do you want me to lace them for you?"

He asked me. He's racking up points now.

"Give me one and you do the other." I hold out a hand and a shoe lands in it.

"Sure thing." He sits down next to me. "We can race."

I have lots of experience lacing shoes but he works here so I'm guessing he'll win.

"Are you a runner?" I ask. "Or is this just a job?"

"Why not both? But yeah, I run."

"You ever run track in school?" I ask. Very smooth.

"Still do. Well, if I make the team, which seems likely. Tryouts are next week."

"Where do you go?"

"I'm a senior at Adams, now. What about you?"

"Ah, you're one of the immigrants. I'm a native."

"Really?"

Now I wonder if he's playing me. Not to be conceited or anything but what are the odds that he's never seen me and my blindfold tapping around school?

It's too much to let go. "You haven't seen me around?"

"No, I guess we don't have any of the same classes."

"Or walk the same halls, or eat in the same cafeteria."

He laughs. "I just walk the track with a granola bar at lunchtime."

I finish lacing. "Time. You finished already?"

"Uhhh..." he says. "Yeeeeeaaaaaah...finished... Here."

"I won, didn't I?"

"You'll never know."

Wow, taking advantage of my blindness in a safe, playful way in the first five minutes.

I put on both shoes and stand.

"You have about three or four clear steps in front of you. If you want more, I can clear out an aisle for you."

"No, this is fine." I bounce on my toes and run the shoes through some paces. They feel odd but in the usual way new shoes do. Otherwise good.

"How much?"

"Seventy-nine ninety-nine."

I pull the credit card from my pocket and hold it out. "I'll take them. I'll be up to the counter in a minute."

"No need, we just got these portable scanners."

While he scans the shoe box (*beep*) and types (*click click*) I change back into my old shoes and pack the new ones away.

"You sign on the screen. I'll put the tip of the pen where it goes."

I hold out a hand and it finds a pen. I grab on and he's holding the other end in space until it clicks on a hard surface.

"There."

I sign my name and he takes back the pen.

"I tucked the receipt in the box."

"Thanks."

"If you check it later, which you should, it actually cost only sixty-eight dollars, or seventy-three seventy-eight with tax."

"They're on sale?"

"No, I have a Friends and Family discount. I think we're friends now. It's just a code we enter—we don't flag your account or anything—so whenever you come here you have to ask for me, Jason Freeborn."

"Cool—thanks, Jason."

"But if my boss asks, I'd better have a name to give him."

"I'm sorry?"

"What's your name?"

Oh. What an idiot. "Parker. Parker Grant. Just like on the credit card."

"I didn't want to assume. A lot of people use their parents' cards."

"I wish."

"Here are your shoes. Promise me you won't run at night, even though you can."

"I promise."

"Good. Maybe I'll see you in the halls at Adams. And since we're friends now, I want to see you run in these sometime."

Strangely enough, I'm thinking I might let him.

Chapter 7

The Doctor is IN.

Except there are no patients in the room, or rather the table where Sarah and I are sitting outside in the Junior Quad. We provide easy access to our patients but not much privacy. Sarah says we can't be overheard if we talk softly but people still have to struggle with whether they want to be seen with us since most people know why we're out here every morning. Well, most Adams natives know, not the Jefferson immigrants.

"Lori's talking to someone I don't know and looking over here," Sarah says. "Either gossiping about us or working up the nerve to come over. Oh, here comes Molly."

"Hey, what's up? You guys usually sit out here in the morning?"

"Every day," I say. "Doing the good work."

"It looks like sitting around to me."

"Looks are deceiving. We provide a rare and valuable service—"

"Here they come," Sarah says with an edge to her voice because Molly's here.

Before I can say anything, Lori says, "Hi, Sarah. Parker."

A girl I don't know says, "Hi, Moll."

"Hey, Reg," Molly says. "How was your summer?"

"Okay."

"This is Regina," Lori says. "She has a problem. I told her she should talk to you."

"Have a seat," Sarah says. "Um...Molly?"

"It's okay," Regina says. "She can stay. She already knows most of it."

There's some scuffling as people sit down.

"Go ahead, Regina," Lori says. "It's okay."

"So...I was going out with Gabe last spring, but we broke up right before school let out."

Silence.

"Regina..." Lori says.

"He dumped me. Then he went to Spain for the whole summer on an exchange program."

"Hang on," I say. "How'd he do it? In person, phone, text?"

"When I was at work he texted me *We need to talk* and I texted back *About what?* and he said *We should talk in person* and I said *You're freaking me out, what's wrong?* and he said I could call him if I couldn't wait and I said I was at work but I'd call him on my break. Then I called him and he broke up with me."

"Did he say why?" Sarah asks.

"He said we were growing apart. That we both knew things were cooling off and he didn't want to drag it out when we only had one more year at school."

"Was he right?" I ask. "Were things cooling off?"

"I didn't think so, but..."

Silence. This is what I need from Sarah later, whether this girl is looking at her hands, looking up at the sky trying to find words, glancing at all the faces not wanting to share with a crowd...

"We can't keep entire conversations confidential because honestly it's too hard to sort everything out," Sarah says. "But if there's anything specific you want us to keep to ourselves, we will. Just tell us."

"It's not that. It's just...well...I guess things weren't that hot in the first place?"

"You're not that into him, or he into you?" I say.

"Oh, we're great together, but…maybe he wants to go faster than I do?"

I say, "He said things were cooling off but he actually meant things weren't heating up fast enough."

"Maybe."

"Did you two talk about it?" Sarah asks.

"No. I didn't say much. I was at work, and I really didn't expect it. I dunno. I just felt like I blew it somehow. I didn't want to make it worse by trying to figure out what went wrong and promising to fix it or begging or whatever. I just wanted to hang up. So I did and that was it. Well, until last week. He started calling me again."

"He wants to get back together?"

"He didn't say that. And I didn't ask. He just said he misses me and wants to catch up."

"And you don't know whether you want to?" Sarah asks.

"I don't know if I should."

"There is no *should*," I say.

"Parker's right," Sarah adds quickly, which tells me to let her follow her line so I clam up. "I asked whether you want to. That's what matters."

"I dunno. I do, I guess. We really get along and stuff. I miss hanging out...but...after he broke up with me...I dunno...I think it'd be weird."

"Weird how?" Sarah says quickly. To emphasize the importance of the question and to get it out before I go off on her which Sarah must know is about to happen.

"I dunno. Just weird. I didn't see it coming the first time so it could happen again anytime without me expecting it. I'd be thinking that all the time. I guess that's true with anyone, though. I just wasn't thinking about it before."

"So what do you want to do?" Sarah asks.

"I guess...I want to be with him. I just don't want to be looking over my shoulder all the time, you know?"

"Yes, definitely," Sarah says.

"So...what should I do?"

"We don't tell anyone what to do—"

"Except when it's obvious," I say, unable to hold back any longer. "You just said it. Go find someone to be with where you don't have to look over your shoulder. Is that this guy, what's his name?"

"Gabe."

"Gabe. Is Gabe a guy you'll have to look over your shoulder with?"

"I guess so."

"Problem solved."

"But I miss hanging out..."

"He said things weren't hot enough for him. Give the guy points for breaking up before he went to Spain to have a fling without cheating, but he loses them again for trying to worm his way back to you now that he's back, to see if a summer alone—were you alone?"

"Yeah."

"To see if losing him for three months might have changed your mind about whether you wanted to put out to keep him."

"He never said that. I don't think he's trying to be sneaky—"

"We already know he's sneaky. He was your boyfriend; didn't he know your work schedule? And he texts you while you're at work saying *We need to talk*. He knows you have to reply to that. And when you do he says you guys should talk in person, knowing you won't be able to wait. Then he breaks up with you on the phone, saving himself the awkwardness of doing it face to face but making it your fault. If he wasn't sneaky, he would've just waited till the next time you were together."

Silence.

"The point is," I say, "if he wasn't happy before, why would he be happy now? Either he's changed or he's hoping you have. Have you changed?"

"I don't think so."

"He hasn't either, sorry to tell you. People don't change. They just learn from experience and become better actors."

More silence.

Sarah says, "I don't know if this helps, but we're here every morning if you want to talk."

I hear shuffling and footsteps.

"They're gone," Sarah says.

"How'd it end?"

"She looked confused. The usual cognitive dissonance. She wants to get back what she thought she had, knows it's not really there, really wants it to be, and is struggling with how much to rationalize to get it back."

"Wait, what the hell just happened?" Molly says. "Regina walked up and told you all that and you've never even met?"

"It's something we do," Sarah says. "Everyone at Adams knows. We listen to anything without being judgmental—"

I snort but Sarah ignores me.

"—and we offer unbiased observations and advice. We do a *pretty* good job of keeping things confidential..."

"Is she looking at me?" I say. "I keep the sensitive stuff quiet, but part of the value we provide is knowing things about other people. For instance, we were helping—"

"Parker!" Sarah snaps.

"Fine!" I say. "I wasn't going to say any names."

"You guys..." Molly says. "Well, I was going to ask if you're serious, but Regina...I mean..."

"She said you knew about her breakup," I say. "She talk to you?"

"A little."

"What'd you tell her?"

"I mostly agreed with whatever she said. It seemed

like what she needed."

"Of course. When he's dreamy, he's dreamy; when he's a jerk, he's a jerk. A lot of people need that, but they also need the truth they usually can't get from friends. Talking the way we do is tough for people to do and stay friends."

"She means the way *she* talks," Sarah says. "And yes, it's *absolutely* hard to stay friends with her talking the way she does."

"Ouch," I say. "But it's what people need; that's why they come to us. They don't have months or years to do it the old-fashioned way, professional-like. So Sarah starts it off right and then I cut to the chase."

"How did this even start?" Molly asks. "You guys sitting out here...How do people know?"

I wait for Sarah to answer. She doesn't.

I pivot my head to face her. "Go on, Sarah. Tell her."

"God," Sarah says in her eye-rolling voice. "The bitchiness I have no problems with...but the smugness...ugh..."

I grin.

"Fine," she says. "One of the unexpected side effects of Parker going blind was how she got...less and less *sensitive* about what she said to people because she couldn't see them flinch. Then freshman year a few people came back and thanked her for being so blunt, saying they later realized she was right and it really helped them. And here we are, two years later."

"See, that wasn't so hard, was it?" I turn back to face Molly. "She even sold herself short. We're a team because those things I say to people, most of them I wouldn't even know if Sarah didn't tell me. It's like I said, she's the eyes and the brains, I'm just the loudmouth."

"Wow, you're like Good Cop, Bad Cop Psychologists," Molly says. "You should charge people five cents a session."

"Yes!" I say. "We used to put out a coffee mug with Lucy on it saying *The Doctor is IN*, but it broke a while ago."

"Maybe it's time for a confession," Sarah says without sounding at all remorseful. "I broke that mug on purpose."

"You did?" I'm genuinely shocked. "Why?"

"She's right about what she says to Charlie Brown

but she's totally heartless about it. That's not us. Lucy's a bitch."

"But that's perfect for you guys," Molly says. "Each of you are half of Lucy. You're the insightful psychologist half, and Parker, you're..."

I laugh. Can't deny it. Don't even want to.

*

My locker combination is easy: zero-zero-zero, and there's a bump on the dial by the zero. I have a separate padlock that takes a key since I can't tell if someone's looking over my shoulder. I asked them to disable the combination lock but they said they couldn't without damaging it—which I don't believe—so I asked if they could at least make it the easiest combination. Now I get the joy of unlocking two locks every time I want in my locker.

"Hi, Parker."

It's Faith. She doesn't normally just say hi out of nowhere anymore so I wonder what else she wants. I'm not worried, though; school's out and Molly has plenty to do in the library till I get there.

"Hey, Fay-Fay, how are you today?" It's an old rhyme from when we were kids. She probably doesn't like that nickname anymore but I'm in a good mood and she's never told me to stop using it.

"You want to go to the mall this weekend?"

There were ninety-nine things I thought she might say—that wasn't one of them.

Faith and I don't hang out, mainly because we have almost nothing in common anymore. We act like we don't get along but we're the opposite of frenemies; we're friends who pretend to be enemies. I guess that makes us *enemends*. We share a lot of serious history without any bumps in the road and were there for each other through the worst of it, just not so much day to day.

"It's only Monday," I say, buying time. "You really plan ahead."

"I go to Ridgeway every weekend. I just thought maybe you'd like someone else to pick out clothes with besides Sarah 'Sweatpants' Gunderson for a change."

"I guess she's not invited."

"She can come."

"We don't really shop together," I say. It's never really occurred to me to wonder what Sarah wore all the time. "Does Sarah wear sweatpants a lot?"

"Only on days ending in *y*. Do you want to go?"

I don't. And, well...I kind of do. I don't want all the hassle, or pressure to get clothes that are too showy or aren't my style, but...since Dad died I haven't done any shopping besides the shoes yesterday. Shoes are about the only things I don't need some amount of help with.

"Don't you usually go with Lila and Kennedy?"

"Not always. It's okay if you don't want to."

I wonder if this is one of those times I should just go with it without over-analyzing everything.

Nope.

"Why are you asking now?"

"What do you mean?"

"We've never been shopping together and suddenly, on a random Monday afternoon, you want to go, but not till next weekend. What made you think of it?"

"Like I said, if you don't want to..." she says.

"I didn't say I didn't want to."

Silence.

"Nothing's easy with you, Peegee. Not one thing."

She sounds resigned, not angry. I feel a twinge because I know she's right. Then a thought occurs to me. "Is this because I'm an orphan now?"

Sigh. The kind that tells me how burdensome my friendship is to her.

"Yes, Parker, it's because you're a hopeless charity case." She closes her locker. "You just have to dissect everything around you like dead frogs."

I laugh. "Today's the first time since we met in kindergarten that you ask me to mall crawl and you're surprised I want to talk about why?"

"Did I say I was surprised?" she says. "Fine, I saw you in the mall yesterday buying shoes."

"Oh, you...Why didn't you say something? Ah...the Dynamic Trio."

She clears her throat—she hates that name. "I was alone. You were talking to a cute guy. I didn't want to break the spell."

"He was cute?" I say.

"Do you care?"

"Ha! See, you *do* know me. Wait, you were shopping alone?"

"There's a time for everything. But I bet you think

all shopping should be solo because you don't want anyone's help. Am I right?"

No way I'll ever admit that. "You're telling me you trust Lila and Kennedy's opinions about clothes more than your own?"

"It's not just about being helped. It's nice. It's fun."

"Nice? Fun?"

"You know what? I've changed my mind. You *do* have to go. Sarah and Molly, too. You can't walk around claiming to know everything if you've never even gone out shopping with friends. We're going this Saturday—it's decided."

Nobody, but nobody tells me what to do. Nobody.

"All right, then," I say.

Chapter 8

When I hear Aunt Celia's car I say goodbye to Molly and walk to the curb. I open the door and plop my bag on the floor and hop in. "It's me," Sheila says. "My mom couldn't come. My dad has work people coming over, so she's making a big dinner. Not for us, though—we're eating pizza in the living room."

It bugs me the way she always says *my* mom and *my* dad. I mean, whenever I talk to anyone about my parents, R.I.P., it's always *my* mom or *my* dad because it's not *their* mom or dad; but Sheila and I are cousins and even though her mom and dad aren't mine, I know them and we live together now and it just sounds weird. I don't know, it just bugs me.

"I'm surprised," I say. "Driving me without *your* mom here means *you're* breaking the law, but *your* mom's still an accessory if she knows about it. I always thought of her as someone who doesn't break the law for convenience."

"*Your* convenience. I told her you could walk home. It's too bad she said no—you could take your buddy Molly with you. She could lose a few pounds."

"What?"

She puts the car in gear and hits the accelerator. "Anyway, it's not against the law if it's to or from school and I have a signed note. Which I have. Wanna see it?"

"I can't...heyyyy, wait just a minute here," I say. "Are you kidding? You must be, since you know I'm blind and all, so I can't see notes or how fat or skinny anyone is. Or are you just being mean?"

"I was being sarcastic."

"Oh, really? You know what that word means?"

Silence.

"School's only two miles away," she says. "You really can just walk if you don't want anyone helping you."

"What I want is to be treated like everyone else. Until you start walking home from school every day, I'm perfectly happy getting picked up, too."

Silence.

"Thanks for the ride."

"You're welcome."

Our moms and dads would be so proud.

The radio turns on. News radio. Commercials. Sheila changes the station till she finds music. It's nothing I recognize but that's no surprise; I don't listen to music much.

"Who's this?" I ask.

"What?"

"The singer, who is it?"

"Ha, ha. We don't have to talk, you know. That's why the radio's on."

"Okay, you don't know either. You could have just said so."

"What are you talking about? It's *Kesha*. 'We R Who We R.' Everyone knows that."

I flop my hands a little—my equivalent of rolling my eyes—but I doubt Sheila understands. "She's the one who used to have the typo in her name, right? A dollar sign instead of an *S*?"

"God, Parker, you're just...so..."

My stomach tightens and I know why. It's this place I go that's somewhere between wanting to wind someone up because of their stupid assumptions and actually feeling bad about missing out on something. There's plenty I miss because I'm blind but a lot of things I don't. I saw rainbows when I was little—I know what they look like—I don't need to see them over and over. But there's plenty of new stuff I just can't keep up with.

"I'm just saying not everyone knows this song."

"You've never heard of Kesha." She says it flatly, like it's so inconceivable she has no idea which emotion to apply.

"You mean Keh Dollar Sign Ha...Yes, I've heard of her."

I don't have anything else to do—and it's playing loud now—so I listen. We pull into the driveway and stop but Sheila leaves the engine running till the song ends.

"Recognize it now?"

"Nope. Never heard it before."

"Wow, you're serious. How is that even possible?"

"What, you think everyone on the planet's heard that song?"

"No, but in every high school in America, yeah. I just figured...Never mind."

"What?" I hear in her voice that it's one of those feeling-awkward-around-the-blind-girl moments. "It's fine, just tell me."

"It's just...if I was...you know...I just figured you'd know more about music than anyone."

I shake my head. Where do I even start?

"How often do you just listen to music and nothing else?"

"I don't know. A lot."

"I mean no leafing through a magazine, no surfing the Interwebz, doing nothing but listening."

"I don't know—does it matter?"

"Not to you, but when you say *all the time* you really mean you read magazines, Web surf, do homework, with music on in the background."

"Of course. That's what everyone does—"

"*Not* everyone. To me, reading is listening. I can't listen to an audio textbook *and* music at the same time. And it takes me twice as long to listen to anything as it takes you to read it. Hell, you can tell right away if you're on the webpage you want while it takes me five minutes just to figure out that I'm not and hit the links to the right page. So I can either spend most of my time reading and working to keep up with school, or I can listen to music a lot and do nothing else and guarantee that when I graduate—*if* I graduated—I'd be fucked with zero education and then what would I do to take care of myself?"

After a moment, keys jangle. "Okaaay."

"It's fine—you didn't know. I don't get mad at people for not knowing. I get mad at people for thinking they do know."

"Well...what'd you think of the song?"

"I don't know. It's all about cutting loose and having fun, and the tune's catchy, but it also sounds like what's probably going through a stripper's head when she sees all these guys turned on by her but knows deep down all they care about is her tits and ass and nobody will ever really love her. So I guess I like how it sounds but not what it says. Do you like it?"

Silence.

"I used to. I think you just ruined it." She leaves and slams the door.

"Don't shoot the messenger."

*

"Faith and I are going to Ridgeway on Saturday to do some shopping," I tell Sarah. "Want to come?"

"Hang on, Parker, the phone garbled you there. Either that or you just said something totally random. If I ask you to say it again, I'll bet you say something completely different this time."

"Faith and I are going to Ridgeway on Saturday to do some shopping. Want to come?"

"Ha. You want me to go shopping. With you and Faith."

"And Molly, but I haven't asked her yet."

"Hang on a second. My world turned upside down. Okay, I'm fine now. Say it again."

"Come on, it'll be fun."

"Who *are* you?"

"You can buy some new sweatpants."

"What?! What did that bitch say to you?"

I laugh. And I keep laughing because she said it to be funny, in a self-aware ironic way, but I can also tell she meant it.

"She has to dress up fancy because she doesn't have a boyfriend. And I'll have you know sweatpants are very comfortable."

I'm laughing too hard to contribute.

"That's...it..." I finally gasp. "I knew there was some deeply buried reason why you're still with Rick. He's your excuse to wear comfy clothes!"

"What's your excuse?"

"Oh, you know I don't need one, Sarah. The real mystery is why the rest of you do."

"Sad but true. I have no answer other than out of sight, out of mind."

"Very funny," I say. "Oh, hey, is Molly heavy?"

"Um, yeah. Why?"

"Sheila said something. And it solves a minor mystery that's been at the back of my mind, why I hear Molly breathe hard sometimes. And her chairs creak. And Rick talks about her lunch in ways that sound weird but I always forget to ask you about later."

"Yeah, he's an asshole but doesn't know it. She's definitely sturdy but not enormous. I think she'd actually be very pretty if she wasn't so heavy."

"Is that what you think?" I say. "Skinnier is prettier?"

"*No.* You know what I mean. Well, okay, maybe

you don't. The point is, there are girls who are crazy pretty who end up going to Hollywood and never pay for anything the rest of their lives. Sometimes they get really heavy and aren't as pretty anymore, but you can still tell by looking at them that if they lost the weight they'd be gorgeous. Bone structure, I guess. I think that might be Molly."

"Okay, this is getting weird."

"Oh? Since when do you not like this kind of conversation?"

"Who said anything about not liking it? But you know I don't care what people *look* like unless it affects what they *are* like."

"Maybe that's true for Molly. I don't know her well enough. She's a tough read."

"So are you, Sarah. So are you."

"Well, some of us have to balance out you broadcasters."

"Moving on..."

"Okay, who's Jason?"

"What?! What did that bitch tell you?"

Sarah snickers. She's so subdued all the time I consider it a victory; I can't even put into words how good it feels when I get her to laugh, or even just her little versions of it.

"She said she saw you at the mall chatting up some hot guy—"

"He was helping me buy shoes! He was an employee!"

"I don't know what you're getting all defensive about. It's just a simple question."

"Wait a minute...I never told Faith his name."

"Maybe he was wearing a name tag."

Damn people and their damn eyes.

"So...tell me about him."

"What's there to tell? I went to Running Rampant, bought a pair of running shoes, and the guy that helped me is from Jefferson. I can't tell you what he looked like, and he sounded...normal, I guess, which is a plus in this world. What do you want me to say?"

"I want you to tell me why Faith stood outside the store for ten minutes watching you."

"Jesus, she spied on me for ten minutes? That's creepy."

"She said when you talk to people you're usually like a little pill bug, all dark and closed up, but with this guy, you were open and glowing—"

"Glowing? She said I was *glowing*?"

"Direct quote. And you were waving your arms around. She was worried you might smack him or knock something over."

"I was not waving my arms around!" Was I?

"She said you were a waving lunatic."

"I wasn't."

"Fine. I'm not going to let you change the subject. Answer the question."

"I forget. What was it?"

"Stop being so coy. What made this guy so special?"

"I never said—"

"Parker!"

"All right!" I take a breath. "I don't know what it was."

"You're admitting to being at a loss for words? Careful, I don't think I can handle my world turning upside down twice in one conversation."

I take another breath. "All I can say is, he knew how to talk to a blind girl."

"Damn, girl, that's all you needed to say."

Chapter 9

Today's going to be a shitty day. Sometimes you just know.

After my alarm woke me up, Stephen Hawking reminded me that a week from tomorrow is Dad's birthday. I have reminders set up early for things I need time to prepare for. I deleted it.

At Gunther Field I have this feeling I'm being watched. I stop at a couple of turns and stand perfectly still to listen. Once I call out to see if anyone's there; I don't hear anything. Just paranoid about that coach watching me last Friday.

As if that's not enough, I get a text from Molly saying she's staying home sick—with symptoms too unpleasant to describe—probably just something she ate so she'll be back tomorrow. Classes will be a pain today.

All leading up to me sitting in Trig before the bell, regretting my decision to come to school at all since

I'll just catch up with Molly on everything tomorrow when she's back.

"Scott," Ms. McClain says. "Molly's not here today. Can you help Parker this period?"

My next heartbeat is painfully fierce and my mouth opens to deflect this request but someone beats me to it.

"I'll do it!" D.B. says, sounding way too eager, but I'm desperate so I'll take it.

"I don't know..." Ms. McClain says. Is she trying but failing to keep the dubious tone from her voice, or is she deliberately injecting it?

"I'm already sitting right here," D.B. says.

"It's okay," Scott says, his voice like a wink. "It's not like he has to *teach* Parker anything. He just has to tell her what's on the board. He's smart enough to do that much."

D.B. laughs. It sounds genuine. Either this is okay trash talk or D.B. doesn't know an insult when he hears it.

"Do I have a say in this?" I ask, invoking a variation of Rule Six.

"I'll leave it to you, Parker," Ms. McClain says, and

starts talking to someone else up in the front of the class.

I point toward Scott, then D.B., and back again. "Eeny meeny miny moe, catch a douchebag by his toe, if he...whines then let him go, eeny meeny miny moe."

My finger is pointing to D.B., as planned. When doing Eeny Meeny with only two choices, always point to the one you *don't* want first.

"Cool," D.B. says. "I'll move to Molly's seat so I don't have to twist around." He executes this maneuver with an amazing amount of clatter, like a one-man band changing seats on a bus. The bell rings.

Ms. McClain talks for a while. Then the squeak of marker on the board tells me she's writing.

"She's drawing a circle," D.B. whispers loud enough they can probably hear it across the hall. People giggle.

"I can't see," I whisper, in an actual whisper, "but my hearing is excellent."

"Uhhh...Oh, am I too loud?" More giggles. Ms. McClain ignores it.

"Well, louder than I need, anyway."

"Sorry," he whispers, just as loudly. "Now she's drawing lines from the middle to the...circle part...I don't know how to tell you where the lines are going... They're like spokes on a bike tire."

"Wheel."

"What?"

"On a wheel, not a tire. Never mind. Just think of a clock. Where are the lines going?"

"Huh?"

"Like, twelve o'clock, three o'clock?"

"Oh yeah. Twelve, one, two, three...like all the numbers, pretty much. Wait, more than twelve... like..." He mumbles some, then, "Fifteen or sixteen."

"So...she's drawing a unit circle?"

"What's that? She's putting those numbers around the outside like she did last week, like square root of two and stuff. Is that right?"

I resist the urge to remind him that I can't verify anything he's describing. "Sounds right to me," I whisper, even quieter than last time to see if I can bring his voice down.

"Why's it called that?" he asks, a bit louder, like he's trying to bring my voice up.

"Well, it's just a circle with a radius of one. It doesn't matter whether it's one inch or one mile, it's just one whatever unit, so they call it a unit circle."

"Yeah but so what?"

"Well, she's writing angles on it, right? And how long the lines are? It's just like in geometry with those special triangles, like a 45-45-90 triangle has a hypotenuse that's the length of a side times the square root of two. Except if the radius of the circle was two, all those numbers would need a two in front of them but that's not the point. It's like reducing a fraction; you divide out the common factors and you're left with...well, a unit circle."

"Okaaay...but so what? What's it for?"

At that moment I realize the room is dead quiet. No talking, no squeaking.

"That's probably what she's about to tell us," I whisper.

"Correct on all counts, Parker," Ms. McClain says. "Have you taken any trigonometry before?"

"No. When Molly and I do homework we look ahead to see what's coming. It makes it easier to follow what's going on in class."

"That's something you all should be doing," she says. "Especially those of you who *can* see the board but *can't* seem to keep your eyes open this early."

Clunk shuffle clatter. "Hey!" Laughter.

I guess she kicked some guy's chair to wake him up—I don't know the voice—there are lots of voices I don't know yet.

Luckily what follows is twenty minutes of talking without much writing on the board. Then she passes out worksheets for us to collaborate on and then it's D.B. reading to me. He's better at describing triangles than circles: "It has a little square in the corner, and the small side is a one, and the slanty side is a two, and the angle is between the little side and the slanty side, and they want to know what the sine is..." I pretty much know the answers right away, but he doesn't, so I walk him through it all. I get him to say *sine* instead of *sin* but I can't get him to say *hypotenuse* at all. I think he's afraid it conflicts with his masculinity, like saying *chartreuse* or *armoire*.

We finish almost at the same moment the bell rings.

"Hey, Parker?" he says while we pack up. He's

actually whispering now. "Thanks for helping me, okay?"

Hearing this makes me flush a bit. Like I've done something wrong. Have I?

"Thanks for helping *me*," I say. "Um, your name's Stockley, right?"

"Yeah. I guess you heard someone else call me that, huh?"

I feel a twinge. He said it in a normal voice so I can't tell if it's a dig from our first conversation or a coincidence.

"Ms. McClain, yeah."

"My name's Kent Stockley but people just call me Stockley, I guess 'cause of football and I wear my jersey a lot. But you can call me D.B."

"But it means…" I'm not sure where to go with this.

"Nah, we all call each other douchebag all the time, me and Scott and Oscar and…well, everybody. But I like D.B. better."

"Okay. Then I guess it's only fair that you can call me P.G."

"Does anyone else call you that?"

"Just Faith."

"Faith...Faith Beaumont?"

"Yeah."

"Wow, okay, cool. Hey, we should hang out sometime."

"Oh, I don't hang out with Faith."

"Yeah, well...I...okay, see you tomorrow."

I can't tell if that was an actual goodbye, as in he's walking away, or not.

"Okay, later," I say.

It occurs to me that he maybe was asking to hang out with me, not with me to get to Faith. I feel myself frowning and relax my face. I'm used to people wanting Faith, not me, which suits me fine, but I don't like it when I misunderstand anything.

"D.B.?" I say.

No answer.

Then Scott says, "He's gone."

I concentrate on closing up my bag. I'm afraid that even saying "Okay" would open a conversation.

"See you tomorrow," Scott says. "Unless you see me first."

The room is quiet enough now that I hear him walk away and out the door.

See you tomorrow…unless you see me first.

That's what Scott used to say to me instead of goodbye, for years. For *four whole years*. A part of me remembers the warmth I used to feel when he said it, a warmth like no other.

My heart pounds in my chest and in my ears.

Damn you, Scott Kilpatrick…You don't get to say these things to me anymore.

*

It's harder to get to the curb right after school, where everyone else is going, instead of the library where usually only Molly and I go. People are hustling toward the parking lot, jostling each other, or maybe just me. As I navigate from the hedges by the office down the stairs I get seven apologies, some of them sincere. At the parking lot nobody speaks to me but that doesn't necessarily mean anything.

"Sheila?" I say in a normal indoor voice.

"What?" she says, not far to my left.

"Were you going to say anything?"

"I just did."

Whatever.

No, not whatever.

"You know it's rude to just stand there without saying anything?"

"You know it's rude to tell people you think they're rude?"

I laugh. That was pretty funny. I don't hear Sheila laugh.

"Are you smiling?" I ask.

"No. Why should I?"

"Oh, I don't know," I say, a bit sad. "If someone makes a joke but doesn't know it's a joke, is it still a joke?"

"What are you talking about?"

"Philosophy, I guess."

"Whatever."

Yes, whatever.

I hear a familiar voice behind me say, "Hello, Parker Grant."

Jason walks up beside me. "How're you doing?"

"Oh, you know—" I catch my arms swinging up and remember what Sarah said about what Faith said and I quickly drop my arms to my sides. I shrug. "Just another Tragic Tuesday."

"Oh? Why tragic?"

I have absolutely no idea why I said that. Maybe because it rhymed? Or alliterated? Well, both words start with *T* anyway. I feel strangely unbalanced, distracted by hearing what I'm saying and wanting it to actually mean something.

"I don't know…" My arms rise and I clamp them down again. "Aren't all Tuesdays tragic, really?"

"Um—"

"Hey," I quickly say to derail this tragic conversational turn. "This is my cousin, Sheila Miller." I gesture a bit and force my hand down again. "Sheila, this is Jason Freeborn."

"Hi."

"Hi."

"We live together." I hear how funny that sounds but I don't want to get into it all now. "So…when are tryouts?"

"Tomorrow and Thursday after school. You coming?"

"Mmmm…" As much as I want to say yes, it just doesn't make sense. "I don't think so. I don't get a lot out of sitting on bleachers."

"Not to watch. To try out."

Okay, something's not right. Treating everyone the same is one thing, playful banter is another, but asking a blind girl if she's going out for track...

"Try out for what?"

"For track. What's your distance?"

"What makes you think I have a distance? Because I bought a pair of shoes? If you think everyone who buys shoes from you actually runs with them I have some bad news for you."

"Oh. You don't run?" He actually sounds disappointed. Maybe just confused. "I thought..."

Damn it, how did I back myself into this corner?

"Well, no, I mean yes, I do. Run, I mean. I just didn't..." *Didn't know how you could know that? Shit, that makes no sense.*

"Are you as confused as I am?" he says.

"Not really," Sheila says. "This is pretty normal for her. I'm used to it. It helps not to listen closely."

"Ja-SON!" a deep voice bellows from across the parking lot. "Let's GO!"

"That's my ride. See you around."

He trots away.

"Shit." *Shit, shit, shit.*

"Parker," Sheila says.

"What?"

"I'm smiling."

Chapter 10

I don't know why my brain does this to me. I occasionally dream things that really happened, almost exactly how they happened, and it's usually things I specifically try *not* to think about when I'm awake. My brain is a troll sometimes.

The dream I had was of that perfect day two and a half years ago. It felt wonderful for a moment when I woke, when I was still the Parker who didn't know what came next, and then reality slapped my face. Yet now my mind keeps trying to think about those good times anyway, to recapture that feeling, but I know the truth and won't let it. As an antidote I try to replay the conversation I had with Jason in the mall.

It doesn't work. The stupid, misfired conversation I had with him yesterday in the parking lot keeps intruding. I try to think of nothing instead, which pretty much guarantees the thoughts I don't want will rush in to fill the void.

I try something else. I reach out with my mind, floating into the hallway like a ghost, passing relatives I barely know, a neighborhood of people who barely know me, out into the wide, blank world...while back in my bed wrapped in blankets I'm crushed and alone. I'm glad for the good friends I have, but they can't fill the space of a mom or dad who will always love me no matter what, and neither friends nor family can provide that special warmth I felt one time and somehow know, deep down, I'll never feel again.

I tap the clock—4:47 AM. I'm unsettled and can tell sleep isn't going to come soon. I can't stop my troll brain from going back to the dream I just had. They were very happy memories once and I only push them away now because of what happened later. Maybe if I can separate them out, to live those moments again the way they felt at the time, when they were still happy, before it all went to shit...

*

It's springtime, dawn on a Saturday. On my way to run in Gunther Field, I hear music.

This happens sometimes, where the city holds an

event or there's a party or a wedding, though usually not this early. Always inconvenient—thankfully rare—seldom lasting more than a day. This time I'm especially disappointed because I really need to run today. It's the anniversary of the crash, when my mom left and took my sight with her.

I wish anniversaries meant nothing to me—after all they're just days like any other. What's the significance of saying *on this day last year* instead of *at this time yesterday*, or *on this day of the week a month ago*...it's all arbitrary. But logic doesn't help. On this day seven years ago I lost more than I thought I could bear, and I can't stop thinking about it.

I almost turn back for home but there's something strange about the music. Not the music itself, but the fact that it's the only sound. No voices, no footsteps, no rustling, nothing else at all. I keep going until I reach the field.

It's the soundtrack to *Grease*.

"Scott?" I call.

No answer.

It can't be a coincidence. His mom plays this

CD so often—it reminds her of Scott's dad—that we eventually learned all the songs and occasionally bust out singing when we're over there.

I walk out onto the field toward the music until I'm standing over it. I reach down and find a CD player. Lying on it is a large piece of heavy paper like a big index card. I pick it up and feel bumps. Braille.

Parker. Are you busy today? I want to show you something. Text me if you want and I will be there in two minutes. Scott.

I smile. Grade 1 braille, no contractions. Made with what feels like little blobs of glue. Must have taken forever. What's he up to?

I text him: *Where r u?*

"Corner of Orchard and Hess." I have his text-to-speech voice set to an Australian accent. It drives him crazy when he hears it.

Just sitting there?

"Waiting to see if you text."

What do u want to show me?

"Lots."

This is taking forever.

Come here.

As promised, I hear a bike, in way less time than two minutes.

"Hey," he says.

"Hey. What are you doing out this early?"

"I want to show you something, but first I want to take you to breakfast."

"I dunno. My dad—"

"I already talked to him. He wants you to text him if you decide to go."

"Go where?"

"Jody's."

I laugh. "That's miles away."

"Seven point two. Should take us about half an hour."

I laugh again. "What, on your bike? There's no way in hell I'm riding double on your bike! Not for seven point two miles; not for seven point two feet!"

"It's not my bike. It's yours."

"Uh..."

"Well, just for this weekend. I rented it for you. It's a tandem bike."

"What's that mean? It steers itself?"

He sings his answer. "It's a bicycle built for two. I'll do the steering and braking. You can do the peddling to get your workout this morning since I interrupted your run."

"You rented...?" And instantly I feel light, as if gravity suddenly turned down by half. My friends and I do little things for each other all the time—well, them more than me, to be honest, because it's harder for me—but this is bigger than most things.

"Want to go?"

I nod. While I text Dad, Scott hides the CD player in the bushes.

It's my first time on a bike since before the accident. It takes a couple blocks to learn to lean together with the turns...Now it's like flying. Riding a bike before was never like this. Without seeing the world go by at a plodding ten miles an hour, only feeling it, it seems so much faster. I've had friends tell me they like to close their eyes on roller coasters, to feel the excitement of moving fast in the dark. They're right; it's exhilarating.

"Having fun?" Scott calls back.

"Yes!" I shout into the wind and pump the pedals hard.

I wish I could trade places with Scott so he could

feel what I feel, but I can't steer for him and I don't want anyone else to.

This unexpected thought, the selfishness of it, shocks me. Why wouldn't I want my best friend to feel this thrill just because someone else would have to be on the bike with him? I know the answer as soon as I ask. It makes my stomach flutter that I suddenly want something so much that it makes me feel...possessive.

As soon as we open the door to Jody's Diner we're greeted by shouts: Sarah, Faith, and Philippa. (This was before Philippa moved back to Greece and before Faith had traveled down her path to becoming part of the Dynamic Trio.) Scott confesses that he texted everyone once I agreed to go to breakfast and Dad rounded them all up and dropped them off while we were pedaling over. For the next hour and a half we eat strawberry pancakes and get sticky with syrup and throw strawberries and shriek and nobody who works there complains at all.

When we've exhausted the possibilities we call Dad for a pickup. Philippa hints that she wants a ride on the bike. I don't say anything, hoping it'll just fade away, but she says it again and Scott says we can all take turns on it later since it's rented all weekend. He says it in a way that makes it nice to Philippa but also clear that I'll be riding home with him.

I pedal slower on the way back and not because I'm tired.

"You said you wanted to show me something. Was it the bike? Or was it breakfast?" I don't think it was either of these—I hope there's more—but I don't want it to sound like I'm expecting anything or ungrateful getting this much.

"Nope," he calls over the wind. "It's at your house."

"What is it?"

"You'll find out."

When we get home everyone is waiting and they make fun of how long it took us to get there. After a few chaotic minutes, including a strange request to make sure we've all gone to the bathroom, Scott lines us up on the long sofa in the living room and turns on the TV.

"We're going to watch TV?" I ask. "You know I can't see, right?"

"There will be no seeing today!" he says.

He plops down on the sofa next to me. "Hold out your hand."

I do and he lifts it to his face. He's wearing a blindfold.

I laugh and he says, "We're all wearing them."

We thrash around so I can feel everyone's blindfolds. Sarah's wearing my White with Blue Polka Dots, Philippa has my Yellow with Smiley Faces, Faith my Solid Scarlet, and Scott my Starry Night. I had chosen Googly Eyes this morning, which now seems appropriate.

We settle down again, sort of, while we wait for the movie to start. I think about how much Scott and I are touching: our arms, our hips, our thighs, smashed together on the couch. This much contact wasn't all that unusual; what's new is how much I'm noticing it.

The show begins. For the next eleven hours it's the *Lord of the Rings* trilogy with Descriptive Audio turned on. It's *hilarious*. Listening to the narrator quickly and dispassionately give deadpan descriptions of Frodo's weepy expressions, arrows penetrating eye sockets, Arwen's soulful looks of immortal love, and the decapitations of countless orcs have us roaring with laughter one moment and shushing each other the next.

Dad makes sandwiches for lunch and orders pizza for dinner and we eat both without stopping the DVDs or taking off our blindfolds. It's night when the final movie ends.

Scott and I squeeze together into the front of the car while the girls sit in the back and Dad drives them each home. Scott comes back with us.

He and I walk to Gunther Field to get his CD player, and after spending so much time squished together on the couch we're freely bouncing off each other as we walk drunkenly down the sidewalk. Halfway to the field, we bump again and he grabs my hand.

This doesn't startle me and I realize I'd wanted this as we walked, touching "accidentally" off and on, but hadn't put words to it. I squeeze his hand.

In the center of the field, I stop. I want to say something but I'm afraid it's going to come out wrong or sound stupid or somehow ruin everything. I'm overwhelmed, and I don't just mean because I'm holding hands with my best friend.

It's obvious what happened today. After four years

watching me be a basket case on this anniversary, he orchestrated a way to keep me busy and laughing all day long. And he did it as though it was just another day, without saying a word about what he was really doing.

I'm so grateful and warm I don't know what to do, yet I have to do something to tell him I understand and how much this means to me.

"Parker?" Scott says. "You okay?"

He's facing me, holding my left hand. I raise my right hand a bit and he clasps it too.

"Thanks," I say.

I want to say more, but I just add, "For today. Thanks for today."

Scott laughs softly.

"What?"

"Your scarf's crooked."

I don't want to let go of his hands so I shake my head a bit to settle it and the two big googly eyes rattle. I must look like an idiot.

"It's like you're looking...I dunno...all cockeyed."

"Straighten it."

I reluctantly let him go and he adjusts my scarf.

He leaves his hands above my ears, and I tip my head till our foreheads touch. We stand there awhile, rolling our heads back and forth a bit, like we're dancing without music. Then he drops his hands to my shoulders and slides his head over till our cheeks are pressed together. He slips his cheek slowly across mine. I stop breathing as his lips skim over my skin until he kisses me lightly on the lips...

I burst into tears.

"Oh Parker, no, I'm sorry! I'm sorry, Parker. Please..."

"No no no..." I put my hands on his cheeks and try to kiss him a few times, clumsily getting closer to the right spot on his lips. "It's okay..."

But my crying turns to sobbing and I can't stop. I want to ask him if he watched a YouTube video on how to kiss a blind girl because if he hasn't, he could make one. Or tell him how I didn't know it was possible to feel like this and how dizzy I am over it. Or how he understands me so well that he could make this perfect day for me, and care enough to actually do it, when I'd expected my annual day of complete misery. And all this is mixed with the unavoidable grief that crushes me on this day every year, which makes it all the more indescribable.

"I didn't mean to—"

"Shhh!" I say, getting back some of my voice. "You knew I was going to cry eventually. Thanks to you I almost lasted the whole day." I wrap my arms around him and push my face into his neck. He holds me while I let out the tears my useless eyes made and need to release.

*

So began the best two weeks of my life before it all crashed and burned. And it turns out I'm not one of those girls who can sit comfortably in cognitive dissonance, enjoying the feelings like they're real while also knowing deep down they're not, like it's just a Hollywood set: a nice-looking house out front but no actual rooms inside. The beauty of that day, at the time, wasn't just what happened, it was what it meant. Only I learned later it didn't mean what I thought it did. That realization didn't just destroy the future, it ruined the past. And like many of my other tragedies, my dreams won't let me forget it.

Lying in bed, I regret letting these memories in. I'm trembling, my face is heating up, my throat is tightening...but the Star Chart on the back of my door has eighty-five stars on it and I'll be goddamned if I break my streak over a stupid boy.

Yet, how can that boy who held me that day be the same one who tricked me two weeks later? It doesn't add up. At the time I shut it all down and refused to think about it or wallow in those tarnished memories, but now sifting through it all again, it makes no sense. And beneath it all I hear a tiny voice I've always refused to listen to, wanting to know *why* it happened, *how* it was even possible.

Doesn't matter. I won't be one of those girls who falls in love with the nice half of a guy and excuses or turns a blind eye, or two blind eyes, to the bastard half. Fuck you, Scott, I don't care how it was possible. It was and nothing else matters. Rule Number One. Rule Number Infinity. Done.

I tap the clock again. 4:58 AM. Still dark out.

Doesn't matter. I throw back the covers and stand up.

I don't need light to run. I don't need light for anything.

Chapter 11

I leave my lunch in my locker—no time for it now; no stomach for it, either—and I grab the duffel bag I hastily packed this morning. I told Molly she didn't have to come but she was happy to ditch her lunch, too. I'd prefer to be alone, to be honest, but I also don't know this side of the school as well and I could use the help. Lunch is only fifty minutes long and I don't know where I'll find Coach Underhill.

"Hello, ladies," Jason says, off to our left. "I'd ask if you come here often but I know you don't. Not this year, anyway."

I start to answer but Molly beats me to it. "Hey, Jason. What happened? That looks painful."

"Oh, pffft...some road rash. Just a stupid fall. I wanted to gauze it up so it wouldn't gross out everyone but Coach says let it breathe."

"Looks like it hurts," she says in a wrinkled-up-nose voice.

"You guys coming to watch or run? Tryouts aren't until after school."

"That's what Parker said. Isn't track in the spring?"

"Yeah, but we have tryouts now to concentrate fall training on people who are on the team, not just anyone who shows up. Want a tour?"

I want to remind him that he's been here two weeks to my two years, though he probably does know this side already much better than I do. He seems to know Molly, too.

Instead I say, "Is Coach Underhill around?"

"Usually," Jason says. "C'mon."

We walk toward the field, I think. I'm kind of disoriented with nothing but grass underfoot and the sun overhead.

"How are those new shoes working out, Parker?"

"You're right, spring-foam is bullshit."

He laughs. "Yeah. Sorry."

There's a moment of grass crunching, and then he says, "I, uh, guess you probably already know your way around here, huh?"

I shrug. "Not really. I did weight training with Coach Rivers and hardly ever go to the field. I'm not much of a spectator."

"But you said you run."

"I do. Every day. Just not here."

"I can't remember from yesterday...we were talking, and I asked you what your—"

"Hundred meters," I say.

"Really?"

"Why? What's wrong with that?"

"Nothing. I mean, I just figured you for a longer distance."

"The way I run, a hundred meters is plenty long."

"How *do* you run?"

"What do you mean?" I'm suspicious again. Am I reading too much into things? Generally yes, but this time?

"Well, you said a hundred meters is long the way you run, so what way is that?"

"Oh. Like the devil's chasing me."

He laughs. "I get it. No throttle. That's cool."

"What—" I stop myself. What am I doing with all these questions? But I can't help it. "What does that mean?"

"Don't be paranoid," he says in a just-joking voice.

"It means you don't pace yourself. For a hundred meters you don't have to. How about you, Molly. Going to give it a try?"

"This isn't what you call a runner's physique," she says. "My distance is from the couch to the refrigerator and back." Her words insult herself but her tone calls him a jerk.

"Fair enough," he says, then he calls out, "Coach Underhill! Hey Coach!"

My stomach tightens. I don't want to have this conversation at all, much less with anyone else listening, and I wonder what I'm doing here. A few possible answers flit around me but I can't tell if they're mine or my troll brain's. I shoo them away.

*

It's not as bad as I feared, though not as good either. Probably because I always have high hopes and low expectations. Either way I'm glad Coach Underhill sent Jason and Molly packing so we could talk alone.

Apparently guide wires are no longer used because they slow you down too much. Sounds like a terrible idea anyway. Having someone stand at the finish line and call out when you're veering out of your lane is another way, but only for practice since it's not allowed in competition. I don't understand why—doesn't seem like it would bother anyone else, but I guess it wouldn't work with more than one blind runner in a race. Only guide runners are allowed, where the pair either hold on to each other or to a short connecting rope.

It stinks. First off, you need a partner or you can't run, which sucks all by itself. Then your guide needs to be able to keep up so already you're admitting you can't win because you can't even enter unless you bring someone who's faster than you. So much for empowering the disabled.

Before I can tell him I've changed my mind, he says the first step is to see how fast I run to match me up with possible guides. He guesses what my duffel bag is for and says we can do it now if I hurry and change since there aren't many people on the track. Somehow the rush of it all leads me through the locker room—which I'd happily said goodbye to forever last spring—and I find my way back to the track with Molly's help, bouncing on my toes and stretching and running in place to warm up. Coach sends Molly into the stands and I don't know where Jason is but as soon as this thought pops into my head I feel unsettled...tipsy...uncomfortable about what I've gotten myself into.

"Just to get a basic time for a hundred meters," Coach says, "it's better for you to run the field instead of the oval. I'll call you from the fifty-yard line and then run backwards to stay ahead. Nothing fancy—I'll just say *right* or *left* if you're veering too much. Just adjust in the direction I say, all right?"

"Okay."

"You ever use starting blocks before?"

"No."

"All right, let's not worry about that now—we just want a ballpark time. Here, take my arm."

I put out my hand and a hairy forearm pushes up against my palm. He leads me a few steps and we adjust till I'm standing in the "end zone," whatever that means.

A minute later I hear him call from far ahead. "Point at me!"

I do. He says, "Turn to your left...stop! Okay, now you're pointing straight at me—that's your direction.

I've got the pistol. Tell me when you're ready!"

What does getting ready look like? At Gunther Field I just *go* without any grand or official starting postures. I'm adrift and something else feels wrong. I realize why. Even on my home turf I walk the length of the field before I run. This seems more important than ever now.

"Hang on!" I call. "I need to do this walking first."

The artificial grass is bristly—not as soft as real grass yet not as hard as sidewalk—but strangely flat. It feels odd to have the surface I'm about to run on be so featureless without being firm.

"Right...more to the right," Coach says.

I veer a little.

"Not so much. You're very good at walking a straight line. Lots of practice?"

"Lots of Dad time."

"We're here," he says. "Touchdown. Ready to run it now?"

No. But I nod anyway. What the hell am I doing? Why am I doing it? And why am I *still* doing it even after asking these questions and having no answers?

"Go, Parker!" Molly calls from the sidelines. "Run

like the wind!"

In addition to my usual black running clothes, I'm wearing my hachimaki today. I hope this doesn't turn into a Kamikaze run...

"I see the devil coming!" Jason shouts. "He looks pretty fast!"

"All right, you two," Coach barks. "And the rest of you in the peanut gallery, stay put!"

The rest of you?!

"Point at me!" Coach calls from ahead. I do. "Perfect. Tell me when you're ready!"

I crouch a bit, right foot back, left foot forward. "Ready!"

What...the hell...am I doing?

"Ready...Set..." *CRACK!*

Divine Wind.

I don't know where I'm going and should be worried running blind in a strange place for the first time but after years of practice my body knows how to do this and I'm not afraid. I'm counting steps and I pass thirty so I'm probably halfway and there's nothing to hit and there are people here to warn me if I get off track—

"Right!" Coach says and his voice is *a lot* closer than I expect...

...and my wheels slip off the rails...

...and the train wreck begins...

I remember something like this from when I was a little kid, running downstairs, feet in a rhythm in time with gravity's pull as your body drops down, down—*thump thump thump*—and then suddenly you think about what you're doing and something changes...Your brain was controlling your feet automatically but then you're suddenly handed the controls and now you're aware of needing to execute every single step one at a time, like thinking about your breathing and then your body stops doing it and you have to take over and do it yourself and wonder how you can *stop* doing it and give control back to whatever part of your brain normally does it when you're not paying attention, but your brain just hands you the steering wheel while you're running down the stairs and suddenly you're driving but incapable of handling this speed and in that moment you either manage to slow down, you stumble, or you fall.

"Parker!" Molly shouts, as if this might help as I fly into the darkness, barely managing to pull in my arms and turn my right shoulder in to take the force of the fall and roll.

My shoulder aches and feels scratched but I'm all right. I want to jump up like nothing happened, to minimize the amount of time people see me sprawled out on the plastic grass...then I remember I don't care. I'd much rather lie here and rest a minute. I roll onto my back and flop my arms out.

And then everyone's around me, over me, buzzing, Molly especially.

"Parker, are you okay? Did you trip on something?"

"Just myself," I say, breathing heavy. "It's hard to explain, but really, you know, since I'm blind, you probably should have been surprised if I *didn't* trip."

"Go on, step back, everyone," Coach says. "Can you stand?"

"Oh, definitely. But I really don't want to."

"Come on, people, back up, let her breathe."

"Yeah," I say. "Give her air. And warm sun on her face. Someone's in her light." Whoever it is moves because now I feel the warmth again.

"Seriously, stand up," Coach says. "Let's make sure you're okay."

I sigh, outwardly, and groan a little. I slowly stand up and people applaud. Too many to count but I guess not more than a dozen so not too bad.

"I was just kidding about the devil," Jason says.

I smirk. "I wasn't."

"You're fine," Coach says. "You're seeping out of that shoulder. It needs to be washed and dressed before you change or you'll get your shirt bloody."

"So how'd I do? What was my time? Do I make the team?" I use my wry voice; I'm not sure I want to do this again.

"Well, you'll have to learn to use a starting block," Coach says.

"That shouldn't be too hard."

"And how to run a hundred meters without taking a dirt dive."

"Dirt would've been softer." I rub my shoulder. It's wet and warm and stickier than sweat. Now I guess I have a bloody hand and I hold it out awkwardly to not get blood on my clothes. Then I remember what I'm wearing and wipe my hand on my shorts.

"That won't be the hardest thing. I knew you'd have a slow start without a block, so I ran two watches to time each fifty meters separately. I stopped the first watch at the halfway point before you fell. Six point eight seconds."

Jason laughs.

"What? Why is that funny?" I don't know what a good time should be—I've never timed myself before. "And show some respect. Have you forgotten that I'm *bleeding*?"

Jason laughs again. "Oh, you'll get plenty of respect, Parker. What you won't get is a good running guide."

"Why not?" I'm getting heated, which is strange because I don't even want one.

"Freeborn's right," Coach says. "Unless there are more surprises this afternoon, we don't have anyone who could keep up with you."

Chapter 12

Molly and I finish our homework. She has to talk to her mom about something and said she'd meet me out at the parking lot in a bit. I'm in the middle of organizing my stuff when I hear the *quack* that means a text from Sarah.

"How's the arm, sugar?" Sarah asks. She knows I have her text-to-speech voice set to Matron, which sounds like a middle-aged woman from the South, and sometimes hams it up.

I text back: *Turns out your ego is kept in your shoulders...Who knew?*

I'm not going to need anything from school at home tonight so I dump the bulky stuff into my locker. I hear footsteps and rowdy voices coming closer. Track tryouts are probably ending about now. I don't hurry. Maybe Jason will see me and come over.

Quack. "Bruised, huh? Well, bless your heart. Glad it's nothing permanent."

Already yesterday's news...at least it will be tomorrow.

"Look who it is," says a guy with a familiar voice I can't quite place.

"Parker Grant," says another, a voice I definitely recognize. The skin tightens across my forehead and down my back. "I always thought you should wear Foster Grants instead of those stupid blindfolds."

Isaac Walters and Gerald Gibbons. Two of the seven who were hiding in the room that day. Their voices changed too, though not as much as Scott's. I take a deep breath and let it out slowly. It shouldn't be hard to ignore them since I can't even see them.

"Sooo," Isaac says, just to my left. "How ya been?"

Dad said that at his high school reunion the bullies weren't bullies anymore but they weren't apologizing either. It was like they thought they'd all been actors in a play called *High School* and they were themselves now, regular people. I can tell Isaac and Gerald are very far from this point. They're still in the roles of Asshole #1 and Asshole #2 in a play nobody else wants to be in.

"Not talking to us, huh?" Gerald says. "Looks like you haven't changed."

"You'd think a couple years of high school woulda loosed you up some."

My phone pops out of my hand.

"Give me my phone, Isaac."

"Hey, she remembers me! Sorry, Parker, *I* don't have your phone."

"All right then, *Gerry...*"

"Gerry? Nobody named Gerry here."

"Fine, Geraldine, whatever the fuck your name is."

"Geez, Parker, no one's gonna want to kiss that mouth."

"Mission accomplished," I say through clenched teeth. "Now give me my phone."

Quack.

They laugh.

"I don't *see* your phone," Isaac says. "But I *hear* a duck!"

"Don't worry, Isaac, she doesn't see her phone either, do you, Parker?"

"Seriously, guys?" I say. "Fucking grow up."

"You got a text from Sarah Gunderson—"

"Hey!" Gerald interrupts. "How is old short and dumpy?"

"She says: *K...call you tonight.* What should I tell her?"

I hear more footsteps. Swell. How many of the other five still hang out together?

Quack.

"Sarah's a duck!" Gerald says and they laugh again.

I do the math of where Isaac's voice and the *quack* came from and I do something stupid; I lunge out with both hands to grab my phone. Nothing but air.

"Whoa, hey now!" Isaac says. "You must really like ducks!"

I've had it with these assholes but there's not much I can do. At least I can stop playing their game. I slam my locker door shut and jam the padlock closed with a loud click.

"When you're done with my phone, bring it to me at the front office."

Under the sound of two idiots laughing, the approaching footsteps are running now.

"Hey, look who we bumped into," Isaac says to whoever's coming. "It's Parker Gr*uumph*!"—*Crash!*

My hands fly up instinctively to protect my face as something bangs hard against the lockers...twice... three times.

"What the hell—" *Crash!* "Cut it out!" *Crash!*

I press back against the lockers and keep my forearms crossed in front of me, hands open to block my face, tucked down. There's scuffling and squeaking shoes on concrete and more clattering metal.

"What's the matter with you!" Gerald squawks, his voice moving down the hall like he's being dragged away.

"Come on," Jason says, grunting from exertion. All the sounds move away down the hall and around the corner.

Quack. It's far away. I start walking toward it, one hand sliding along the lockers to keep me oriented. One set of footsteps returns.

"It's me," Jason calls. When he gets closer, he says, "Here's your phone."

I hold out my hand and the phone touches it. I quickly slip it into my bag.

"Sorry about that," he says. "Those guys are... they're just jerks. It was Isaac—"

"I know who they are. We went to Marsh together."

"Oh. Well, it's over now. I don't think they'll bother you again."

"Was bleeding involved?" I ask with my hopeful voice.

"No," he says, chuckling. "That would lead to questions nobody wants to answer. Street justice is about bruises, not blood. Deterrence is more about threats than actual violence."

"Sounded violent to me," I say.

"Only as much as it needed to be."

"Thanks for my phone."

"No problem. Where are you going? I'll walk with you."

I unfold my cane and we head for the parking lot.

"I heard you work in the library after school," he says. "I was coming to see you."

"What about?"

"Oh, it hardly seems right to ask now, after I just saved you. It might bias your answer."

My heart beats harder. It occurs to me that during the scuffle my heart rate didn't go up much at all, but *now...*

"You want to ask me something?" I say. "About homework, or...? We don't have any of the same classes."

God, I can't believe I said that.

"It's okay, we can talk about it later, maybe tomorrow."

No. Now. Right now.

"If it makes you feel better," I say in my sorry-to-have-to-tell-you voice, "the only thing you saved me from was more inconvenience and exasperation. I was headed for the office. Mr. Sullivan would have sorted it out pretty quickly. Those assholes can't hurt me with their one-syllable words, and they weren't actually going to bust out any real sticks and stones to break my bones."

"Uh...okay..." he says, like I'd given him a math problem. "I was just wondering if you wanted to do something Saturday. Night, I mean. Well, afternoon and then...I'm working till five, but after that—"

"Sure," I say. I swear my mouth said it before I even thought about it, all on its own. "What do you want to do?"

"Well, I can pick you up when I get off work—"

"Oh, I'll be at the mall Saturday. I can just meet you there. Five o'clock you said?"

"Perfect," he says. We arrive at the parking lot. "My ride's here. See you Saturday. Well, I'll probably see you tomorrow, and Friday, then Saturday."

"It's a date," I say. I feel a little corny but I don't care.

Jason trots away as other footsteps approach from behind.

"Did I hear the word *date*?" Molly asks.

"You did. Because I said it. And yes, I just wanted to hear it out loud."

"When?"

"Saturday night."

"Cool," she says, but she doesn't mean it.

This could mean any number of things and my troll brain is going to run through the entire list of possibilities unless I stop it the only way I can.

"What?" I ask.

"What?"

"You said *cool* but you meant *not* cool."

Silence.

"I hate it when I'm missing something," I say.

"How well do you know him?"

"Just a bit. He's fine."

I hear her sit down on the stairs. I join her.

"Do *you* like him?"

"No, he's not my type."

"What then?"

"I don't think he's your type either."

I don't like being pigeonholed, especially by people who barely know me. "What's my type?"

"I don't know," she says quickly. "Forget it. He's fine. I hope you have fun."

"I can't forget it. What do you mean?"

"It's just that you're...quick...and clever. But Jason... he's...very literal."

"So?"

After a moment, she says, "Jason doesn't operate on as many levels as you do so I don't think he'll get you, that's all. Maybe I'm wrong. I hope I am."

This might mean more to me except I had a boyfriend once who "got" me and that didn't work out.

"Sorry," she says. "Sometimes I don't know what I'm supposed to say."

"You're not *supposed* to say anything."

"I know, it's just..." She breathes a few times. I wait her out. "There are things you might not know because you can't see them. How am I supposed to know what to tell you and what's none of my business?"

"Ah, okay, what'd you see?"

"Just...everything. A million quiet things happen all around all the time. I'm supposed to be your eyes but I can't tell you every single little thing. How am I supposed to decide?"

"What's there to choose from?"

"I don't know, lots of stuff. Like...do you know I'm not white?"

"White?"

"Caucasian?"

"Oh, um...I hadn't thought about it."

"No one's told you?"

"No, nobody's said, *Hey Parker, Molly's black, just thought you should know.*"

"*There,*" Molly says with some relief. "If you could see, you'd just *know*, without it being, I don't know, a thing. But if someone specifically tells you, you'd think they were trying to tell you something and you'd probably say, *What's your point?*"

"Okay, so no one's gone out of their way to tell me you're black—they don't think it matters."

"Oh...yeah, well, maybe...but also since I'm not black."

"Jesus, Molly!"

"But I'm not white either."

"Asian? Peruvian? I don't *enjoy* being blind you know! *Molly Ray* isn't much to go on."

"Have you been picturing me as a frizzy ginger with freckles?"

"I don't picture anyone much anymore except people I saw before the accident. It's funny because I know Sarah doesn't look seven now but I can't help seeing her like that sometimes."

Molly laughs.

"Glad to entertain you, but can we skip over screwing with the blind girl to the part where you tell me what *color* you are, if that's where this is going?"

"It's not, but my mom's from Nigeria and my dad's a blue-eyed-blond mishmash of every European country there is. Most people aren't sure whether I'm black or white and say I look like my parents merged their faces in Photoshop, except my eyes are all brown and my hair is just wavy and not quite black. Technically I'm biracial, but I never say that—"

"Why not? I mean—"

"Oh, it's just because when guys hear the 'bi' part it revs them up. Don't want that."

I laugh. She doesn't, but maybe that's just modesty, not laughing at your own jokes?

"So your face is exactly half of your mom's and dad's faces and they look nothing alike...That either looks really great, or..."

"My big sister's a model," she says in a smirking voice. "She got the good halves—I got the leftovers. I don't know what that leaves my little sister—she's only twelve."

"A model? Like runways, stuff like that?"

"Some, but mostly photo shoots. She was in *Vogue* last spring—March, I think. In the lower right corner of some page in the middle, wrapped around some shirtless guy like a snake. I don't even remember if it was an ad or part of a story...It's hard to tell with *Vogue*."

"Wow. Sounds very glamorous."

Molly snorts. I can't tell what it means. "She's coming home this weekend—maybe you'll meet her. She's not one of those big sisters who's too important to notice us. She wants to be in on everything right up to the moment she disappears on a plane to Italy and doesn't call again for weeks."

Aunt Celia's car bounces into the parking lot. It's an awkward time to leave, but…I grab my bag.

"When you fell today," Molly says quickly, "if you could see, you'd just know who ran over to you. If I tell you now, it's like I'm also trying to tell you something else but I'm really not."

"Who was it?"

"You see what I mean, though?"

"Was it Scott?"

"Yeah. He was first. When you asked for someone to get out of your light, that was him."

"Then what?" I ask. "He stick around?"

"No, he backed off. I guess he knows you don't want him around."

Smart guy, that Scott. That was one of the things I liked about him, back when I liked him. Back when him caring about me might have been something other than guilt or obligation or some kind of lingering regret.

"I'm not saying it means anything, right? It is what it is."

"I get it. And I'll never get mad over something you tell me but I might get mad over something you didn't. Just tell me anything you're not sure about and let me worry about what it means."

Chapter 13

It's almost one o'clock on Saturday and I'm riding Aunt Celia's Silent Shuttle Service to the mall. There was an awkward moment when she suggested Sheila go with me but before I could open my mouth, Sheila said, "Can't—homework" and ran upstairs. My disbelief was silenced only by my agreement that I didn't want her along. The conversation about me going on a date and having Jason drive me home took longer, but in the end it was settled by promising to reply to any texts and getting home by ten. I complained about that last one mostly for show. I'm meeting Jason at five so that's still plenty of time.

For whatever reason I never bumped into Jason Thursday or Friday. He was probably at tryouts or at least at the track. I promised myself I wasn't going to wander out there hoping he'd see me, and I can't look for him without asking around. I talked to Coach

Underhill again and we decided to meet a week from Monday, after the chaos of tryouts and the aftermath had ended, to talk about what we might do. After my tumble, though, I'm even more ambivalent about the whole thing.

It was Thursday night when I realized Jason and I didn't have each other's cell numbers, but I convinced myself that if anything had changed, he'd have found me. By Friday night I wasn't so sure. Logically, everything was fine, but I'd be lying if I said I was logical all the time. Sarah tried to help by talking casually about it, but Sarah going out of her way to talk casually about anything puts me even more on edge.

Despite all this uncertainty, though, I'm surprisingly optimistic. Sarah and Faith are waiting for me at the curb, and Aunt Celia drives away without throwing out any more rules or reminders or anything.

I'm struck by the oddness of how this outing is so ordinary and yet so striking. I see friends every day, and we talk and text a lot outside of school—though mostly Sarah and I—but we hardly go out to do anything. A lot of it's me not wanting to bother with movie theaters and restaurants and all that, but we used to do more as kids when our parents drove us around and organized stuff. It stopped when we got to high school.

Sarah says it's me, not just that I'm blind but also that I changed when Scott pissed away any hope I ever had of trusting a guy who wasn't my dad—her words. I don't deny it, but what we don't talk about is her parents' divorce, which happened around the same time, and how her dad mostly disappeared. It really dimmed the light in her. Once I said it broke her laugh box and that conversation ended so fast I promised myself I'd never bring it up again. But I did hear a note of genuine interest in her voice when we talked about going shopping with Faith so I'm hoping for the best, that afterwards we'll kick ourselves for having gone so long without doing this.

"Aren't you going straight to a date from here?" Faith asks.

"What's wrong with this?" I hold out my arms, slowly so I don't whack anything. I'm wearing jeans with a dark-blue cotton collared shirt, both of which actually fit instead of being a more comfortable one size bigger like usual. For my scarf I'm wearing Autumn Leaves—it's fall after all—and I'm wearing my army vest loaded with buttons, of course.

"Should I start at the pile of leaves on your head and work my way down," she says, "or from the bottom up starting with those black basketball shoes?"

"Jason sold me these shoes! And they're not high-tops—they're for running!"

"Maybe we can get something for you here. Something less—"

"I'm not going to change!" Though I look into the future and suspect I might.

"Here comes Molly," Sarah says. "She looks pretty sour. And she's not alone."

"Hey," Molly says. She doesn't sound sour to me. More resigned. "Parker, Sarah, Faith...this is my sister, Danielle."

"Call me Dani," says a higher-pitched voice that sounds nothing like Molly. "I just landed early this morning and have some things I need to pick up. Mind if I tag along?"

"Of course not," says Faith, utterly sincere or

acting brilliantly; the only one of us classy enough to answer instantly and save us all from an awkward silence waiting for someone else to answer. "The more the merrier. Are you away at college, or...?"

"What? No!" Dani laughs. "Molly's the smart one."

"And Dani's the pretty one," Molly says, like she's said it a million times before.

Dani laughs again. "That's not true! I just have an army of experts working on me all the time. It's hard work, trust me!"

And we're off. Into the mall, Faith and Dani up ahead, outpacing us already, or at least me, with Faith coming up to speed on what Sarah and I already know, that Dani's a professional clothes hanger slash walking coatrack just back from Milan and heading out to Chicago and then New York as soon as...well, I lose track at this point because Sarah startles me by breathing into my ear, "Oh. My. God."

"It's fine," I say. "It'll be fun. It's not like we have a routine she's going to mess—"

"No, I...That's not it...I...I wish you could *see* this... She's...she's..."

"Jesus, Sarah." I stop walking. This is weird. Sarah

sounds flustered. She's *never* flustered. "She's *what*?"

Sarah grabs my upper arm with both hands and leans in. "She's *gorgeous*."

"Yeah," Molly says. "A real curve buster. Without the curves, anyway. She caught me by surprise. When she offered to drive I knew she'd—"

"I thought this stuff only happened in movies," Sarah says like Molly isn't talking. "Heads are actually turning. Two guys by the fountain just bumped into each other. Three other guys pulled a U-turn and are following us. Following *her*. Holy shit, *look at all this!*"

"Whoa," I snicker, trying not to laugh, keeping my voice down. "What's wrong with you? It's not like you've never seen a pretty girl before, even if just in movies—"

"Pretty? *Pretty?* She's not *pretty*, Parker. *You're* pretty. *She's* from *another planet*. It's not the same thing. I didn't know till now but it's not the same at all. I'm having a *physical reaction*. I'm seeing the Theory of Evolution. I'm beginning to understand the Trojan War. I'm starting to question my sexual orientation—"

"Sarah, *shhh!*" It's hard to whisper when trying not

to laugh. "Pull yourself together!"

"I know Rick would be okay with her in a threesome and I'm pretty sure I'd be too—"

"Sarah!" I can't hold back anymore and start laughing. "Sarah! Where are you? There's someone here pretending to be you and doing a really crappy job!"

"Shut up! Shut up! *Shut up!*" Sarah whispers and tries to cover my mouth and I bat her hands away. "They're coming!"

"Is everything okay back here?" Faith asks in a voice that's trying to tell us something, probably related to maturity.

"Absolutely, yeah," Sarah says. "We're all fine here. How are you two?"

"I thought you said Sweatpants was the quiet one," Dani says.

"She usually is," Faith says suspiciously. "Maybe she's having a stroke."

"My *name*," Sarah says emphatically through clenched teeth, "is *not…Sweatpants…*" and I hear her trying hard not to laugh.

I squeeze her in a bear hug and lift her off the

ground, so happy to hear this. She squeals and thrashes and I set her down.

"Are you okay?" some guy says. Probably our age or a bit older—I can't tell for sure.

"Yeah, do you gals need some help?" another guy says.

"Gals?" Sarah says. "Are there *gals* around here?"

"Are some random guys we've never met talking to us?" I ask her loudly. "That's weird."

"We're fine, thanks," Faith says. "For some people it's never too early to drink."

*

None of us had lunch before we came so we head for the food court. Despite this it still takes an hour to get there because someone—well, Faith or Dani—stops us at every store along the way to go inside and not buy anything. I can't even begin to describe how much blind people love window shopping, but despite Sarah calming down some, she's still entertaining me.

I get a burrito at the intersection of best tasting and easiest to eat of the food court options. I demand reports and hear that Molly got enchiladas and beans at the same counter, Sarah got a sourdough bread bowl full of cream of mushroom soup, Faith got a wispy spinach salad, and Dani got some Thai food. My nose confirms the truth of these reports and we dig in.

"Excuse me," some guy says to us.

"Private Party!" I say. "Thanks anyway!"

"Go ahead, it's fine," Molly says to him. Then to me, "He wanted our extra chair to sit with his wife and kids."

"Oh." Maybe I should be embarrassed, but no, I'm not.

"Dani," Faith says. "We were having a disagreement earlier. About Parker's outfit. She's going on a first date tonight."

"Oooh!" Dani says. "What are you going to wear?"

I frown.

"I win," Faith says without a hint of gloating. I don't know how she does it.

"This isn't far from what I was wearing when he asked me out so he must like my look."

"It's what you wear every day of your life," Faith says. "But this isn't a day, it's a date. It's okay to wear something special. It's more than okay."

"Like what, a dress? A gown? Glass slippers?"

"Maybe something that's seen the inside of a washing machine recently."

"That's just hurtful," I say, lifting my vest. "You know this doesn't wash easily. How often do you wash jackets anyway." I sniff the fabric—it does smell the tiniest bit musty.

"I'm not saying you need a makeover," Faith says, her tone saying the opposite. "Maybe you're right; maybe he asked you out because he likes the way you clash blue and green. I know you aren't going to care or even know whether he shows up in overalls or a tux, but I'm sure he'd like to see you cleaned up a bit, even within your own...unique...style."

"I resent that! Just because I can't see doesn't mean I don't care what he's wearing...which...I guess I don't really...but anyway he's at work so he'll be wearing work clothes!" I spin my head as though looking at everyone triumphantly.

"I'm sure he'll change," Faith says in her yes-I'm-being-patient voice. "He's not going to wear his uniform out with you. I don't even think they're allowed to wear them off duty."

"His uniform?"

Molly says, "They all wear black T-shirts with *Running Rampant* printed on them in white. The two letter *R*s are wearing running shoes on their legs or whatever."

"This is all beside the point," Faith says. "And it's not a philosophical discussion. It's shopping. Shopping means buying clothes. Finish your lunch and let's buy some clothes."

"I think it's bold," Dani says.

"Here we go," Molly says in her eye-rolling voice.

"What's bold?" I ask.

"Your look. It doesn't follow the rules, but...it's like you're just one step over. That's how new trends happen. I like it. Especially the scarf as a blindfold. That's brilliant."

I lean toward Faith. "The *professional* likes my style."

"Here, stand up and step back a bit," Dani says. "And stand up straighter."

I do. I'm ready for anything.

"Have you thought about hanging your scarf down

front instead of behind?" Dani asks. She touches my shoulders and then adjusts my scarf and drapes the tails, about a foot long, down the left side of my chest.

"You've got some curve and this highlights your contour. There. Your sex appeal just went up a whole number."

I stand perfectly still. No one says anything. I don't want to be the first to speak.

"Damn," Sarah says. "Let's go shopping."

*

For days I've thought more about seeing Jason than this shopping trip, yet here it is almost five o'clock and I want to stay with the group. Everyone except Faith was on my side about my jeans and black running shoes being okay, but now I'm in a dark-blue cotton top with a V-neck that stops just north of my white sports bra, and over that I'm wearing a light-blue plaid shirt unbuttoned...which I'm still not too sure about but everyone, Faith included, said was perfect and exactly my style as the girl who usually wears an open army vest every day. I also have a new scarf that's longer than my usual: a solid navy blue that Faith said was too dark but Dani said was striking and that settled it. Molly is helping me out by holding my old clothes for later. I can't really explain it but in my new outfit I even feel a bit taller.

I try to keep track of what everyone buys but it's hard to remember just being told once and having no reminders of what stuck and what didn't in all the chaos. I do know Sarah bought a few pairs of yoga pants under the premise that they're as comfortable as sweatpants but, as Dani said, easier on the eyes.

"Who do you normally shop with?" Molly asks while we wait for Dani, who's doing God-knows-what.

It takes me a moment to answer. "My dad."

The silence tells me the conversation isn't likely to continue, but then she asks, "How was he in the fashion advice department?"

I laugh. "He just described things. Colors, shapes, whatever. He'd tell me what other people were wearing, though I know he only told me what he liked, or at least didn't hate. I also get help from salespeople, looking for my size and then talking about what to get."

My phone beeps—my reminder.

"I have to go," I say. "Where is everyone?"

"Dani's holding court by the makeup counter. I bet those people never saw so many guys stay by the counter this long before."

"Sarah and Faith?"

"Basking in her light," Molly says. Then she shouts, "Hey! I'm walking Parker over. Back in a few minutes."

The chorus of *goodbyes* and *good lucks* in a higher pitch than I've ever heard out of Sarah especially disturbs me as we walk away.

"I know you don't need my help," Molly says. "I just need a break."

"Actually," I admit, "I've gotten so turned around I don't know where we are. Walk me to the fountain and point me in the right direction. I can take it from there."

We don't talk as we navigate out of the department store—Macy's, I think, or maybe Nordstrom—an obstacle course of clothing racks designed to stop you from walking in a straight line. I'd set my reminder to give me plenty of time, figuring I'd be solo, so once we're out in the main mall we relax and stroll. Okay maybe not relax. My stomach is tightening up and

I'm feeling shaky, but we're walking slowly at least.

To distract myself I say, "I can't imagine what it must be like to be Dani."

"I can," Molly says in a voice that's, well, kind of dark.

"You can't be jealous," I say lightly. "That's like being jealous of Einstein or Mozart..." I immediately regret this. In my head it sounded like comforting perspective.

"Jealous?" Molly says. "I feel *sorry* for her. All those guys talking to us today—"

"That was only because of her."

"But they weren't talking to *her*, either. Sometimes they were talking to the four of us—*Blind Girl, Sweatpants, Tubby,* and...I dunno...*Fashion Insect*—but they were really just trying to get to *Cheekbones*. If they could get her without having to talk, they would."

"Some of them, sure. I guess it could get annoying—"

"No. Imagine winning a billion-dollar lottery and suddenly everyone's talking to you, being nice, seeking you out, constantly, all the time, never a break. One day nobody, next day everybody, just

176

because of your bank account. It's not annoying, it's... it's like drowning."

"Well, when you put it like—"

"When you look like her, ninety-nine percent of everyone who talks to you, male *and* female, is just trying to get you or get something from you. They're lying or saying what they think you want to hear so you can't trust anyone or even find the one percent who aren't. It's horrible to even think about but that's her every day."

"Molly..." I don't know what else to say.

"Sorry, Parker. I...I know this isn't what you wanted to talk about now. It's just that she calls me on the phone from all over the world, usually crying... She's done it more times this year than I've cried in my whole life. It's exhausting just being her sister; I could never survive actually *being* her. Everyone thinks Dani is *sooo* lucky but she's the saddest person I know. I'm *glad* no one can see my cheekbones under all...*this*. I wouldn't trade places with her for anything."

Chapter 14

It's twelve minutes after five and I'm sitting alone on the bench outside Running Rampant. The fact that I haven't heard from Jason is at the bottom of the list of things I can't stop thinking about.

I had a lot of fun today but what Molly said about Dani has me feeling like someone turned up gravity a few notches. I feel like I was no different, using her like everyone else. I know it's not true—I'm obviously not wowed by her looks—I liked hanging out with her for the same reasons I like Molly; she's fun to be with and talk to. Yet there's no denying a lot of it was the craziness that only existed because she's crazy beautiful. What if my friends only liked me because they thought it was fun watching me fumble around and bump into things all the time?

And if that's not enough, now I wonder why anyone talks to anyone. Not later, after they know each other, but why the first time? When someone you don't know just starts talking to you without actually needing something like directions to the bathroom, why are they doing it? I don't know—I've never done it. I guess it's just based on what people see. Because they find someone attractive.

Why did Jason ask me out? First he helped me buy shoes, but after that we talked, what, three or four times, never more than sixty seconds each. Why did he want to talk to me again or ask me out? Does he think I'm cute? He can't like my personality—I haven't really unleashed it on him yet—if anything, the way I've fumbled around every other time we've spoken, he's had plenty of reasons to *not* talk to me. And if I'm cute, wouldn't a lot of other guys have asked me out by now? Maybe they don't because I'm blind, or it's because of my personality and Jason doesn't know any better yet. Once he gets to know me he'll change his mind. Or what if he's just got some bondage fetish and my blindfolds turn him on? God, now that I've thought that, I really wish I hadn't. Damn, that's creepy. Troll brain in action.

Even more mysterious is why I like him and said yes to this date so fast and why I've been excited about it. I could claim the high ground and say it's nothing as superficial as thinking he's hot to look at, but without that, what have I even got? Because he's charming and treated me with lighthearted respect? That's all it takes to give me butterflies? Jesus, that's pathetic. A kind word delivered in the right tone that properly navigates my disability minefield and I'm all aflutter? God—

"Hey, Parker," Jason says. "Sorry I'm late. My shift supervisor literally had us pinned down for the last twenty minutes going over stocking procedures. We were all standing together so I couldn't even come out and tell you."

I stand. "It's okay. Do you have to change or anything?"

"Uh, no, I did already. It's just the shirt. You ready to go?"

"Yep."

"You look really nice."

"Thanks," I say. "I'm sure you look nice, too. But really it'd be fine if you didn't."

"Um, okay," he says. "You hungry?"

Wow, that was poor planning, eating a burrito

three hours ago. "I can eat anytime," I say, surprising myself with this level of evasion. I mean, I certainly *can* eat, just not much..."Are you hungry?"

"Starved," he says. "I didn't get lunch. I made dinner reservations for six."

"Reservations?" I say. "Fancy. Where?"

"It's a surprise."

I don't actually like surprises much. But I guess that's not fair. The day Scott kissed me was full of surprises and I liked that at the time.

"Okay."

"Here, let's go out the front, to your left."

"Can I take your arm?" I hold out my hand. "It'll be faster than caning."

"Of course," he says. His sleeve touches my fingers. Thin, smooth fabric...maybe a dress shirt of some kind.

"Also fancy," I say. "Your shirt, I mean. Long sleeves and cuffs."

"Yeah, this being a special occasion. I even showered today."

"Thanks!" I say, starting to feel more at ease. "It's true what they say about blind people developing stronger other senses. My nose would tell me if you were lying."

"I wouldn't lie to you, Parker," he says, and he really says it, not just playing. It warms me. I can almost believe this is going to work out.

"Promise?"

"Promise."

I remember he made me promise something, too, when we first met. I promised him I'd never run at night, a promise I broke only three days later after I dreamed about Scott.

*

For the next five minutes he talks about his job, prompted by a question I asked but already forget. Something stupid like, "So what do you do besides carry shoes in and out of the back room?" I'm only half listening to him describing the logistics of tidying up shelves and displays, stuff like that—I'm not dreamy-eyed enough to find that interesting. Plus, I'm distracted wondering where we're going since there isn't any parking at the front of the mall where we're heading.

I can't take it anymore. "Are we going to walk

there? The parking lot's the other way."

"Oh, they don't let employees park there. We have to park in another lot. I don't usually take the shuttle, but I figured...well, I mean, we can walk there if you want to. I didn't mean—"

"It's okay, we can ride. It's not like I don't get enough exercise."

We get to the curb just as the shuttle does, and after some stair navigation fun and games, we're sitting on the bench seat at the back of a smallish bus. For whatever reason the driver has the AC on max and it's freezing, but I don't hug myself because I don't want Jason to feel bad.

"You cold?" he asks.

"I'm fine," I say, surprising myself again.

"I don't have a coat or I'd let you have it. I didn't know these buses were so cold."

"It's okay."

Something touches my shoulder, the one away from Jason, and I jump, startled, and I really jump because my muscles are tense from the cold—my arms fly up and my forearm bounces off Jason's nose but thankfully I don't squeal. My heart pounds as I realize Jason was putting his arm around me.

"Sorry!" I blurt out. "Sorry, I..."

"No, no," he says. "*I'm* sorry. I didn't mean to scare you."

"No, it's okay! It's...it's okay..."

The bus bounces us around a bit; I can feel his arms down at his sides. I want him to try again but I'm not going to ask.

"Really, it's okay," I say.

"Don't worry—soon we'll be in my car instead of this refrigerator."

"Okay."

Silence. No arm around my shoulder. An unnecessary reminder that Rule Number Two is as much for me as everyone else.

We stop after a couple minutes. With a little more help from Jason than I need, I leave the bus and his car isn't far. It's a short drive to the restaurant that we spend by him asking me what food I like to eat, which seems strange to be asking now after he's picked a restaurant and won't tell me what it is. I give vague answers—I don't want to say I don't like sushi if we're headed for a sushi bar—and I can tell this frustrates him but I'd rather be safe.

"Surprise!" he says, pulling into a parking lot. "We're at Andino's."

"Okay, cool," I say, trying to sound enthusiastic. The surprise value of not knowing the restaurant till we got here is lost for the very reason I knew it would be; Jason telling me now is no different from telling me at the mall a half hour ago. You can't blindfold someone, lead them somewhere, and then have a surprise moment if they never take the blindfold off.

Now I understand why he wasn't loving my answers to his food quiz. I hadn't mentioned Italian food. I like it fine but it's messy and seldom my first choice.

We're seated immediately and from what I can hear around me the reservations weren't necessary. That's okay.

Jason says, "I called around but couldn't find a restaurant with braille menus."

I bite my tongue. If he'd asked me I could have told him a half dozen good restaurants with braille menus. That's the price you pay for surprises. I'm torn between feeling special that he's trying to do romantic things and me not really liking them much.

But how was he to know?

Exactly. How was he to know? He doesn't know anything about me.

"So…how hungry are you?" he asks. His voice is strong, like he's goofing a little. Does he know I ate recently?

"Medium."

"Okay. Would you care for soup, salad, appetizers, or garlic bread?"

I get it. He's playing the waiter, making the menu into a game.

"I'm not hungry enough for appetizers or soup or salad," I say. Not to mention there's no way I'm going to eat soup or floppy dressing-soaked lettuce.

"Very good," he says. "Pasta or pizza?"

Pizza would definitely be easier, but it seems wrong to order in a nice restaurant…

"Pasta."

"Excellent! Choose from the following list: Linguini Mare, Spaghetti Carbonara…"

His reading falls into a rhythm, and then a bad Italian accent…

"…Cap-pel-lini Pomo-doro, Fettu-ccine Pri-ma-ver-a…"

Now he's nearly singing the choices. I lean forward and whisper, "Jason…"

"…TOR-tel-LI-ni MAR-i-NAR-a, or some VE-al SAL-tim-BO-cca—"

I giggle at him inserting words to fit the meter of his menu song. I hear how it sounds and cover my mouth to stop and not disturb other people. That plus I feel a little stupid giggling, like Sarah at the mall.

"…and there's AL-so SCALL-o-PI-ne OR some CHIC-ken PARM-e-SAN…eee."

I laugh. "Jason!"

"I'm not even halfway down the page yet," he says. "There's also AN-gel HAIR with A-i-O-li, RIG-a-TON-I A-bruz-ZI…zi…"

"I don't even know what half these things are!"

Silence. Or at least as soon as I stop laughing.

"Then may I recommend the Beef Lasagna?" he says, deadpan.

"Too messy," I say, sneaking in a bit of honesty. "Do they have any gnocchi? With Alfredo sauce?"

"Never heard of it…I don't see it anywhere…"

"The *G* is silent. It's spelled g-n-o-c-c—"

"Oh, here it is. Gnocchi Del Giorno. A delightful

platter of potato—"

"I'll take it. With garlic bread."

Oh wait, garlic breath—

"Are you ready?" a woman asks. "Oh!"

"It's okay," Jason says. "Fine dining is about taste and smell. What it looks like is just distracting."

"Oh, well," she says, playing along. "I know Chef would disagree. He definitely believes in presentation—the first bite is with the eyes, he says. But he doesn't have to know."

"We'll both have Gnocchi Del Giorno and garlic bread. What about a drink, Parker?"

"C-6, please."

"We only have soda, lemonade, cranberry juice, grapefruit—"

"Oh, I mean Coke or Pepsi or whichever, with caffeine and sugar. And a straw. Please."

"Me too," Jason says.

When the waitress leaves, Jason says, "What's C-6?"

I feel funny about this but I'm not sure why. Am I embarrassed? No, that can't be it. "Cold Carbonated Caffeinated Caramel Colored Cane sugar. I'm sure they'll only have C-5 here—only a few sodas have cane sugar instead of high fructose corn syrup, but I was already having trouble communicating and didn't want to make it worse."

The waitress is back in record time with garlic bread.

"Have some," I say, for more honesty, "so I'm not the only one with garlic breath."

"Okay. I've never heard of gnocchi before. It's potatoes? That doesn't sound Italian."

"They definitely are. Not my favorite, exactly, but pretty good."

"Why didn't you order your favorite? Were you hurrying to get me to stop singing?"

"No! No, it's just...well, like the waitress said, some people care what food looks like but I care how easy it is to eat. Gnocchi is easy, but spaghetti? Forget-y...it."

Jason laughs. "Fair enough."

I eat a bit of garlic bread and enjoy that the silence feels comfortable, at least to me.

"Hey," Jason says. "Sorry about the bus ride."

"No, it's okay. I get startled when people touch me since I can't see it coming. It's...well, sort of a rule about blind people. Next time just say something like *Hey, let me put my arm around you*, then next time I won't punch you in the nose or anything."

Shit, I just said *next time* twice...

"Oh, okay."

"Or—and here's a pro tip—if you just bump into me first, that works too."

Enough already!

"Okay. I meant the whole bus ride. I don't want you to think we took the shuttle because I don't think you can walk a couple hundred yards..."

"Oh, that's...okay...I didn't..." I can't think of what else to say. Maybe in part because my face is heating up since he wasn't talking about putting his arm around me.

"Are you blushing?" he asks.

"No! Why would I be blushing?"

No answer.

"But if I was, a gentleman wouldn't notice."

"Notice what?"

"Exactly," I say, and I smile. Outwardly.

Chapter 15

"So where are we going?" I ask. I haven't checked the time because I can't do it without Jason knowing. I can't imagine we were at Andino's for much more than an hour, an hour and a half at the most. Then we drove to Ice Cream Explosion to share some dessert—I made him choose, and I'd never had a butterscotch sundae before, but I liked it—and I could eat less since we were sharing. God, between the burrito, most of my gnocchi, and half the garlic bread, even a small portion of sundae had me feeling very roly-poly.

Add all that up and I think it's maybe nine o'clock at the latest. I don't have to be home till ten and honestly, if I'm late, what'll Aunt Celia do? Ground me? I hardly leave the house as it is, except for, well, like now...so I guess I do have something to lose after all.

"Any place you'd like to go?" Jason asks.

"I don't need to be back till ten," I say. "What time is it now?" Smooth.

He laughs softly. "Eight-thirty."

"What's funny?"

"You have to be home by ten?"

A lot of answers occur to me. This is my first date... Maybe girls have earlier curfews than guys...I haven't lived with Aunt Celia long so she doesn't trust me yet, or maybe never will, it's too soon to tell...

"Give me a reason to stay out later," I say. I hear how this sounds...but instead of trying to clarify, I leave it alone to see what happens.

"How about we go to the Bluff?"

"What's there?"

"Nothing, but it's either sit there or sit somewhere else. If you're still hungry—"

"No! The Bluff is fine. Not that I'll be able to see a sunset or anything..."

The car turns.

"The sun already set. Parking on the Bluff is about who you're with, not the view."

"You park there a lot?"

"I wouldn't say a lot."

It's not far. Soon we're parked and the engine shuts off.

"Is that a new...is it a scarf?"

"I bought it today. How'd you know? You can't have seen all my scarves yet."

"They usually have a little braille flag sewn in on one end except this one doesn't."

I smile at this nice attention to detail, and what it means. I'd been worried he wasn't much of a thinker or a noticer.

"Are you cold?"

"A little. It's okay."

"I'd put my arm around you to warm you up but the console's in the way."

Ummm...

"So..." he says. "Want to sit in the back?"

Oh boy.

"Won't that look funny? Us sitting in the back?"

"Maybe if anyone was looking. There're only two other cars here. One's empty—probably hikers. The other one, well, they're probably more worried that we can see them if you know what I mean. There's a bench we could sit on, but it's getting even colder out."

"Backseat it is, then."

I feel for the door handle, let myself out—he's right, it's getting colder—and I let myself in the back and close the door behind me.

I don't like wondering if he's going to kiss me. If he doesn't, I'll feel stupid that I thought he might. Yet he wouldn't ask me to go into the backseat just to put his arm on my shoulder, right? It strikes me as funny that this is what I'm thinking about, not whether I want him to, because, I realize, of course I want him to. I mean, why wouldn't I? Jason's nice, and safe, and—

"What are you smiling about?" he asks, playfully suspicious.

Was I smiling?

"If you prefer a frown, I'm not sure I can help you, but I can try."

"No, smile's good."

He bumps his shoulder against mine then slips his arm around my shoulders.

"Pretty slick," I say. "I bet you bump all the girls..."

Damn, that's not how I thought it would sound.

"No, I just need to know the rules," he says. "I'm guessing you have lots."

"The list goes to infinity." I lean into him a bit. It turns out it's actually warmer, too, not just an excuse to touch.

"All right then, let's hear it. Your rules, I mean."

His voice is soft and low, with breath that has just a hint of garlic. I like it. Who'd have known? I turn to face him.

"I'm not really thinking about rules right now," I say.

"What are you thinking about?"

"Well..."

I'm thinking it's strange that I'm not thinking much. My mind is usually churning all kinds of nonsense, but it's happily quiet now, soaking it in, enjoying itself for a change...

Chemistry.

That's the word that escaped me this afternoon. What makes you talk to someone, to want to talk to them some more, or to feel their hand on your shoulder, even though you don't really know them. It's more than a kind or charming word from a stranger; it's the right word, or words that play well with your words. I don't know if Jason and I will be compatible as we get to know each other, but now, on the surface, we have chemistry.

"I can tell you're thinking about something," he prompts again, not impatiently.

I'm thinking how despite the fact that I just climbed into the backseat of a parked car with a senior I barely even know, in unfamiliar surroundings, I feel comfortable. Maybe it's chemistry and intuition. It has to be, because I'm pretty short on facts.

I'm thinking I must be crazy but if I could see, I'd be the one taking the chance, leaning in to kiss, hoping it's not too soon. But I can't see so all I can do is...I slide my hand up to his collar to get a sense of where things are, and I tip my head and lean forward...If he doesn't get it, I'll have to walk my hand to his jaw and guide my—

Something touches the tip of my nose. His nose.

Perfect.

I push forward and lightly kiss his lips. Again. God, it's like being cold and blowing into hot cocoa and feeling warmth waft over your face, then sipping it and the warmth spreads to your cheeks and down into your chest, lower and lower, filling you. My head spins with nothing but simple thoughts like *warm* and *soft* and *exciting* and *wonderful* and *mmmmm...*

"What?" he whispers when he takes a breath.

"What, what?" I whisper back and kiss him again.

"*Mmmmm...what?*"

"Oh." I guess I said that part out loud. "*Mmmmm, garlic...*"

"Oh!" He draws back. "Sorry, I..."

My hand finds the back of his neck and I pull him back to me. "Don't you know what *mmmmm* means?" I kiss him again. And again. And again. Firmer but not harder.

The tip of his tongue fleetingly touches my lower lip—a star bursts in my head, a thrill that no other word can describe. Like when you're running at a comfortable pace and push yourself to go faster but instead of getting more tired you get a surge of energy. I feel just a flick of tongue again and now I'm sprinting along...

I have no sense of how long we've been in the backseat, kissing and breathing and touching...hand on my back, and then down to my waist where it fits just right...and I know I could do this all night without a break or getting tired or bored...his hand sliding up a bit...then a bit more...

I know where it's going and my brain wakes up. The troll brain that thinks and double-thinks and triple-thinks and overthinks and acts like I'm a committee instead of a person. It asks me what the hell do I think I'm doing, French kissing this guy I met less than a week ago and considering letting his hand slide up—no, not *considering* it, but *anticipating* it, *wanting* it, expecting to *enjoy* it...My troll brain wants to ask why I'm letting it happen but it can't because I'm not *letting* it happen, I'm *willing it* to happen. What does it mean that I want to be touched by this guy now?

It hits me, clear as ice-cold water, how for three months I've had almost no physical contact with anyone. Faith hugged me on the first day of school and aside from that I've had a pat on the shoulder here and there but that's it. Dad hugged me every morning before school, and when I came home, and before bed, and lots of other times just because, and many nights we'd listen to a book on tape or a podcast and we'd sit together on the couch with his arm around my shoulders and I'd lean on him like a warm cushion. Dad was the exception to Rule Number Two because him *not* giving my shoulder a squeeze when he walked by would've been more of a surprise. Then he was gone and in the following days of stunned disorientation all sorts of people tried to hold me and comfort me but I wouldn't let them, wouldn't allow strangers or relatives I barely knew to touch me, and finally they stopped trying. Of course you want this guy all over you, my troll brain says. You used to be hugged and touched several times a day and now you've gone three months with nothing around you but voices in the dark. You're starving—

"Parker?"

We aren't kissing anymore. Jason's hand is back down on my hip, having never strayed very far.

"Are you okay?"

I don't want to tell him any of this. Not that I need to keep it a deep, dark secret; it's just some things you only want to share with people who know you. Jason would listen and be sympathetic but he wouldn't really understand.

"Yeah...yeah, I'm fine..." I say, sounding groggy.

"What time is it?"

"Only nine-thirty. Well, almost nine-forty. But we're only ten minutes from your house."

"Let's...let's head back anyway," I say, slowing my breathing. "I don't want to give my aunt anything to bitch about."

"Okay," he says. I can hear he's disappointed. I don't know how I feel.

We climb out our separate doors and back into the front. He starts the car and we back up.

I'm sort of numb. We drive for a while before he says anything.

"So...you live with your aunt? What about your parents? If you don't mind me asking."

"My mom died when I was seven. She drank a bottle of wine and wrecked the car and that's why I'm blind."

"Oh. I'm sorry."

I'm glad it's all he says, understanding that it's long past and not trying to get into it all now when we have so little time left.

"Then it was just me and Dad till he died in June."

"Which June? This past June? Three months ago?"

"Yeah. Then my aunt and uncle and cousins came here to live with me."

"Oh, man...Parker...I'm...I'm sorry. I didn't know."

"It's okay," I say. "There are lots of things you don't know about me. I don't know much about you, either."

"That'll change," Jason says.

"I hope so," I say, but it's my flat voice. It's the only one I can seem to find.

"Does that mean you want to do this again?"

"Only if you do."

"We're agreed then."

The car gently stops.

"Ten minutes early. Someone's peeking out the blinds. Looks like a little kid."

I take a deep breath and let it out. "My cousin Petey. He's probably been bored to death without me tonight. I don't know what he did for entertainment before he moved in with me."

I hear myself sounding mostly normal now but I don't feel normal. It's like I'm on autopilot, holding the same trajectory from the past hour but not feeling it anymore. I mean, I like Jason, and I do want to get to know him, but that time in the car feels like something weird now, something not me, like I was under some spell that's now broken. A voice in my head is saying that the past hour didn't have much to do with Jason other than him being warm and willing and within reach. I try to silence it, but I have a feeling it's not the troll talking.

"I'll tell you my work schedule next week when I get it," Jason says, sounding far away.

I just nod my head. I don't trust my voice. My throat is tightening up.

"Are you okay?" he asks.

I nod again. I force a cough into my hand to be able to talk without squeaking. "Yeah. I had a good time."

"Me too."

But he knows something's up. It's not his fault and I don't want him to feel bad. I try to think of something nice to say, something not generic...

"I, uh...don't know if I said it at the time, but thanks for pulling Isaac and Gerald off me. Just because I could have handled it myself doesn't mean I don't appreciate your help. I do."

"Glad to do it. I have to be honest, though…I can't take all the credit."

"What do you mean?"

"I was walking with a friend after tryouts and he suddenly took off running. He had Isaac up against the lockers before I caught up and saw what was going on and grabbed Gerald. Then I had to pull Scott and Isaac apart. He's never liked those guys—I think he was going to get into it for real if I hadn't stopped him. What they were doing was shitty, I know, but not really worth…Hey, Parker, you okay?"

Dizziness is making my stomach churn.

"Parker? What's—"

"I have to go."

"Let me walk you to the—"

"No. I got it. It's fine. I know the way." I claw for the door handle. "Talk to you later."

And I'm out and across the sidewalk and find the lawn and sidestep right to the path and up to the porch but the door's locked goddamn it even though they know I'm here and now it's open and I'm stumbling up the stairs and Petey's saying something but I can't hear it and I'm in the bathroom with the door closed and now it's locked and I wish to God if there was a God that I could throw up and make this feeling go away but I can't I can't I just can't...

Chapter 16

Is this still your number, Scott?

It's Anime Sunday with Petey again. I really don't want to be sitting on the couch in front of this blast of electronic noise but this has become a thing with Petey and I'm not up to trying to break it off now either. I successfully added a gold star to my chart last night but it's a good thing I'm not keeping track of my running. I only ran a couple half-assed sprints and then jogged home. No one was up to see that I'd been gone less than half my usual time. I took a long shower and by then Petey was up and our routine began like last night never happened.

But it did happen, and today is happening. So I plugged my phone into the ear opposite Petey and did something I hadn't done in years.

The answer comes quicker than I expect.

"G'day, mate."

He's right, I never changed his voice from

Australian Male.

"You're missing it!" Petey says. He's not angry, he just doesn't want me to miss out.

"It's just for texting," I say. "But really, I'm missing most of it anyway unless you tell me what's happening."

He tries for a minute or two but he's so caught up in the action he doesn't make a lot of sense, or maybe the show doesn't make sense. That plus a lot of Japanese names and words and all these made-up things, like super-sayings, which only mean something to true fans. Petey's explanations thin out and stop without him realizing it.

I wait to see if Scott will say more on this momentous occasion but he doesn't so I press on. Whatever he was trying to tell me in eighth grade, I need to hear it now.

Why did you do it?

This feeling I have is a rare one. It's like how I felt when Coach Underhill almost outed my morning sprints to the cafeteria and then told me he'd watched me run. It's a kind of...dread, I guess. Yes, what I'm feeling now, texting Scott, it's dread.

Enough time for a complete anime battle goes by—at least I think it's a battle—before Scott answers. I didn't delete him from my phone back when it happened but I did switch him to Silent to stop the incessant ringing. Now my phone just vibrates a bit.

"Sorry I ruined your date."

Huh?

What are you talking about?

"Jason told me you ran out of his car last night after he told you what happened with Gerald and Isaac. He's confused but I didn't tell him anything. I figured you didn't want me to."

He's right, of course...damn it. I *don't* want him to tell anyone about any of it, except...

Jason needs to know but I don't want to be the one. You tell him. Today.

"That won't be easy to admit, but I will. I'll do it tomorrow to tell him in person. He's a good guy. I'm glad you're together."

I want to answer that but need to stay on track.

I want to know why you did what you did at Marsh.

Minutes go by without an answer.

I've lost track of time and now I want Petey's show

to last longer. It's perfect cover for this conversation. I could go hide in my room like Sheila, but that's not like me and I don't want to draw any more attention than I did last night, which I blamed on something I ate.

"Why ask now?"

That's not the answer I expect, especially after minutes of thinking he was typing. It's strange since he wanted so much to explain back when it happened and I wouldn't let him.

I'm finally ready to hear it.

This is true, even though the whole truth is more complicated. As much as I want to ignore it, I see now that it's going to keep following me, jumping in front of me, slapping me like it did last night. For some reason it's all feeling different than it did back then and I need to figure out why...either that or I just have to face it down.

"I don't think it's a good idea to dig it all up again."

My dread shifts toward anger. I'm shaking a bit from adrenaline seeping into my blood and have to retype my next text a few times to get rid of the typos before sending.

Maybe you buried it but I haven't.

His answer comes quickly. "Can I call you?"

My answer goes out even quicker. *No.*

Now I'm waiting again, wondering if it's taking a long time now because he's typing or just thinking. What I get is a bit of both.

"Explaining it will sound like I'm making excuses but there's no excuse and I'm not trying to justify it, okay?"

Fine. Just tell me.

Now I figure I'm in for a wait and it looks to be true. I try to make sense of Petey's show, even asking a couple questions, but it's hopeless; I can't concentrate, and I'm not sure it would matter if I could. When Scott's text finally comes it's so long it's broken into fragments.

"Us getting together was like a kid getting to be an astronaut. Not when he grows up, but right now, today, pack your suitcase, you're getting on a plane to NASA. When I told my friends they wanted me to prove we were more than friends. I said that was stupid, but we weren't trying to hide that we were together and other people kissed in public and it was no big deal. So I told them about us going into Ms. Kincaid's room at lunch and if they looked in the window they might get lucky. I thought this was okay, since there was always a chance someone might look in anyway and we never worried about it. I didn't know they were hiding in the room until Isaac started laughing. But when you pushed me away, I saw the look on your face and knew none of that mattered. It felt like a crazy dream where dumb things make sense and as soon as you wake up you think back and see how stupid it all was and wonder why you ever believed it. It felt a little iffy telling the guys where we'd be but mostly fine, but following you out of that room I saw how obviously stupid it was, and how it must have looked to you. I knew my astronaut days were over. I also knew I'd do anything for as long as it took to try and make it better because I'd never get over how Parker Grant could have had anyone but she chose me and I ruined it."

"Big P?" Petey says and I jump. "You're breathing funny."

"Yeah, Little P...I mean...is the show over?" I struggle to even out my breathing and wrap my head around what the Australian Male just said in stiff and awkward intonation.

"Just that one. Another one's starting in a minute. Wanna watch—I mean listen?"

"Okay."

"Cool!"

The commercials are loud—I turn up the volume on my earbud and listen to Scott's text again. And again. And again.

He thought being with me was like getting to be an astronaut. That I picked him when I could have had anyone. The anger I felt coming earlier has fizzled out and...I miss it. I feel lost in endless darkness. I never would have guessed in a million years that my anger disappearing would make me feel this intensely alone. Alone and wretchedly sad. More than sad.

He also said he'd never stop trying to make it better.

I text him, *You did stop trying.*

I get a text the instant after I send mine—he must have sent it at the same time.

"Just because I didn't know they were there doesn't make it okay. I told them where to find us without telling you and that's what matters. I hope you never forgive me."

I play it again, "I hope you never forgive me."

Is that a typo? No, even autocorrect wouldn't change *can* into *never*.

Am I supposed to feel sorry for him? No...it'd make things easier to believe that, but I can't. Despite what happened, he never lied or tried to manipulate me. He's not fishing for anything. I think he really *doesn't* want me to forgive him—

Bzzz.

"I haven't."

It takes a moment to work out that he means he hasn't stopped trying to make it better.

You stopped after you came to my house that last time.

"I just stopped trying to make excuses."

What did my dad say?

"He told me I fucked up. And he was right. He said I wasn't welcome at your house anymore and to leave you alone or I'd just make things worse. So I did. I've been trying to give you as much space as I can but they wouldn't switch me to a different Trig. I'm trying to keep things normal and not weird for you."

You don't want me to forgive you? Or was that a typo?

"Don't forgive anyone who breaks your trust. Rule Number Infinity. Some things are unforgivable."

Unforgivable.

I...

"You're breathing funny again," Petey says.

Quack.

I fumble with my phone to play Sarah's text and Southern Matron speaks for her.

"Rick and I broke up last night."

*

I leave Petey to his cartoons and I run up to my room and call Sarah. She answers on the first ring.

"What happened? You okay?"

"I'm fine," she says, and she does sound fine.

"How'd it happen?"

"I called him and told him we should end it, though there wasn't much of *it* to end."

"You broke up on the phone?"

"Yeah, I know. We've been saying that's cowardly but when it came to me doing it, I realized if someone breaks up with you, do you really want to be stuck with them in a café or someone's house? Better to give them the option to hang up and be out as quickly as they want. And that's what happened. He wanted to get off the phone pretty fast."

"What'd you say was the reason? What *was* the reason?"

"We were just together out of habit. He tried to argue, but...he'll be relieved later if he isn't already. Deep down I think he knows I'm right."

"Wow," I say. "I had no idea."

"You had *some* idea. You've been calling him my Sort Of Boyfriend."

"Just by Hollywood standards. Compared to movies you guys were pretty lukewarm but movies aren't real. I thought you guys were just...more real, I guess. Nothing had changed in a while, at least as far as I knew."

Silence.

"You sure you're fine?" It seems like there's something she's not telling me.

"Yeah. How was your date with Jason?"

"What? It was...it was okay. We can talk about that

later. You've been together with Rick for almost two years—aren't we going to talk about it more than thirty seconds? I mean, why last night?"

"It was just a long time coming and it finally did."

"But you never said anything."

"It's not like we fought or did anything worth talking about. Things have just been blah. Then running around the mall all day, it reminded me there are plenty of guys out there, you know, so I thought it was time to try something else."

"Those guys weren't after us."

"I know, but you were out on a date with a guy you just met, and other stuff."

"What other stuff?"

"You know, just...stuff."

"I *don't* know. Why didn't you tell me?"

"We don't talk about Rick much."

"Because you don't. How you're feeling about Rick isn't something I would just bring up without anything happening. I tell you everything...I just figured you...told me everything, too."

Silence.

"There's nothing to tell. It's really not a big deal."

"But…" I can't tell if her breakup *is* a big deal and she's trying to be cool about it or if it's really not a big deal for her but is for me. Not that she did it but that it happened without her even giving me a clue.

We talk a lot every day but not about everything. She doesn't like to talk about her deadbeat dad, so I don't ask and I try not to talk about my cool dad too much. We didn't talk about Rick for the same reason, I thought, just the other way around, that she didn't want to rub it in that she had a boyfriend.

But Sarah's not just my best friend—she's my only really close everyday friend. Faith and I go way back and I can count on her but we don't know each other's details anymore. Now I'm realizing that we don't talk about Sarah's life outside of school much at all. Not her dad who pretty much only sends her cards on her birthday and Christmas except when he forgets. Not her mom who struggles as an accountant to afford to stay in their house and not move to an apartment. And, apparently, not her boyfriend even though she's been thinking about their relationship a lot lately and last night called him and broke up. The fact that she went through all that without sharing even a hint of it with me...it's making my stomach twist into a hard, cold knot.

"But what?" Sarah asks.

Something's shaking loose inside of me. I feel maybe angry but definitely sad that Sarah and I aren't as close as I thought...Am I being selfish, thinking about myself when my best friend just ended a two-year relationship? And my normal impulse to ask about this directly, to blurt out cold hard truths, it's failing me and I don't know why. It's like all the other truths I toss out easily mean nothing but this one means something and that's making it different.

"Parker, is something wrong?"

Something's definitely up. She isn't using her normal questioning voice. She sounds suspicious, or guilty, I don't know, like she knows I'm upset but doesn't want to acknowledge it.

"No," I say, impressed that I sound normal. "I'm just thinking about you and Rick."

"It's fine, really." She sounds relieved. "Tell me about your date with Jason."

"Actually, I was in the middle of something with Petey. I just wanted to make sure you were okay. I'll tell you about it later."

"Oh, okay. But it went fine? You're going to see him again?"

"I think so."

"Okay, well...talk to you later?"

"Yep."

Silence.

"Are you sure nothing's wrong?" she asks.

"Yep, all fine, talk to you later," I say in my easy-breezy voice despite the ice-cold ache in my chest. I hang up.

And unless I'm forgetting something trivial from when we were little kids, it's the first time I've ever lied to Sarah.

Chapter 17

I feel like I'm falling.

I'm told I'm not much of a bobber; the rocking many people do when they can't see. People don't realize how much their ability to stay still and upright is not just in their inner ears but also depends on seeing the room or the horizon. Maybe it was that I could see for the first seven years of my life, or maybe it's the way I lost my sight, but I don't feel floaty much.

Until now. I'm disconnected from the Earth. I know I went into shock when Dad died, and by the time I came out of it enough days had passed that I could more or less transition to being normal, or at least seeming normal. I think I might be in a different kind of shock now. When Dad died I lost my main rock but I had Sarah and I hung on for dear life. How much of my stability is based on people I cling to? A lot more than I thought because now that I've lost my last rock, I'm physically dizzy...floaty...with an unpleasant swoopy-ness. Like falling.

I can't call Faith. I mean I could, and she'd listen, and I don't have secrets from her, but these days there's plenty we don't know about each other and it would take too long to tell her.

The rest of Sunday went...Well, it was weird...At any given moment it felt like time was crawling by, like night would never come, and when it did, it felt like the day had flown by. I mostly hung out with Petey, playing games, and sitting in front of the TV like a zombie. When my phone quacked around nine, I didn't answer and then I texted Sarah that I was busy with Petey and we could talk tomorrow and she said okay, which was an unusually short answer for her given how we never miss our nightly phone calls even though I'm often playing with Petey and usually just put the game on hold.

My Monday sprints were a mess. Twice I felt the grass by the sidewalk and had to slow to adjust my direction. Then on my first sprint I lost count of my steps. I run too fast to actually count all the numbers; I just count one to nine over and over, then say ten, twenty, thirty...except I lost track of whether I had just said forty or fifty...?

I assumed fifty so I wouldn't run into the far fence, but when I finished the leg and walked to the fence it was farther than usual so I'd probably been counting right all along and just second-guessed myself. Like they say for taking tests, stick with your first answer.

The second sprint went okay but I lost count again in the third. After that I ran instead of sprinted, counting out real numbers, but even then I felt off so I quit and went home.

At school now I'm just standing here in the hall by my locker, bobbing, stuck.

I've heard that lying gets easier. Not for me. The lie I told Sarah yesterday is growing and I can't figure out how to get around it. If I go meet her at the Junior Quad like always, either I pretend nothing is wrong and try to have a normal conversation, which feels like lying on a scale beyond my ability, or I tell her what's wrong, which seems equally impossible. Yet if I don't go at all she'll definitely know something's up.

I'm being childish. Selfish. Stupid. Something, I don't know. Whatever it's called, I'm making a big deal out of nothing. I just have to stop.

But I can't. It's *not* nothing. I thought Sarah was my best friend, not my psychologist. Not that I was her project. Not that I was someone she could keep in her pocket because it's hard for me to get close to people and we've known each other so long she has a monopoly on me and doesn't have to share anything really intimate to keep us together. That she could just peer into my life but keep me out of hers.

None of which helps me figure out what to do now. Stand here or walk...go left or right...

"Hey, Parker," Jason calls, some distance up the hall. "What are you doing?"

"Huh? Oh...just...nothing."

He's next to me now.

"That's what it looks like. You coming or going?"

"Um...I'm done in my locker, if that's what you mean."

"Yeah. Do you have anywhere you need to be, or do you want to go for a walk?"

"Walk? Sure. Where? The track? Is that what you usually do?"

"Not in the mornings, just lunchtime. I thought we

could take a walk over to the Bio Garden."

Saved.

"Okay. Let me text Sarah so she doesn't wonder where I am."

"Sure thing."

Jason found me and we're going for a walk. Heal the heartsick without me.

I stow my cane in my bag and take Jason's arm.

Quack.

"Okay, have fun," Matron Sarah replies.

I'm not sure fun is in my future but miracles do happen.

*

"You know I still don't have your phone number."

"And this is crazy," I say.

I say my number to type into his phone.

"So call me maybe," I add.

"That's the idea..."

He doesn't get it. I don't think I want him to now.

"I mean now, so my phone will get your number without me having to type it in."

"Right."

My phone rings but I think he's had enough—I

know I have—so I don't pretend answer it. He hangs up.

"Sarah's a duck? Will I get a special sound, too? Or is that only for certain people?"

"Everyone gets one. That way I know who it is, to see if I should answer right away or if it can wait."

It's only after I answer that I realize he probably wanted to be called special. I say, "I'm thinking you're going to be one of the right-away people."

"Seems like a lot to remember. What everyone's sound is."

"Maybe your contact list is longer than mine. But is it really hard for you to remember what all your friends' voices sound like? It's not much different."

I can hear I sound bitchy but isn't this obvious? He doesn't answer.

We head toward the Bio Garden. I vaguely know where it is from last year when I took bio, but it's a remote corner I don't otherwise go to so I let Jason steer. I try not to think about how most of my wanting to be with Jason right now is to avoid Sarah.

"You okay?" he asks.

"Why?"

"You just seem...tired, I guess. Like you usually drink coffee but didn't today."

"I'm fine."

This lie is spreading. And I feel no rising urge to stop it. Jason's right, I am strangely tired.

"Scott told me everything this morning."

I don't reply. I completely forgot about telling Scott yesterday to come clean with Jason. It seems like days ago.

"So I guess I know why you ran out of my car Saturday. I'm sorry about all that."

"You couldn't have known. When did you see him?"

"This morning. We're jogging buddies."

"He runs?"

"Yeah, he's on the team with me. We run a three-point-two-mile loop from his house every day before school—we live just a few blocks apart."

"Oh."

"I'm kind of pissed at him. We talked awhile after he told me—then I turned around and went home but he kept going. He knows he screwed up; he took off running pretty hard."

I don't say anything.

"He should have told me when he heard we were going out."

"It was years ago…He probably didn't know I was still…I don't know…"

"He still likes you."

"He said that?"

"He didn't have to. I don't know why I didn't see it before. Now I know why he can't stand being around some guys, especially Isaac who's kind of a tool anyway. He said you texted him yesterday for the first time in years. That true?"

"Just to clear the air. We hadn't talked since it happened, and…well…I didn't have to think about it with him at Jefferson…so it was time. I let him have his say and now it's done."

"I don't know what to do."

"About what?"

"Scott."

"Because of me? Don't do anything. If you guys are friends—"

"We are, but…I don't know…He said he was sorry, but—"

"Don't stop being friends over this. It's got nothing to do with you and it's over. Okay?"

He doesn't answer. I decide not to push him.

"We better head back," he says. "The bell's going to ring."

*

I don't text Sarah that I'm not coming to the cafeteria, I just tell Molly in class that I'm meeting Jason at the track for lunch and let her deliver the news. Molly doesn't ask me anything all morning but I can tell she knows something's off kilter. Sarah finds me in the afternoon at my locker but with only a couple minutes between classes we have what sounds like a normal conversation. She tells me no one came to Office Hours and how she wants to hear about my date with Jason, and I say I'll tell her about it later and then we have to go to class. As we walk away from each other she calls after me to be sure to call her tonight, that she doesn't want to go another day without knowing, and to call her, okay? This is unusual; we always just call each other naturally without saying up front who's supposed to call who.

I don't answer. It feels terrible because I want to,

but I don't want to lie to her anymore. I want to tell her all about what happened with Jason, and Scott, and Jason and Scott...but...I also don't want to be anyone's project or entertainment. Most of all I want her to come tell me everything she's been keeping from me, though my brain hurts from the conflicting feelings of wanting this while thinking it makes me selfish and pathetic.

Pathetic. How did this happen? Of all the things it means to be Parker Grant, how did it come to *pathetic*?

God, I want to be angry. I want to feel betrayed. I know how to deal with those things. But lost, adrift, alone, and sad?

I already know I'm not going to call Sarah. I know it's going to make me feel stupid and petty and yes, pathetic. And I know that knowing this won't change anything—I still won't call her. The thing I don't know is what I'll do when she gives up waiting and calls me. I was willing to just ignore Scott trying to talk to me, but I could never in a million years do that to Sarah.

Chapter 18

Sarah hasn't called. No texts either. My phone hasn't quacked in over twenty-four hours. I'm with Jason before school again, at the Bio Garden. He texted me a couple times last night just to say hi and ask what special tones I assigned him on my phone. I hadn't even thought about it so I told him he'd just have to wait till morning. Maybe this is what people mean when they say lying gets easier. I'm doing it more but hating it just as much. I think he's disappointed that I assigned him Male With Deep Voice but there really aren't that many choices. He should just be glad he's not Chipmunk or Leprechaun or Martian. I think he likes that his ringtone is running footsteps, though—I did make a little effort.

He says he didn't run with Scott this morning, that he needed to think about things. He says Scott said he understood, but Jason isn't sure what that means.

I see it as more evidence that everything around me is falling apart. My morning run was as clumsy and cut short as yesterday's.

I'm also a no-show at morning Office Hours and Sarah still hasn't texted me. I'm not planning to go to the cafeteria for lunch. If I get to the end of the day without a quack, that'll mean the pretending is over.

Jason walks me to Trig and then runs off to his first class, U.S. History, I think, I'm not really sure. Shouldn't I be interested?

Molly isn't there when I sit, or at least I assume this since she always says something. Yesterday, after my texting with Scott and him talking to Jason, I was tense about what might happen, but I barely heard Scott at all, and what few times D.B. said something to him, he gave one-word answers. This morning no one's saying anything so I don't even know who's here.

"D.B.?" I say.

"Hey, P.G. What's up?"

"Nothing, I...I just don't know who's around if no one says anything."

"Oh, yeah, well, I'm here. So's Scott, but not Molly. Nathan's here—"

"Huh?" Nathan asks from in front of D.B.

"It's okay, I don't need a roll call. Just who's nearby."

"Oh. You finish the homework?"

"Like always. You?"

"I wrote down answers for everything but they're probably wrong."

"I wouldn't worry too much. There are more important things in life than trigonometry."

"I still need passing grades even if I get a football scholarship. Hey, maybe if Molly's sick again—" He stops. Then he says, "Hey Molly, what's up?"

"Not Parker," Molly says. "Unless by *up* you just mean not in bed anymore."

"What?" I say.

"You." She sits down. "You're not up. As in you're *down*. Like you were all day yesterday. It's okay. You can't be up every day. It'd be weird if you were."

"Well..." I try to think of something Parker would say if she weren't down. "There you go. I wouldn't want to be *weird*."

D.B. laughs. It surprises me how much I appreciate it.

*

I reach the library after school but as I approach our table I don't hear Molly's usual greeting. Maybe I've finally beaten her here for once.

"Hey, Parker," Sarah says.

I stiffen, outwardly. I can't take it back.

"Hey, Sarah. Where's Molly?"

"I asked her at lunch if she could be five minutes late today so we could talk. I know texting during the day is a pain."

It is for me. I put down my bag and sit. I try to relax but can't. "About what?"

"About whatever I did that you're mad about."

"I'm not mad." I throw in a shrug. It's true. I wish I were mad. I just found out I liked her more than she likes me, or at least trusted her more…Talking about it would just make it worse, make me even more pathetic.

"If you're not mad you're still *something*. I can see wanting to hang out with Jason, but you're not talking to me at all anymore. Why didn't you call me last night?"

There it is, the direct question. So far my lies have been slippery. I just don't have it in me to completely make up some bullshit reason why I didn't call. I might not be able to tell her the whole truth, but at least I can say true things.

"I just didn't feel like talking. Is that not okay?"

"Of course it's okay, but..." She takes a deep breath. "Something's happened. I don't know what, but..." Her voice drops to a near whisper, not angry, more like she's hurt. "You're treating me like I'm stupid. I might not be taking all honors and AP classes like you but it's just that I don't want to bother with subjects I don't care about. It's not because I'm stupid. I'm not stupid."

My throat closes. These past two days seem like forever and God I miss my Sarah. But I missed Scott, too, and just like now, I was actually missing what I thought I had, not what I really had. I miss the Sarah I thought I had. I feel like I'm melting.

I cough to clear my throat. "I know you're not. You're the smartest person I know."

"Next to you," she says. I can't tell if it's a Sarah-style joke or a jab.

"I know I'm not as smart as you. I've actually been feeling pretty stupid lately."

"Why?"

"Just...stuff. You know."

"No, I don't know."

Silence.

"This is about Rick, isn't it?"

"Why would I be upset about you breaking up with Rick?"

"Not that I did, just that I didn't, I don't know, tell you I was going to do it beforehand? I told you I decided while you were out with Jason. Did you want me to call you at the restaurant during your date?"

"You could if you wanted to."

"Just so you'd get to hear about it before it happened instead of after?"

I concentrate on slowing down my breathing, to stay calm.

"I didn't know you thought I was that petty," I manage to say.

"No, Parker, I'm sorry." She sits across from me and puts her hands on mine. I flinch but I don't pull back. I don't want to do anything to make things worse.

"I didn't mean that," she says. "I just...I don't understand. Please, whatever it is, just tell me. You know you can tell me anything don't you?"

"I know. And you can tell me anything, right?"

"I know I can. Believe me, my next boyfriend, when I'm going to dump him, you'll hear about it first. I promise."

I take my hand from hers, but to make it less glaring, I start unloading my bag for when Molly comes.

"Only if you want to," I say. "It's not a new rule or anything. You don't need to run everything by me first."

"That's not...that's not what I meant. I just mean..." She doesn't finish the sentence. I don't think she knows what she means if it's not what it sounded like. I don't know what else it could mean.

The door to the library opens.

"I hope that's you, Molly. We have lots to do today."

"Only if you're taking different classes than I am," Molly says. Then she adds, "Oh, or...I mean, except Trig I guess, that could take a while."

Sarah gets up. "I'll ca—" She stops herself. Then, "See you, Molly."

When she's gone, Molly says, "Should I ask, or...no?"

I struggle to think of a way to say no that isn't

rude. None of this is Molly's fault and has nothing to do with her, but we're getting to be friends, so even just saying no would sound...unfriendly.

"I'm not ready to be asked yet. But thanks for asking...about asking..."

*

Molly walks me to the parking lot to wait for my ride. She asks if I want to be alone and I say definitely not. She sits next to me but we don't talk. Maybe I'm not petty but I guess I can be selfish.

Aunt Celia's car arrives. I know Sheila's driving since Aunt Celia texted that she's at a parent meeting for Petey's field trip to the tide pools tomorrow; I would've known anyway because the radio is really loud. I say goodbye to Molly and climb into the car.

Sheila's favorite Alicia Keys CD is on full blast. It's good but soulful and I'm not sure I can take it.

"Can we have the music off?" I shout.

"I want it on!"

Damn. "How about not so loud? Maybe turn it down a notch?"

I hear the music go from what sounds like volume 95 down to 92. I don't know the name of the song but

I'm wobbly and it's starting to tip me over.

"Please, Sheila, I'm asking!"

It turns down to maybe 89.

"No, seriously, I can't take it!" I reach out to find the knob though I've never touched it before in Aunt Celia's car and have no idea where it is. I feel some buttons and move my hand to the left—Sheila's hand bats mine away.

"We'll be home in a couple minutes!"

"I don't have a couple minutes! I'm having a shitty couple of days and I can't stand it! You can live without your goddamn music for two minutes and when we get home you can crawl back into your room and lock the door and listen to whatever as loud and as long as you want!" I lunge out and drag my hand across all the buttons and the CD ejects—

"Hey!"

—and I yank it out and hold it to my right in case she tries to grab it.

She pulls the car over violently and we bounce against the curb and stop.

"Jesus!" I say. "What the hell's wrong with you? It's just a fucking song!"

Silence.

Well, not exactly. Over the idling car engine, Sheila's breathing heavy. No, she's breathing funny, like she's trying not to cough, or sneeze, or...

Oh shit, she's crying.

"I...I'm sorry. Here." I hold out her CD.

It's yanked from my hand and clatters against the windshield. She sniffles and coughs twice.

"I didn't mean to..." To what? I didn't really say anything personal. "It's okay."

She snorts and growls, "Fuck you, Parker."

The car lunges forward—we're driving down the street again. She's not sobbing or anything but her stuttering breaths tell me she's still crying.

"I wasn't really yelling at you. I was just talking loud over the music. I didn't mean anything—"

She coughs again. "God, Parker, you think this is because you yelled at me? Everything isn't about you! Other people have problems and...and...fuck, whatever."

I get it now, finally. She was crying when she picked me up. The music was so I wouldn't hear.

"What's wrong?" I ask.

"It's not about you!"

"I know, I'm just—"

"Ha! What do you know? Tell me! Tell me what you know!"

"It's not about me—"

"I hear the words but everything else tells me you *don't* know! Yeah, you got big problems...You really *are* blind! You can't see you're not the center of the universe! That other people have lives and things happen to them all the time and you know nothing about it!"

"How can I if nobody tells me?"

"You think everyone runs around telling everybody everything? Or that we can all read each other's faces? That's not how it works!"

The car jerks to the left and we bounce into the driveway and stop hard enough that my seat belt locks down on my collarbone.

"No," Sheila says, loud but hoarse. "You just don't care. Say whatever you want but in your head it *is* all about you. Except it isn't, Parker. It really, really isn't."

She kicks open the door and it crashes shut. Her footsteps trot to the door, keys hit the ground, get picked up, the door opens, and then it slams.

After a minute I slide my hands across the dash until I find her CD. It seems okay—no scratches I can feel. I search some more and find an empty case. I put the CD inside and stow it in my bag to give her later.

I know why I'm so sure of everything all the time; it's because I can't stomach the alternative, that I can't be sure of anything ever. But when my breathing calms down and I think it through, honestly, the hard truth is clear. I was wrong about pretty much everything that happened in this car ride. And if I let myself think about it, I might be wrong about a lot of other things too.

Chapter 19

It takes me an hour to cane to Sarah's house. It used to take less time but it's been a couple years since I walked it. She would have picked me up if I called her but I needed time to think, to meditate even, which is what cane-walking can be like. Besides, I want to do all the work myself this time, just in case.

I ring the doorbell.

It's strange but I'm here hoping to learn I'm wrong, and I hate being wrong, except this time I'd give anything to be. If I'm not, well...I don't have a Plan B.

The door opens. Sarah says, "Parker? Did you walk here?"

"Do I talk too much?"

"What?"

"I dunno. We talk about me more than you...I thought it was because I had more...drama...but maybe I don't. Maybe I just...don't listen enough."

"That's not true," Sarah says. "You always listen when I need to talk."

"But?"

"But nothing. I just...don't need to talk about things as much, maybe."

"I don't tell you everything because I *need* to," I say, feeling prickly. "I thought we were friends, not that I was one of your patients." I try to use my bitter voice—it comes out sounding pathetic instead.

"Hey, Parker, no. *No.* Is that what's going on? Jesus..." She leans in and her voice deepens and gets hoarse, something I rarely hear. "Don't you *ever* think *anything* like that! Get in here!"

She jostles me and uses the contact to take my arm and pull me inside and close the door and now she's hugging me and whispering loudly in my ear. "I *love* you, Parker. You're my *sister*. No, better than that; real sisters you're stuck with—we're sisters because we *want* to be."

I don't know what to say or even think. She doesn't loosen her grip.

"You hear me? I love you more than family. We've known each other so long I can't even remember when we met. If we don't get prom dates, we're going together. We're going to each other's weddings. We're babysitting each other's kids. We're going to get drunk and complain about our husbands. When we get divorces we're moving in with each other to get back on our feet and find better guys. We're driving each other to the hospital for chemo when we're seventy. Right? *Right?*"

"Right," I whisper.

"It's just, you've been through so much, I feel stupid complaining about...anything."

"Sarah, no!" My voice squeaks and I pull back to talk to her face. "If I can talk to Marissa about Owen I sure as hell can talk about your problems with Rick, even if it's just that it's boring, or...or...or how you feel about other stuff, like...like your dad leaving—"

"*Fuck* him. He *left*. Your dad *loved* you and he *died*! Why talk about my asshole dad?"

"Because he's your dad! We can talk about losing a bad dad and losing a good one but it's not a contest! You know how I feel because I tell you. And I...I have guesses but I don't really know what you think about your dad. I want to know everything, like why you've been with Rick so long when he just seemed like a check mark in the Boyfriend Box, and why now you've suddenly erased it. It...it *kills* me to think...God, not telling me stuff doesn't make me feel special, it makes me feel like I don't matter to you!"

"I'm sorry," she whispers. "You matter more than anything. I'm really really sorry—"

"Stop being sorry and just tell me. What happened with Rick really?"

More silence.

"I can't, Parker. I..."

"Did he do something to you—"

"No, no, nothing like that..."

"Sarah, I've been walking around in a funk for two days thinking there's important stuff you're not telling me...and there is! We're never going to get through it if you don't tell me. I...I...I won't go to prom with you if you don't!"

The joke works and she snorts, not quite a laugh, but her voice is serious when she says "Let's sit down."

She leads me to the couch and we sit. She doesn't speak right away. I slide my hand out on the cushion.

She takes it loosely. Her hand is clammy and shaking a little.

"You're scaring me now," I say with no joking in my voice. "Is something really wrong? Did something happen?"

"No, I just...I don't want you to shut me out again."

"I won't, I promise. Why'd you break up with Rick?"

"I told you. We were just...blah. Habit."

"Then what's all this about?"

"It's...it's Scott."

What??

I try my only guess, a bad one. "What...I mean...do you *like* him?"

"No."

"Then...oh...wait...*wait*...Is he looking at *you* now?"

"No, Parker," Sarah says. "He's looking at you."

"Well...okay...but I don't see how..."

"With him away at Jefferson these past two years, I kind of forgot what it looked like. Now I see him looking at you again...Rick's never looked at me like that."

I don't know what to say.

"He still looks at you like he used to, even before

you got together, like you're the most important thing in the world. Like if you were trapped on railroad tracks he'd break every finger to get you free without even noticing...and if he couldn't, he'd sit on the tracks and hold your hand and watch you instead of the train."

I take a deep breath and feel like I have to defuse this. "That's kind of extreme, isn't it?"

"Nope. Intensity isn't creepy from people who really love you. Don't you think your dad would have gone blind instead of you if he could have?"

"I know he would've."

"Scott too. He doesn't have a crush on you or just want to get in your pants or think you're better than nothing. He *loves* you. And I couldn't watch that any more, when you're not even *together*, and see Rick barely look at me at all. I was just a check mark to him, too. I don't believe in soul mates either—"

"God, if Scott was my soul mate, I'm screwed."

"But it still showed me you can get a hell of a lot closer than I was with Rick. Then goofing around in the mall put me over the top."

And just like that, I understand what this is really

about. God I'm an idiot sometimes.

I pull my hand back.

"You think I should have stayed with him." I hear my voice and it's freaky. Flat. Dead.

"Parker, no, I'm on your side!"

Hands grab at mine and I pull back, more because I instinctively don't like being grabbed than not wanting Sarah to touch me.

"Please, Parker, it doesn't matter what I think—"

"Of course it matters! If it didn't I wouldn't be here!"

"Parker—"

"Wait, just...just wait." I dig my phone out of my pocket.

"You asked about my date. I found out Jason and Scott are friends. And when Jason stopped Isaac and Gerald, it was Scott who came first and Jason followed him. He said he thought Scott was ready to beat the shit out of them if he hadn't stopped him."

"I know."

"What?! How the hell do you know?"

"Other people saw and word got around."

"Why didn't you tell me!"

"Why would I? You hung up on me just for telling you he was in your Trig class."

Shit...I *did* hang up on her then...That's not how it seemed at the time. I thought I was just...

"Sorry."

"You don't have to be sorry—"

"Yeah I do." I swallow. "Anyway, I texted him."

"Really? When?"

"Sunday." I hand her my phone.

I lean away and rest my head against the arm of the sofa. The coarse weave, like burlap, is rough but somehow pleasant. It's nice to feel something, to keep me grounded while I sort this all out.

"Wow," she says.

"You were always on my side, but if it were you, you'd have forgiven him. Wouldn't you?"

"If it were me, sure I'd have been mad, I'd have frozen him out awhile. Then I'd have probably thawed out and made him buy me an expensive dinner or something. That doesn't mean I think *you* should have. Maybe I'm wrong—maybe staying with him would have been weak and you did the right thing. Do you know what I mean?"

"Sort of. You're still not telling me everything, though. I can tell." I sit up straight but don't turn to face her. "Just say it."

"Please," she says in a small voice. "Can't we just forget it?"

I hear that she's doubled over, face on her knees. I bow my head from the weight of it. I'm more than an idiot sometimes. Sheila was right; I can be totally blind.

I slide off the couch to sit on the floor at her feet and clasp my hands together on the back of her neck. I whisper into her ear.

"I love you, Sarah. I'm not going to throw you away."

She sniffs. Is she crying? Sarah crying is more rare than Sarah laughing.

"You threw Scott away."

This hits me in the chest like a physical blow.

"That was because of what he *did*, not what he said or believed. It's not the same."

"He was my friend too."

Oh God. This never crossed my mind. Never. "I didn't make you throw him away."

She doesn't answer. Her breathing is ragged. I open my mouth to say more, to convince her, but now I just want to un-say it because I see what a gift she gave me back then and how hard it must have been.

I let go of her and hold up my right hand, fingers spread.

"Face," I say.

"Mm-mm."

"Please?"

She knows it's not fair to hide her face from me just because my eyes can't see it like anyone else's would, and I don't abuse this request by making it often—it's been years in fact. She lifts her head and presses her face lightly against my palm, her nose between my index and middle fingers. Her face is tightly scrunched up, her eyes squeezed shut, her cheeks damp.

"Oh, Sarah..." I climb up and wrap my arms around her. She pushes her face into my neck and gasps.

"He...he was...he..."

"Shhh..." I say. "We have all afternoon."

"He was...so...upset..."

"Scott? Yeah, I—"

"No, *Rick*. He was really, *really* upset. I...I almost changed my mind."

She starts really crying, shaking and sobbing. I've never heard her cry like this, not even when her dad left. I hold her tightly and try to keep from crying myself. It's not easy. If Sarah were trapped on railroad tracks, I'd break all my fingers for her too.

She slips down to lie across my lap and words start pouring out of her along with the tears. "And... and...and it made me think that if Rick felt that bad breaking up, when he didn't even really *love* me, how did poor Scott feel? But I couldn't tell you that...I couldn't...because I'm on your side..."

I feel strangely hollow except for how much Sarah means to me, how much I depend on her, and in a way that makes me feel good, not weak or dependent or pathetic. I reach out and feel her hair lying across her face. I tuck it behind her ear.

"I was so happy for you back then," she says between sobs. "I wasn't even jealous. I sometimes wondered why I wasn't but I wasn't. Maybe if I wanted Scott...but he was yours and I was happy for you and I just hoped I'd find someone like that someday. I even...I even hoped my dad would help me like yours did...but...but..."

Sarah stops talking and struggles to breathe. I hold her and try to think about how much I love her and not about how much her dad doesn't.

*

I wish these weren't all one-way conversations. I need someone I trust to tell me if I'm going crazy. Thank God I have Sarah back, but everything else is quicksand. Jesus, Dad, I'm bobbing, even now with the weight of Sarah on my lap I still can't tell exactly which direction is up. I never thought there was anything psychological to that but the more I lose my grip on what's going on around me the more I can't stay steady.

Scott said seeing me cry in that classroom back then was like waking from a dream, wondering how he could have ever believed what he had before. That's how I feel now. He was my best friend, closer than Sarah as impossible as that seems, maybe because of that extra spark we had...How could I have thought this one stupid thing was more true than everything else? How could I have been so goddamn paranoid I immediately thought the worst and never questioned it again?

He didn't know they were hiding in the room. He didn't know...

He must have told me, through the bathroom door, or later when he tried to talk past the Sarah-Faith blockade. I don't remember but he must have and I wouldn't listen. He says now he doesn't think it matters but it does because he's right; I didn't care if anyone saw us. It never occurred to me that people might look in the window—it's easy for me to forget about things like windows—I never thought we were hiding. It's just obnoxious to do in the middle of the cafeteria.

It's so clear now I can't even remember what it was like to not see it. When someone tricks you, like taping a sign on your back or sneaking up behind you to dump water on you, or tricking you into a room to kiss in front of a secret audience...all those things hurt because they mean the people doing it don't give a shit about you. Not just indifferent, but cruel.

But when I ran away crying, he didn't waste a single word on them. He ran out the door after me, trying to explain that he wasn't one of them. Not an asshole. He loved me, he cared about me, and two and a half years later he's ready to pummel those same guys just for playing keep-away with my phone, enough that Jason needed to get between them.

I've always been so worried that everything around me is just one big setup...In my head Scott became an asshole like the rest of them and I shut him out until you told him to leave me alone.

I was grateful for that, but you knew him, too...Did you know I was overreacting? That my freak-out would end and then you'd help me understand that the problem wasn't just that Scott was only thirteen but that I was only thirteen too? And when I grew up I'd see people can't be defined by just one thing? Were you waiting for the right time, but months turned to years and then...? If you were really here now, would we be having this conversation for real, now that I'm ready?

Thank God for Sarah. For asking me to imagine how Scott felt. I wish I had asked it myself...that I were a better person...

I want to think about it now, about what it meant to him to lose not just me but also his friends who turned out to be assholes, plus Sarah and Faith when they chose my side...but it's too much to hold all at once. And if that's not bad enough, this isn't the person I've become, it's apparently the person I've always been.

*

I don't know how long it takes, maybe half an hour, before Sarah quiets, sprawled across my lap, her breathing steady. She takes a deep breath, holds it, and lets it go.

"Wow," she says.

"You held that in way too long. It's a wonder you didn't explode."

"I did explode," she says and snorts a little. That's closer to a laugh than it deserves and I'm glad for it.

"It's ironic that you broke up with Scott over something he didn't tell you," she says in her miserable voice. "Then I didn't tell you all this because I was afraid you'd break up with me, too."

"We'll never break up. But I don't want us to get cancer either. Let's just drive to Bingo when we're seventy, okay?" I lean over and hug her, awkwardly since she's lying crossways on my lap. She squeezes me back tightly.

"Jesus, Parker, I think I'm going to cry again."

"Go ahead. You're already not getting a gold star today."

She snorts. "Ha, ha."

"Sad, but true. And I intend to. Number ninety-two."

Sarah shifts her head in my lap. "I told you all this stuff but you haven't said anything. What are you thinking?"

I feel like I'm made of lead. A twisted lump of cold lead.

I hug her. "I'm thinking I have the best friend I could possibly have."

"Me, right?"

I nod, my cheek pressed against her forehead.

"Good answer," she says. "But that's not what I mean."

"I know."

"So what else?"

Thinking it is one thing...saying it out loud is another...

I whisper it into her ear. Maybe saying it as quietly as possible will keep it under control.

"I think I've made a terrible mistake."

Chapter 20

Ten minutes later we're in Sarah's car but I can tell she's driving under the speed limit.

"I said this is a bad idea, right?" she says. "I didn't just think it?"

"I'm going to start counting. Your ass is covered, and not just by those new yoga pants."

"How'd you know I'm wearing them?"

"Lucky guess. You remember how to get there?"

"Yeah, but there's still time *not* to. We can turn around and text him instead. He might have friends over or not even be home. Or he might be working; I think I heard he has a job."

"Where?"

"I don't know—don't change the subject."

"I want to talk to him face to face. I want to hear his voice and his answers without him getting time to think about them too much."

"That's what phones are for."

"What are you so worried about?"

"I'm worried that you're not worried."

"I'm plenty worried."

"Then let's go back. I mean, two and a half years of nothing and now...what's the rush?"

"I'm not rushing. I'm just not waiting anymore. Are we there yet?"

"God, are you twelve?" She pulls over. "And yes, we are. I'll wait around the corner till you text me."

"Are you sick of me telling you how good of a friend you are?"

"Keep trying, I'll let you know. His path is directly in front of your door."

I get out and then unfold my cane while Sarah drives away. The path is flat concrete with grass on both sides, just like I remember. I find the doorbell and press it. The silence tells me they still haven't fixed it, so I knock. I hear footsteps inside and I adjust my scarf. I chose Peace Symbols this morning because I wanted some peace; maybe now it can mean something else.

The door opens.

"Parker!" It's Scott's mom. "Parker Grant! Oh, look

at you! Let me give you a hug!"

Before I answer she hugs me warmly, which feels strange because she was always very nice to me but seldom hugged me.

"You must be half a foot taller since I last saw you! How did you get here, did you walk? Come inside!"

"Sarah dropped me off," I say, folding my cane.

"Come into the kitchen. It's still straight ahead and then left, I'm sure you remember."

I do. Six steps, left, three steps, table, chairs...I sit without incident.

"I wish the furniture in my house stayed put this much."

"Old habits—" She stops herself. Then she sits and her hands grab mine and I manage not to flinch. "I'm so sorry about what happened, Parker. Martin was a wonderful father. You must miss him terribly. What an awful time for you."

"Not so good for him, either," I say and instantly regret it. I don't want to sound glib, I just don't know what to say sometimes when people talk about Dad. "But thanks. My aunt's family moved in with me because..." But my usual answer, how my house was just better than theirs, won't come out, not to Scott's mom. "They moved here so I wouldn't have to move in with them. It takes me a long time to learn my way around new places and they didn't want me to have to go to a new house and a new school and town right after..." I stop talking—it feels like someone is squeezing my throat. It's awful saying all this out loud.

"That was very nice of them. So now you have cousins with you? Your aunt has kids?"

I clear my throat. "Two. Sheila's a junior like me and Petey is eight."

"Oh, it must be hard for her moving in the middle of high school. That happened to me and, well...well... it's not nearly as hard as what you're going through, of course." She pats my hand to comfort me but only emphasizes how Sheila's life was ruined so mine wouldn't be. "When terrible things happen, it's hard on everyone. When Scott found out...well..."

She squeezes my hands again and lets go. "Let me get you something to drink. You still like iced tea?"

I haven't had any since...well, Dad was the one who made it.

"I do."

"It won't be as good as Martin's. I don't know why his was always so much better."

"Put baking soda in the water while you're boiling it."

"Baking soda? Are you sure?"

"It counteracts acid in the tea and makes it taste smoother. A quarter teaspoon per quart."

"Well...I'll certainly try that...baking soda..."

She sets a glass in front of me and I take a sip. Yes, it needs baking soda.

"Thank you."

"I thought Scott would have heard us by now. I'll go get him."

Maybe he just doesn't want to come out. Sarah was right; he's going to feel like I'm cornering him. It's stupid—I didn't even think about his mom being here. It's surreal sitting here having a normal conversation with her like the last couple years never happened.

She's gone longer than it takes to walk down the hall and back. What am I going to say if he won't see me? How much does she know? What am I going to say if he does come? I really haven't sorted this out.

I hear shuffling and doors opening and closing. Then footsteps. He's alone.

"Hey." He sits down.

"Hey. Where's your mom?"

"In her bedroom."

"Oh."

I hear the soundtrack to *Grease* start playing, muffled by the intervening walls and closed doors... The sound wraps itself around my heart and squeezes.

God, I should have thought this through. I usually just say whatever I think but my mind is blank. Now I wish I'd planned something.

"I guess I should have texted you instead of just coming." My voice surprises me at how quiet it is, like I'm talking to myself. "I just wanted to hear your real voice, not texts or over the phone. I know that's not fair...I didn't let you do that..."

"It's fine, though I need to go to work in a few minutes."

"Oh? Where do you work?"

"I...do building maintenance and some landscaping at Ridgeway Mall, for the owner, not just any one store. But...that's not what you came to talk about."

"No. I came to tell you..." What?

Silence.

Then something comes out without me even thinking about it, in a whisper.

"I miss my dad."

"I..." Scott says. "I know. I'm sorry. I wanted to... when it happened, but...you know. I...I mean..."

He's using what I used to call his boyfriend voice but I don't think it's deliberate. To me it's like a cat purring.

"What?" I ask.

"Nothing. I'm just sorry about your dad."

"You were going to say something else."

"It's nothing. I'm just sorry."

"It's okay, Scott. Say it. You...you can say anything."

"It's just...I miss him, too."

Scott's dad died of a heart attack when Scott was just a baby. I never really thought much about how all that time Scott spent at our house was time with my dad as well as me. It never occurred to me that when I cut him off he lost my dad too, long before I did.

"I'm sorry." I can barely hear myself.

"You don't have anything to be sorry about."

"I do. I...I should have let you explain. It wasn't fair that I didn't even listen."

"It doesn't matter."

"It matters! I...I don't want to be someone who doesn't listen! And...and I think it would have made a difference."

He says nothing. There's definitely something I'm missing, but I don't even know how to ask.

"You know they think he killed himself?"

"What?" He sounds like this is a complete surprise.

"He OD'd on prescription drugs. I know it was an accident. The police report said the amount of drugs made it impossible to say for sure but they strongly suspected suicide and that was enough for the insurance company."

"Of *course* it was an accident, Parker. He'd never do that to you. *Never.*"

"I know...except...I didn't even know he was taking anything in the first place. For depression or anxiety or both, I don't know. It's like those things are all tangled up in ways I don't understand."

"It doesn't matter. It was an accident."

"But what if it wasn't!"

I'm holding the half-full glass of iced tea on the table and with all the moisture it slips out of my grip when my hand squeezes—it slides across the table and stops. Scott takes my hand with his, puts the glass back into it, and lets go. My throat closes up.

"It was an accident," he says. "It was."

I cough. "But he was taking drugs and I didn't know, since he felt...I don't know, depressed or something, and I didn't know that either. What else didn't I know? It's like he was just another secret like everyone else."

"What does *that* mean?"

"Everyone is a secret. There's no way to know what's in anyone's head."

"Ummm...what's in my hand right now?"

"What? I...I don't know. How could I?"

"Check it out. It's right here."

I find his hand, palm up. He gently closes his fingers and now we're holding hands.

"There's nothing in it," I say.

"Sure there is." He squeezes. "People are full of things you don't know but that doesn't mean they're secrets; you just don't know everything yet." He lets go. "And that's good, otherwise you'd have no reason to talk anymore."

There's a lot I don't even know about myself, apparently, like why I've been such an idiot. All I can think about now are things I *do* know, like how much I want him to keep talking, and how much I want him to touch my hand again.

Scott stands up. "I have to go to work. Was that why you came, to talk about your dad?"

"No," I say. I hear my wretched voice and hate myself for it. I stand and sway a bit and grab the back of the chair for support. "I came here...to tell you I'm sorry. I should have listened to you back then. It wasn't fair to shut you out. I hope you can forgive me. I want to be friends again. Can we?"

"I wish we could. It's not really possible. And I can't forgive you when you did nothing wrong. I really have to go. How'd you get here? If you need a ride—"

"No, Sarah will pick me up." I unfold my cane while trying to orient to walk to the front door with him. "Why can't we be friends?"

"You need to be able to trust your friends."

"I...I trust you."

He opens the front door and we step through. "You used to trust me without hesitating. I can't forget what that was like."

He closes the door. "I'm going to be late. You need me to call Sarah?"

"I'll do it."

"Okay, I have to go." His voice fades as he crosses the yard to the driveway and opens a car door. "I'll see you in Trig tomorrow."

"Unless I see you first," I say, like a reflex. It surprises me. A lot of things I'm saying and doing lately are surprising me.

The door closes, the engine starts, the car backs up, and he drives away.

Chapter 21

"Hey, Parker."

I jump at Jason's voice almost right next to me at my locker and my hands spring open and drop my bag. I hear the tumble of my stuff spilling out on the concrete. I'm willing to bet that includes the few loose tampons I have in there.

"You jumpy this morning?"

"No," I say with my patient voice. I squat by my bag and turn it upright. "I pretty much always jump when someone sneaks up on me." I sweep my hands and scoop everything into my bag.

"I didn't—" he says, crouching next to me. "Oh… sorry."

"It's fine," I say. "Do I have everything?"

A couple things land in my bag. "Now you do."

"Thanks." I stand up and close my locker.

"Hey, you talk to Coach Underhill yet?"

"We decided to give it a week to let everything else sort out. I'm meeting with him next Monday afternoon."

"Cool. You ready to walk? I thought maybe somewhere besides the Bio Garden this time, but I guess it doesn't matter much."

"Oh, I'm sorry, I promised Sarah yesterday I'd meet her this morning."

"What, for homework, or...?"

"No, nothing for school. We just...sort of hang out together in the yard every morning."

"You've been with me all this week."

"I know, it's just..." Okay, what do I say now?

A better question is how did I become this person? It's time to start being myself. If he doesn't like it, that'll suck, but better to know sooner than later.

"It'll take too long to explain now but Sarah and I sit outside and listen to people who want to talk, for advice about all kinds of stuff. Only we sort of got into a fight earlier this week...well, more like a misunderstanding...Okay, I was being an idiot. Then you asked me to walk at the same time so I went with you instead, but now Sarah and I have patched things up. Make sense?"

"Not really. I just thought we had this thing going with morning walks."

"No, I mean yeah, it was nice, I just usually sit with Sarah. We can still have lunch today. What do you normally do here in the morning?"

"I'm not usually here. I came early Monday to talk to you and then we started our walks."

He lets this hang there and I'm confused. Is he trying to guilt me, or get me to cancel on Sarah—like two days in a row constitutes a recurring date?

"Sorry, I didn't know. I thought you were here anyway. I better get going."

"It's just, I had something to tell you."

He doesn't go on—I guess he wants me to ask. "What is it?"

"After school let out last year my family went beach camping in Baja. When I got back, Scott had changed to a different route. He didn't really say why and it didn't matter to me; I just liked that the new route was longer. I didn't notice it Saturday night in the dark, but this morning I started running with him again and saw we go right by your house."

"Oh. Have you..." I say. "I run in the morning too. You guys ever see me?"

"No. We pass by around quarter to six."

"I leave at six. Usually, I mean. Not today." After Monday and Tuesday were such a wobbly mess, I felt even worse this morning and skipped going out entirely.

"Okay. Maybe it's not spying since we never see you, but it's still creepy. I thought I should tell you."

Wait...Scott started running by my house sometime in the middle of June?

"It's not creepy," I say, dizzy again. I have to swallow before I can continue. "He's...he's checking my route. You know, for any new stuff I might trip over."

"Why would he need to?"

"Because my dad can't anymore. Every night before bed my dad and I would take a little walk. He said it was the only exercise he got being a desk jockey all day but he was really checking my route for my run the next morning."

"Wait...you actually run alone? No one's with you?"

"I told you I don't run with anybody—"

"I figured you had someone on a bike or something!

That's crazy—you can't run by yourself!"

"Well, actually, I *can*, and I *do*. Every day."

I feel a shiver, an actual shiver, across my shoulders and back. "Do you remember ever seeing a big van parked across the sidewalk near my house? Back toward the end of June?"

"I was still in Mexico. Why?"

"Nothing. Never mind."

Silence.

"You don't think it's creepy, Scott running by your house every morning...what, three years after you broke up with him?"

"Two and a half," I say, my voice quiet. "It's not creepy. It's..."

"It's what?"

He says it like a challenge and it irks me, but I try to look at things from his side. Truth is one thing; it's another to rub people's noses in it.

"Whatever the opposite of creepy is."

He blows air out of his nose. "You still like him, don't you?"

"I broke up with him, remember?"

"Part of you still likes him though."

"He was my best friend for years. Some things you can't just switch off." Even though I sort of did. "What does it matter anyway? We're not together now."

"Maybe you want to be."

It's unsettling how his words are provoking but he talks in an easygoing voice. I don't know what to make of it.

"Are you asking a question?"

"I just want to know where we stand."

"Um...we met a week ago...then we went out Saturday night...and it was fun...and...we should do it again sometime? How's that?"

"Are you going to call him again?"

"I don't know, maybe?" This is getting weirder. I try to defuse it with a smile. "Is that a problem?"

"I'm just saying, either we're doing this or we're not, it's up to you."

"Doing what? Liking each other? Having a good time?"

"No, you know...seeing each other."

"Isn't it a bit soon to be talking about being exclusive?" Wow, if I could go back in time, Parker back in August wouldn't believe the conversations she's having now only a few weeks later. "We've only been out once."

"You climbed into the backseat fast enough. Is that normal for you?"

"No! Is it normal for you? You drove us to the Bluff fast enough! It was my first time there—how many girls do you bring up there?"

"None while you and I are going out."

"Well don't do me any favors. You can park with anyone you want and so can I until we agree otherwise, but it's going to take more than one night out, I'm just telling you now."

"Yeah, you're telling me a lot."

"I'm just being honest."

"Things aren't that simple."

"Really? I think they are."

Silence.

Quack.

"That's Sarah wondering where I am. I gotta go. We can talk about this more at lunch if you want." I sure hope he doesn't, though. I unfold my cane.

"Fine. Okay. Later."

*

I sit down at the usual table with Sarah. I'm still buzzing inside.

"I didn't listen to your text—I just came straight here."

"Just asking where you were."

"Having a shitty conversation with Jason. He somehow thought it was our new routine to spend mornings together so when I said I was coming here he got all twitchy, like I was flaking on him to be with you."

"Bitches before...britches?"

"Jesus, Sarah, did you just make that up?"

"Yeah, sorry, that sucked. You think I'd memorize something that lame?"

"It's true, though."

"You still like him?"

"As far as I know him, but...well, it hasn't been the smoothest ride."

"Does he know what day it is?"

I face her. "Do you?"

She scoots closer to me, bumping my hip, and puts her arm around my shoulders.

"Of course I do."

Yesterday we spent the rest of the afternoon mostly talking about her stuff. Not much about Scott other than telling her everything that happened at his house. She tried to get me to talk about it more but I'd said all there was to say. I'm not sure how I feel and said so. I didn't mention my dad's birthday.

"You doing okay?"

"I got my gold star last night if that answers your question."

"It doesn't, but that's okay." She squeezes my shoulder and lets go.

Sarah doesn't approve of my Star Chart. She thinks it's about stifling emotions that should be let out. She's one to talk.

"You seem tired. You sleep last night? Or run extra hard this morning?"

"I didn't run."

"You..." She shifts to face me. "You didn't run?"

"No. I was...I was too...I don't know. Too wobbly."

"That's...too bad..." Her voice softens. "You're going to need your strength."

I hear someone approach and sit down. A hard landing. Then a sniff. A *productive* sniff.

I'm only ninety-five percent sure who it is.

"Hey Marissa," Sarah says.

Sarah's right, I don't have the strength for this. I just waggle my hand.

"How are you doing?" Sarah asks.

Sniff.

Sarah tries again. "Is there something you want to talk about?"

Sniff.

"I have a question," I say, surprising myself, since two seconds ago I was sure I was going to sit this one out. "Why?"

"Why what?"

"Why do you love Owen?"

"What do you mean? Why does anybody love anybody? You just do."

"No," I say, and Sarah is already clicking her tongue but I keep going. "There are always reasons. Does he know how you like your coffee? Does he take you to stupid romantic comedies just because you like them?"

"No, we don't—"

"Is it the way he combs his hair, or how he wears

socks that don't match—"

"He doesn't mix his socks."

"Then what?"

"I don't know...It's everything."

"It's okay," Sarah says. "Parker means—"

I don't let Sarah interrupt me.

"You like *everything* about him? *All things?* Name ten. No, name three."

Sniff.

"Okay, one. Just one thing. We can start with that."

"He...he laughs a lot. I love his laugh."

"Okay, good. Do you love the sound of his laugh, or how much he laughs, or...?"

"All of that."

"How about what he laughs at? What does he think is funny?"

"I don't know...stuff. He laughs a lot, like he's happy and having fun all the time."

"You're not, though. I don't think I've ever heard you laugh."

"Parker," Sarah says. "I think—"

"It doesn't matter—those were trick questions. Knowing how someone likes their coffee isn't love or you could be a barista and problem solved."

"Marissa," Sarah says. "I—"

"For a year I've been telling you what love *isn't* but maybe I should've been telling you what it *is*. I have the perfect example right here; I love Sarah. I don't want-to-have-sex-with-her love her, but I love her like crazy. I wish more than anything I knew how to make her happy again. If a genie gave me three wishes I'd use one to bring back my dad, another for my mom, and the last one wouldn't be to see again; I'd wish for Sarah to be happy like she used to be. That's what love is, Marissa. It's not magic or voodoo. It's *real*. You *can* explain it. I can tell you *exactly* why I love Sarah."

I hold my hand out and, thank God, Sarah gently interlaces her fingers with mine.

"I had lots of friends when I was little but by the time I turned eight they were mostly gone. It turns out blind Parker with a dead mom wasn't nearly as much fun as she was before the accident. I couldn't run around and play and I cried all the time and knocked over everything and turned into a royal bitch and one by one my friends disappeared until there were only two left. I'm not saying they were the only ones who understood me or were nice, just that they were the ones who didn't go off and find easier people to be friends with. I love Sarah because she's been my best friend *and* stayed that way when it got really *really* hard to be my friend at all."

Sarah lays her head on my shoulder.

"It even happened again this week. I had a bad couple of days and didn't treat her very well but she didn't just stomp off and sulk. She called my bullshit and we solved it. And this might sound strange but part of why I love her so much is that I don't take it for granted. I don't like to admit it but whenever I put my hand out a part of me worries that maybe she's not going to be there this time, that she's finally sick of all my selfishness and drama..."

Sarah squeezes my hand tightly and presses her temple on my shoulder.

"...and that's why I freaked out, but then she's always there for me and I'm so goddamn grateful I wonder what I could have possibly done to deserve her. If you want to know what a soul mate is, Marissa, that's it. Sarah's my soul mate. I would stand in front of a train for her, and I love her because she'd do it for me too."

"Yeah, but it's not the same—"

"It *is* the same! Wanting to kiss or have sex, that's later, another layer. It has to start with a guy who actually loves you, not just says he does, or doesn't even say it, or doesn't even look at you! A guy who looks at you like you're the most important person on Earth! Who doesn't think you and all your problems and baggage are a pain in the ass or just dead weight to carry around but worth it because you're pretty or the best he thinks he can do! A guy who knows how fucking crazy you really are inside and doesn't *tolerate* your bullshit but *loves* you for it! Someone who...who... who would do anything to help you and protect you and...and...and take a crappier job at home to be there for you and teach you how to take care of yourself no matter what anyone else says, or who sits and drinks iced tea with you every single day and listens to all your *stupid* little stories and actually *cares* about all the dumb things that happened at school and...and... and who lets you say *anything* without getting mad as long as it's the *truth*!"

I'm standing and shouting and waving my arms and Sarah is hugging me tightly and maybe crying and there's scrambling and stuff getting knocked over and others are calling my name but it's really important Marissa hears this but I'm being pulled somewhere and it's not just Sarah but other arms too and it's all I can do to keep up and not stumble and I've completely lost track of where I am or where I'm going until I smell cigarette smoke and pot and hear Faith snarl *"Get out!"* in a voice I've never heard before and know that we're behind the custodian's shed and I'm slipping to the ground sandwiched between Sarah and Faith and I'm not sure who else because I can't hear voices clearly over all the sobbing and wailing and the oddly late realization that the hoarse and wretched barking and howling that sounds like a dying animal is coming from me...

Chapter 22

I'm not sure how long I've been asleep. The morning's a blur...a longish while behind the custodian's shed...a few minutes of calm, or at least less hysteria...being led somewhere interrupted by another breakdown...some curling up on grass, sobbing hard enough that I threw up breakfast, or maybe that was still behind the shed, I'm not sure...another attempt at walking with no sense of direction until the stairs tell me it's the parking lot...crawling into the backseat of Sarah's car, being driven home to an empty house, hands fishing in my bag for keys and then being propped up and half carried up the stairs, aching with exhaustion and wanting to crawl into bed, getting help pulling off my jeans and burrowing under my comforter, coughing as much as crying until finally losing consciousness.

"Is anyone here?" I call, or try to; it comes out a feeble croak.

"We're all here," Sarah says. The bed shifts as she lies down behind me and spoons me as much as she can with me under the comforter and her above it. "It's me, Fay, and Molly."

"You guys missing school?"

"I don't miss it much," Sarah says. "You guys?"

"Don't miss it a bit," Molly says from my desk chair.

The bed wiggles from someone leaning against it. "You're the one we miss, Peegee," Faith says, only inches away. Her thin fingers wrap around my exposed hand. "You went away. And you don't have to come back yet if you're not ready. We're not going anywhere."

Her voice is so worried and tender a sob grows in my throat. I start to clamp down on it, to force it back wherever it came from, like always, but I remember I already lost my gold star today so I relax and let it out...and another...and she's right, I'm not ready. Faith's hands squeeze mine and Sarah's arm tightens around my waist and I cry again. Just my throat and face this time, not the body-quakes like before. My eyes and scarf are wet and sticky but it's not time to get a dry one yet. Faith lets go with one hand and strokes my head like I'm a cat.

"Thank you," I whisper.

Faith kisses my forehead.

*

I guess I fell asleep again soon after Faith kissed me. I have no idea how long it's been. Sarah's still nestled in behind me, her arm across my waist. I can feel her breath on the back of my ear. She's breathing slow and steady and even a bit loud. I realize she's asleep and it makes me smile a tiny bit. I'm amazed that I can smile even this much now.

"Faith?" I whisper. Sarah rouses and stretches.

"She's downstairs," Molly says. "Your aunt was on a field trip or something with your cousin Pete and they picked up Sheila on their way back. They all got home a few minutes ago."

"What's she telling them?"

"Faith said, 'I'll go tell them Parker's having a bad day.'"

I hear Petey—it can only be Petey—pound up the stairs, but other footsteps catch up. Then slower steps thump back downstairs again. Two other sets of footsteps come and stop outside my door. After some murmurs one keeps walking and I can tell it's Sheila and she goes into her room and shuts the door. My door opens and closes again.

Faith kneels down and takes my hand.

"Everyone's home," she says, "but they're going to let us be. They're all worried about you. Especially Sheila."

"Sheila? Why?"

"Why not?" Molly asks. "It would take a pretty hard case not to worry about you after this morning."

"Molly!" Sarah says in her scolding voice, but I shake my head.

"It's okay. She saw? Or heard? Everyone did, didn't they?"

No one answers. I reach out of the covers to clamp Sarah's arm onto my waist and snuggle in and smile a tiny bit again.

"I don't care. I'm glad I saved everyone from another boring Wednesday."

"And, she's back," Molly says.

"But you don't have to be, Parker," Sarah says in her trying-to-tell-me-something voice. I think I'm going to be hearing a lot of special voices for a while.

"I want to be."

"I know, but you don't always get to decide. It's only been three months. You walked around like a zombie for a week afterwards and then made that stupid Star Chart and you've been a ticking time bomb ever since..."

"And I exploded."

"You *did*, and it was *epic!*" She squeezes me. "It'll be the top story at all our high school reunions. But I think we have some work ahead helping Marissa recover from the trauma."

I laugh and it hurts. It feels weird to laugh after so much crying and my body aches all over: my stomach, my throat, the muscles in my face, and my eyelids feel swollen.

"And this is just the first time," Sarah says. "Not the last. You gotta let it out when it comes, not bury it under all those stupid stars if you don't want to explode every few months. It's been how many years since my dad left and I still cry sometimes."

"You do? Why don't you tell me?"

"It's not a secret. Your furniture moves around

now with new people in your house and you don't tell me every time you bruise your shin. It's just the way things are now. There's no point in saying oh yesterday I heard the ice-cream truck drive by and it reminded me how my dad would always say that it only plays music to say they're out of ice cream, but if I said *nuh-uh* and *please* enough times he'd say okay and buy me a Neapolitan ice-cream sandwich, so I sat on the couch for a few minutes and my eyes got a little wet, but it wasn't a huge thing, just one of hundreds of little things happening all the time."

"But you know you can tell me, right?"

"I'm telling you now. Exploding today wasn't you getting it all out, it was just getting the last three months out. More's coming and you need to let it out when it does. Don't store it up or you'll explode again, and again, and again..."

"No more gold stars?" I sigh. "I don't know, every time I get one it feels like I'm coping."

"Hiding. Burying. Adding a little more gunpowder to the keg that blew up today."

I sit up and hug Sarah as tightly as I can. "How'd you get to be so smart?"

"Experience," she says. "Experience I wish I didn't have."

I let her go and lean against the headboard.

"Did something happen this morning?" Molly asks. "I mean, why today?"

"It's her dad's birthday," Faith says.

"And other stuff," I say. "You know some of it about Sarah and me...and...well, I guess I need to catch you up on a few other things."

"First," Faith says, "I've been hearing a lot about standing in front of trains. You know I certainly would if it came down to it; I just think it would be better for all of us if we didn't have to."

"Okay." I smile. "No trains."

*

Aunt Celia tries to get everyone to stay for dinner but nobody wants to, myself included. They all leave to go home and explain why they weren't in school today.

I offer to help with dinner and Aunt Celia of course says she can manage, especially today, but this time I refuse her refusal. I ask what she's making and when I hear it all I insist on making the mashed potatoes. After enough stubbornness, her desire to do something for me turns into letting me have the counter to the left of the sink. I need to ask where every single thing is since she's rearranged everything and I haven't been in the pantry for a while. She gives me whatever I ask for except garlic and she starts to say something about needing it for spaghetti later in the week—then she stops and says she can just get more later and hands me all the cloves she has.

Dinner is unusually quiet. Uncle Sam specifically compliments the potatoes as better than usual. Aunt Celia tells him I made them and he's surprised. It all sounds sincere so maybe she didn't put him up to it. Does that mean I'll get to help cook more? Time will tell. Most of the conversation is Petey talking about the tide pools, and it's Uncle Sam and I who talk to him the most. Sheila doesn't say a word and goes upstairs as soon as she can. When I offer to help clean up and Aunt Celia says no thanks I let her win and head upstairs.

I pick up Sheila's CD from my room and head to her door. I knock twice. I'm nervous and really hate it but this is long long *long* overdue. I have a lot to make up for, starting at home.

"Who is it?" she says in her annoyed voice, so, her normal voice.

"Just me." I almost add *your nemesis* as a joke but successfully hold it back. Too soon.

When she opens the door I say, "Can I come in?"

"Um, sure...but..." She doesn't sound annoyed now; I guess annoyed is not her normal voice. "Hang on, there's crap all over the floor..."

She kicks at what sounds like books and laundry and who knows what else.

"There, you can sit on my bed, straight ahead."

I step through, close the door, and slowly walk forward sweeping my arms until my hands hit the bed. I sit. She doesn't.

"I just came to say I'm really sorry—"

"Don't. Don't be sorry."

She doesn't say it like oh, it's okay, you don't have to be sorry. She sounds angry like she really doesn't want to hear this.

"But I shouldn't have yelled at you yesterday—"

"I deserved it. Cranking up the music was a shitty thing to do."

Which it was, but...this is nothing like how I imagined this conversation might go.

I hold out her CD. "I can understand you not wanting me to hear you."

The case pops out of my hand with some force. "So I blasted music at you to plug up the one working sense you had? I was yelling at you for not knowing I had stuff going on, stuff I was *trying* to keep you from knowing, and then I didn't even know it was Uncle Martin's birthday today! So now I'm a hypocrite, or just blind—fuck, I mean...Jesus, you know what I mean."

"Hey, Sheila, it's okay—"

"No, I *saw* you this morning. I...*saw*...you. And you were...you were..."

I'm not sure what this means. "You probably heard me, too. Along with half the school. I'm not embarrassed about that. I had a good reason—"

"But I've never seen...I...I watched you at the funeral...You just *sat* there. And for another month you just sat around or argued with my mom, and...and...you just acted *normal*."

"That wasn't normal. And I wasn't just *sitting there*.

I was *frozen*. Losing Dad was bad enough but for a while I thought I might lose *everything*. If I had to move away from everything and everyone I've ever known, I'd have lost my mind. Seriously. Thank you. Thank you for doing it instead of me. I'll never be able to repay it but I want to try. Whatever I can do, just ask."

She doesn't answer right away, and then she whispers hoarsely, "Please..."

I really wish I could see her face. "Just say it. What can I do?"

"Please go..."

"Go where? I—"

"Just go," she says in a steadier voice. "Away. Anywhere that's not here. Or didn't you mean it when you said you'd do anything?"

Ouch. I want to make her understand how much this means to me, how hard it is for me to learn new places and people, and to trust them...but...that would be trying to make *me* feel better.

"If that's what you want. I really am sorry." I stand and retrace my steps to the door—

"Wait," Sheila says.

I stop. After a moment she says, "Left...more to the left."

I course-correct and find the doorknob.

"I won't keep bothering you about it," I say. "I know what it's like to have people constantly offer you help you don't want. Just let me know if there's anything I can do."

She doesn't say anything. I open the door. I'm halfway through and she clears her throat.

"The only way the past three months makes any sense is if one of us was a heartless self-centered bitch. Right?"

I think for a moment, trying to decipher her words, her voice, what she's really asking.

I get it. This is a bullet I can take for her. It almost makes me smile. Faith doesn't want to talk about trains anymore; I wonder what she'd say about bullets.

"I'm definitely a Certified Heartless Self-Centered Bitch. But I can say from experience that acting like one sometimes isn't the same as being one. So there's hope."

I hear her trying not to sneeze again, so I leave her be.

Chapter 23

Sheila doesn't bolt as soon as Aunt Celia's car stops in the parking lot; she walks with me to my locker. We don't talk though. I've been up for at least an hour longer and ran my sprints, and she's not really a morning person. She's also not really a Parker person, so there's that. One step at a time.

Faith gets to her locker at the same time and they talk, starting with Faith making some crack about how the smiley faces on my scarf are upside down and can't Sheila take some responsibility for dressing me in the morning. It's embroidered so I can tell which side is up but I just didn't think about it today. I had a fifty-fifty chance and lost. I hope it's not a sign.

Faith and Sheila are still talking clothes when Molly says, "Hey, you getting back on the horse today? Out in the quad with Sarah?"

"Definitely. I wouldn't want anyone to think I'm afraid to show my face."

"Like you care what anyone thinks."

"Damn right." I nod. "But the Doctor is definitely IN, and by that I mean Sarah. Her loudmouth bitch partner is still en route. What are you up to?"

"I'm going to check Lost and Found for a sweater I lost yesterday. It's chilly out today."

"Is it? You should take up running. It warms you up."

"Funny. So I guess you ran this morning?"

"I did. It was great. It felt weird not running yesterday."

"I bet a lot of things felt weird yesterday."

"That's true. I blame it all on the not running."

"Not months of suppression and denial?"

"No, that know-it-all Gunderson doesn't know what the hell she's talking about half the time. I'm going to run every morning and never miss a day again and have a wonderful life. I'm a new woman. You'll see."

"You're an inspiration to us all."

"Damn right."

"If only your tone matched your words."

"Still a work in progress."

"Speaking of which, you talk to Jason?"

"Not yet. Someone switched off my phone yesterday—"

"That was Faith."

"Oh, well, I had no missed calls or texts from him. I thought I'd have at least gotten a *Where are you?* at lunchtime but I guess he was still bent out of shape and figured me a no-show."

"He knew where you were. Or at least that you probably weren't at school. He saw our fun times yesterday morning."

"He didn't come over?" Or even text or call me later?

"I guess he decided to leave it to us."

"That's one way to look at it. Was Scott there?"

"I didn't see him. I doubt he would have come over, though."

I'm not so sure. Either way, I look into the future and see finding Jason at lunch to tell him we won't be dating anymore. But I'm going to be nice about it. That's my new plan. Honest but nicer.

"I don't suppose you know what schoolwork we missed yesterday?" I ask.

"No. I was just going to pick it up as we go. I'm not too worried about it. Are you?"

"Not specifically, I just hate missing a day. It's hard enough to *keep* up without needing to *catch* up. Mostly I worry about English, but I can crank up the speed on my text-to-speech...though *Count of Monte Cristo* will sound like it's being read by the Chipmunks."

"What a pain. It must suck to...you know...read..."

"As slow as I do? Yeah, but math is the hardest since it's more than just talking and reading. Geometry was like walking barefoot on broken glass."

"Trig's not so bad," Molly says.

"It must be boring since it takes so long to go through it all with me. If I don't say it enough, I really appreciate it."

"It's no problem. I think I learn it better by going through it so methodically."

A part of my brain searches for a comeback to her calling my coping mechanisms *methodical* but the other part sticks to the plan.

"Speaking of which, you knew D.B. before? At Jefferson?"

"Stockley? Just the way everybody knows Stockley. Why?"

"I told you he was my seeing-eye-buddy when you were out sick—oh, by the way, did I thank you for abandoning me that day?"

"Many times, and again, I'm *so* sorry you were put out by my painful bout of diar—"

"*Aaand*...he was having a lot of trouble, and I helped him as much as he helped me. Then after class, I'm not sure, but I think he was..." How do I say this?

"He's wanted to hang out with you since the first day of school. Tell me you knew that."

"Well...sort of?"

"I don't think he's crushing on you, though," she says to rescue me, and I like her even more for it. "If that's what you're worried about."

"Oh, I'm not worried."

"You seem worried. I figured it was for the usual reasons, not wanting the awkwardness of not liking someone who likes you."

"It's not that I don't like him."

"Oh, wait...*do* you like him?"

"I don't *like* like him, but he's not the douchebag I first thought he...might have been. I don't usually peg people so wrong and...I don't know..."

"Is it hard to imagine a guy might want to be your friend without falling in love with you? Wow—"

"What? No! That's not what I mean! Jesus, ninety-nine percent of the guys here don't talk to me at all—it hardly ever happens—so sue me if I don't know what to do when it does."

I'm not joking but Molly laughs. This makes me smile. It is pretty funny.

"Anyway, I feel bad that I was mean to him before."

"I doubt he even noticed."

"It doesn't matter. My dad used to say if you're mean to someone then you're a mean person, period. You can explain forever why someone deserved it and it'll never add up to you being nice. Like two wrongs don't make a right. If you see someone being mean, even if they're being mean to Hitler, you might say *Good for you* but you'd never say *That was nice of you.*"

"Your dad thought you should be nice to Hitler?"

"Hmph, now you're just being thick. I just don't want to be mean."

Silence. Well, except for Molly's breathing and the cricket on my shoulder whispering in my ear that I'm a bad person.

"When I say I don't think he noticed," Molly finally says, "I mean you're talking like you've shot him down or something and I don't think he sees it that way at all." She drops her voice to a whisper. "I think he might be gay."

"What? Really?"

"I don't know if he's ready to admit it, even to himself, but it's what I think. Maybe I'm wrong. Doesn't really matter, though, if you don't *like* him."

"No, but maybe it helps. The point of all this is I was thinking we could invite him to study with us. He really needs help in Trig—"

Molly laughs. "Why didn't you just say so?"

"Screw you, Molly—I *am* saying so!"

"I guess you did get around to it eventually. Sure, yeah, you can invite him."

"I mean can *you* invite him? In case we're wrong, I don't want him to—"

"To take it the wrong way, I get it. Leave it to me; I can make it work. And don't let anyone say you're a mean person, Parker Grant. Sometimes you can be downright...nice."

"Why, thank you, Molly Ray. But...how *exactly* will you make it work?"

"I'll tell him you already have a crush on someone—"

"Don't you dare! I do *not* have a crush on anybody! Crushes are..."

"I know: empty, superficial, like with Jason—"

"Hey! That's..." I sniff at her. "Truth can hurt, you know."

"Okay...I'll tell him you've already given your heart away. Better?"

"Well, don't lie to him."

"It's not a lie, though, is it."

She doesn't say it like a question so I don't need to answer.

*

I stand near the track at lunchtime, eating, waiting for Jason to see me. If he hasn't by the time I finish my sandwich, I'll text him.

"Hey, Parker," he says, from a better distance today

so it doesn't startle me.

"Hey. Granola bar lunch?"

"Yeah. You feeling better today? Did something happen to set you off like that?"

"I don't usually break down and fall apart for no reason. It was my dad's birthday yesterday."

"Oh, I didn't know. I'm sorry."

"I'm better now. If you saw me upset, why didn't you come over?"

He doesn't answer right away. I wait him out.

"I don't know. It looked like your friends had you covered..."

"You're not my friend?"

"I am, but...we don't know each other very well yet...They were your best friends...I didn't want to get in the way."

"I met Molly a week before I met you and she stayed in my room with me all afternoon."

"Oh. Well...girls usually want to be with other girls when they're really upset. Should I have come over?"

"There are no shoulds. But if you're asking if I'm grateful that you didn't come or call or text when you saw me sobbing in the yard and get dragged behind the custodian's shed and then disappear from school...No, I'm not feeling all that grateful."

"I just thought...Yeah, you're right. Let me make it up to you. Saturday night. You pick the restaurant. Okay?"

I think for a moment, for the nice way to be honest.

"I don't think so..."

"Not Saturday? Or not ever?"

"Not ever is a long time. But that's probably closer. It's not all your fault—"

"Oh, here it comes."

"What?"

"The *it's-me-not-you* speech."

"It's *us*, Jason, and it's not a speech. I like you but when we talk it feels more like stumbling than dancing. And the more honest I am the worse it gets. Before you I've kissed one guy and that was years ago and not for very long, so I was a little starved and moved too fast and now I got my head straight and want to pull back. So yeah, that's mostly me not you but yesterday was all you and I'm not a cliché, I'm a person, a person who's not happy you thought the best thing to do when I fell apart was to hang back and wait for me to get normal again—"

"I know, I know, I'm sorry! Can't you forgive me?"

"I do. But I want a guy whose first impulse is to be with me when I need help, but that doesn't mean we can't be friends. I have friends who I wouldn't go running over to if I heard them break down crying because I know I would just get in the way of their closer friends, like you said. That's okay—everybody can't be closest friends with everybody else. I think we can be very good casual friends."

"Now it's the *let's-just-be-friends* speech."

I snort a bit, the nice kind, or at least I hope it sounds that way. Somehow I'm not really upset by any of this.

"You know why I like you? You're nice, and charming, and from the moment we met you've treated me like a normal person who just needed a bit more information than other people. That's extremely rare and *exactly right*, so you made a great impression. I think we could be great friends. For dating, though, I'm looking for something else."

"This is about Scott."

"Um...*no*. We've barely talked in years, and when

I asked him if we could just be friends, he said no. If you say yes, you'll be miles ahead of him."

Silence.

"As far as boyfriend material goes," I say, "yeah, he was a tough act to follow. Unfortunately for you. Even more unfortunate for me."

More silence. I listen for breathing or shuffling to make sure Jason hasn't walked away.

"It's funny," he says in a bitter voice. "When I talked to Scott about you, I think we liked you for opposite reasons."

I want to ask, I *really* want to ask, but I'd rather he just tell me so I try waiting him out.

"He says the problems other people have, like being petty or liars or snobs or whatever, they could fix them if they wanted to, but they just don't do the work or they blame everyone else. And even though your problems can't be fixed at all, you're the one who needs taking care of the least."

"And you think...what, the opposite?"

"No, just...I don't know. It doesn't matter. You're smiling so I can tell he's right and I'm wrong."

"But I really do want to be friends. All those good

things I said about you, I mean it. I wish more people in the world were like you. I'd have more friends if there were. Can we?"

"I guess."

"Hmmm...That's fine for being in the outermost circle of friends. If you want to be better friends, what's the more honest answer?"

Silence.

"Come on, it's okay to tell me how you really feel. Just try it once. What's the worst that could happen?"

"No," he finally says. "I don't think we can be friends. I'm starting to think you're...demanding, exhausting, and...high-maintenance. There, happy now?"

I laugh. "Yeah, I am. Because it's all true. I think we're already better friends now than we were a minute ago. Don't you?"

"Not really."

"Don't you at least feel better getting that off your chest?"

"No, it makes me feel like a dick. Look, I...I'm going to go walk the track. I'll see you around I guess."

"Okay. But you're not a dick, Jason. You're a good

guy and a quick study. It gives me hope. Thanks for that."

*

Sarah and Faith decide they need to keep an eye on me despite my amazing performance of normalcy today, so they come to study with us in the library after school. I don't think they understood that Molly and I need to talk the whole time, and our talking makes it hard for them to get anything done, so they talk too and nobody gets anything done. By the time Stockley comes after football practice we've done nothing but we're having too much fun to stop.

"Hey P.G., Molly, sorry I'm late," Stockley says. "Coach loves to hear himself talk."

"Hey," I say, "everybody, this is Stockley—*Kent* Stockley. That's Sarah and Faith."

Greetings are exchanged as Stockley sits down hard on the other side of Molly. I'm hoping to use this interruption to bear down on some homework. It would be lousy to invite him here to work on trig and then not do any. I'm glad he dives right in.

"What was all that Sacagawea stuff? I didn't get that at all."

Molly laughs. I swat at her arm but my hand finds nothing but air and this makes others laugh.

"It's SOH-CAH-TOA," I say. "Sine, Opposite, Hypotenuse; Cosine, Adjacent, Hypotenuse; Tangent, Opposite, Adjacent—"

"Whoa, word blizzard!" Sarah says and everyone cracks up again, including Stockley, but not me. I'm trying to keep it together here.

"Jesus, you guys, Asshole Hour is over." I use my teacher voice if not teacher vocabulary. "Can we set a good example for the new student?"

"Does she mean us?" Sarah whispers. "We're the assholes?"

"I'm not sure," Faith says quietly, like they're having a private conversation we can't all hear. "I'm usually called a bitch."

"Who calls you that?" Stockley sounds shocked and endearingly protective of someone he's only just met. "Give me names and I'll—"

"It's nobody you can hit," I say. "Unless you're willing to hit girls."

"Oh," he says. "Sorry. Can't help you there."

"It's fine, D.B., you're—"

"What's D.B.?" Faith asks. "I thought your name was Kent."

"Everyone calls him Stockley," Molly says.

"We're getting off topic," I say, hoping to avoid explaining to Faith what D.B. stands for. "The topic is SOHCAHTOA."

Stockley starts reciting, "Sine, Opposite, Cosine, Adjacent—"

"No. Molly, write it down for him."

"Look, it's here in my notes," Molly says and notebook pages shuffle.

"It's easy to remember *O* means Opposite and all that," Stockley says, "but remembering SO-CA-TAHOE..."

"It's easier with a rhyme," Molly says. "Like...Some Old Hippie Caught Another Hippie Tripping On Acid—"

Now everyone's really laughing, *loud*. I'm trying not to but Molly didn't tell me that rhyme before, so I'm caught off-guard.

"Guys, shhh!" I hiss. "Ms. Ramsey's going to come over here!"

"Oh my God!" Sarah says. "Oh! My! God!

Somebody help us! We're in Opposite World! *We're* embarrassing *Parker*!"

Everybody completely loses it. I put my forehead down on the table with a hard *thunk*, playing my part, but really I'm breathing in the sound of everyone laughing like it's my first deep breath after nearly drowning. I haven't heard Sarah or even Faith laugh like this in years.

It's okay, isn't it, Dad? It's not too soon, right? You'd want me to be okay, not falling apart anymore, I know it. This is my real birthday present to you, a day late...

Tears are coming. I don't think it's sadness trying to crash the party like it sometimes does. I'm just happy, whether or not I have a right to be, though in a desperate, unstable kind of way. I don't want this all to go sideways.

The laughter calms and before anyone has a chance to say anything to kick it off again I lift my head and lean in.

"Everybody, shhh! Radius check. *Radius check!*"

Sarah and Faith quiet first—they know what this means. Stockley next, since he probably understood the least why we were laughing in the first place.

Molly stops last. "What's radius check?"

"We're alone," Sarah says. "Except for Ms. Ramsey. She's watching us through the glass but she can't hear if we whisper."

"There's nobody else here," Faith adds, "or she'd have come out by now."

"What is it, Parker?" Sarah whispers. "Spill it."

"Okay. So...there's this guy I like—"

I'm interrupted by a lot of *oooh*s and I wave my hands.

"Okay, okay...*shhh!* I'm pretty sure he likes me, too, but...well, I screwed up—"

"*He* screwed up," Molly says.

"Who?" Stockley asks.

"Yeah," I say. "But I screwed up too, and worse. I want to fix it, but I need some help."

Everyone is saying *yes* and *of course* and *anything you need* except for Stockley. He says in a voice that tells me he's just realized something profound, "Oh, man...I've been here for like ten minutes...Am I one of the girls already?"

Silence.

"I didn't plan it this way, D.B.," I say truthfully. "But

312

for what I'm thinking, I might need your help more than anyone's."

Silence.

"Are you in?" Molly asks. "Or out?"

Silence.

Sigh.

"In."

Chapter 24

I'm having doubts now. Big surprise.

This seemed like such a good idea yesterday. I even set my alarm twenty minutes early to listen at the window; sure enough, a few minutes later two sets of footsteps jogged by. Seems like Jason and Scott are still friends, or at least running partners.

I held on fine stopping at my locker to drop off my stuff first thing this morning, and then walking to the field with Molly and Sarah. I didn't even waver when they left me alone on the far bleachers to wait and Sarah called back, "This is batshit crazy Parker but good luck!" and Molly added, "You'll do fine! See you at lunch!"

No, it's the waiting that's doing me in. My troll brain shifts into overdrive imagining how it could all go wrong. I try to stop that by imagining it all going right in as much detail as I can.

D.B. asked Scott for a lift to school this morning, saying he needed to get here early. I picture them pulling into the parking lot right about now, as planned, and D.B. gives Scott a printed note that I folded and taped shut, to give D.B. time to be gone before Scott reads it.

The note says, "Scott, please come meet me at the track? I need to tell you something. Thanks. PG." The *PG* isn't typed; it's a secret symbol I invented when we were kids, drawn with a ballpoint pen, to prove that a typed message was really from me. It's like a capital *P* where instead of the round part I make a capital *G*.

Maybe he sits for a minute, wondering what's up, or looks around for D.B. to ask him. Then he gets out, heads for the stairs, crosses the school seal, turns right at the pillars by the office, takes the second left into South Hall, fifty-two steps to the courtyard, passes the tables of the Junior Quad, and walks across the field to the track.

Although I've meticulously imagined it all in real time, he arrives in my mind but not in reality. But it's reasonable things would happen faster in my head, maybe ten or twenty percent?

I start again.

And Scott arrives again...except he doesn't. Maybe they stopped on the way to school and got here later, or not yet? Or...?

Wow, this was a bad idea. I should have just texted him to meet me and then had a simple adult conversation, but I wanted to talk away from everyone and was afraid if I asked directly he'd have said no or found some way out of it. My stomach is growing queasy, that I arranged this to steer him into meeting me even if he didn't want to. Maybe I really am crazy.

I just need to be patient but I'm much too nervous to sit...

I start mapping the bleachers. I feel around to get a sense of how high each bench is compared to the one in front of it, how far apart they are, and I count them. In a few minutes I have a picture of how it's all put together and I walk up and down, all the way to the top rail, all the way down to the bottom rail, stepping only on benches like wide stones across a stream, one foot on each, counting, feeling for edges that would tell me if I'm off track with strides too short or too long.

I walk faster, up and down. I can never be sure enough to trot—even I'm not that crazy—but I'm walking pretty fast now. Up. Down. Up. Down. Up. Down—

"Parker!" Scott calls from across the field when I reach the bottom bench, at the rail, about to turn to go back up.

My heart pounds but not from being startled; his voice was far enough away. I climb under the rail to stand on the ground. It's breezy this morning and my scarf flutters. I'm wearing solid white and I pull the tails forward to lie on my chest, then I snort and throw them back over my shoulder. *God.*

"Jesus, Parker, was that some kind of test?" he says, closer.

"What do you mean?"

"When was I supposed to tell you I was here? You'd fall if I startled you so I waited over there till you got to the bottom rail but even then—"

He stops. Maybe because I'm grinning.

"Damn it, Parker—"

"No, no, it wasn't a test. Really, Scott, I was just... killing time. I'm sorry, I didn't think about all that.

But *you* did. And that's—"...*why I love you.*

We said it to each other plenty of times before so it's not that big a hurdle, but now...too soon. I even resisted signing my note with *Love, PG.*

"That's what?"

"Nothing. I'm sorry. Forgive me?"

"Okay. Jesus, stop smiling like that, you're freaking me out."

"Sorry." I manage to stop. "You were there when I almost ran into the Reiches' van back in June, weren't you?"

"Um..."

"That's a yes, isn't it? Her coming out right then was too big a coincidence."

"Yeah." He's embarrassed...no, more like worried.

"You told her not to tell me?"

"She didn't know. I threw the newspaper from their driveway at their door. That didn't work so I threw it at their window. Then I heard you come out of your house. I was about to run over and pound on the van so you'd hear, or call your name; I wasn't sure what I was going to do. Then the door opened and I hid around by their trash cans. Sorry."

"God, don't be sorry. Thanks for saving me a trip to the hospital."

"I wasn't spying on you, I promise. I—"

"It's okay, I know what you were doing. Jason told me."

"Jason...?"

"Do you like running now?"

"Not at first but I do now. It's not really a passion like with you, but being on the track team will look good on college applications too."

"Will you be my running guide so I can join the team?"

"Um..."

"You know what I mean, right?"

"Yeah, I heard Coach Underhill talking about it. I'm not a sprinter. I know someone who is—I could ask. I'm not fast enough for you."

"No one is. That just means I'll get slower times but so what? I can run alone at Gunther Field but track events are all over the place—I won't be able to do it unless I'm with someone I'm comfortable with. That's a very short list and you're the only runner on it."

Silence.

"Besides," I say, getting wobbly over him not answering right away. "If you practice with me, you'll get faster. Maybe you'll be a good sprinter too when the meets start."

"I don't know…"

"I…this isn't about being friends or anything, it's just about being safe."

More silence. I was afraid this might happen. I really hoped it wouldn't…

"You don't have to tell me now. Just think about it. Okay?"

"Okay."

"Thanks. Now…" I take a deep breath. "When we talked at your place, I got so hung up on…well…my dad…I didn't really say the most important thing."

"Parker, I don't think—"

"It's okay," I interrupt him before he can derail me completely. "I want to tell you—"

"It's just that I—"

"Just let me say it! You've tried to talk me out of it, but…I forgive you anyway. You did something dumb, but it's okay. I understand it better now, and

I forgive you. Okay?"

Silence.

"Okay?"

"Okay," he says. "But I don't know what you mean by understanding it better."

"I thought you tricked me but really you just...you told people something that was private, but just the where and the when. The *us* part, that wasn't a secret. I'd have kissed you in the middle of the cafeteria if you'd asked."

"That would have been a crappy thing to ask."

"Now, yeah, but not for a thirteen-year-old. And I was just a kid, too. If this happened now, when all those assholes started laughing, I'd ask you if you set me up and when you said no I'd say to them all, 'Take a good look, guys! This memory and a bottle of lotion is all you'll have tonight!' Then I'd go back to kissing you until they got bored and went away. Imagine what things would be like now if I'd done *that* back then?"

Scott blows air out his nose. I hope it's the laughing kind but I can't tell.

"It could have been like that," I say. "If I wasn't

thirteen and afraid of everything."

"You're not afraid of anything."

"You know me better than that. Or you used to."

"What then? What are you afraid of?"

"Well, certain dates on the calendar. Anniversaries."

"That's not being afraid," he says in a soft voice, not quite his boyfriend voice.

"I'm afraid of what people are thinking, or might be thinking."

"That's just not trusting people. If I were you I'd have a hard time with that too."

"I'm getting better but I still worry all the time that my whole life is just something I'm imagining...that if I could actually *see* it, I'd see that everyone's either humoring me or worse, playing this big elaborate joke on me. With you it was worse than ever. I felt like I was living in a dream like you said. I was so worried I'd wake up and find out it wasn't real...so the first hint I got that it wasn't I grabbed on and wouldn't let go and I'm so sorry, Scott! It was just this one thing and kind of a misunderstanding and I...I just freaked out!"

"You had every right to."

"But I didn't have to! I lord it over everyone that

people don't think about how others see things and I did it to you! I didn't listen, I didn't even think about it…and if Sarah hadn't talked to me…"

"It's okay." His tone is even softer but still hard to read…

"No it's not! You slipped up once on one lousy day, but I…I really screwed up and wasted two and a half years! And you're a better person than I am because you don't want to be forgiven but I do!"

"You didn't do anything—"

"I did! I did everything I could to *not* think about your side…When I think now about how you must have felt with me not even willing to listen to you for one minute…" I'm having trouble talking with all these lumps growing in my throat.

"Hey," Scott says. "It's okay…" His hands take my shoulders. I lean forward for a hug but his hands stay firmly on my shoulders. Is he not getting the hint or is he keeping me away?

"I forgive you," he says. "All right? We can just stop worrying about who actually needs to be forgiven. It's all done. Okay?"

I nod, concentrating on his hands.

"So..." I say. "You don't have to stay away from me anymore, right? We're good?"

"Yeah, we're good."

"I'm sure my dad would be okay with it if he were here. I'd have made him understand."

"I know. He told me."

"He...what?"

Scott lets go and I'm back to standing alone in the dark.

"On that last day he said it would be bad if I talked you into forgiving me because you'd learn to let people get away with hurting you as long as they apologized. But he also said if I let you be, *then* if you came back, it'd be okay."

"Is that why you said before we can't be friends?"

"Partly. It's complicated."

"Everything's complicated, but..."

Just say it.

"I really miss you."

My voice cracks but I keep going—it's okay for him to hear me like this. I'm *safe*.

"You were my *best friend*, Scott. And I...I want it all back. I really, *really*...miss you."

"I miss you, too," he says, but his voice sounds like acceptance, not hope. "Or at least who you used to be. It's been a long time. We're different now."

"Not that different," I say. I want to add more, to turn this around, but I can't think how...

"I don't know. I'm having trouble imagining this Parker Grant who'd get caught kissing me in a dark room and laugh at the crowd and keep on kissing."

"You don't think that sounds like me?"

"About other stuff, sure, but that's not what you did. I guess you're saying you've changed. I've changed too."

"So tell me." I bend my arms a bit at the elbow and fan out my fingers, the way I used to for him to take my hands. "We have time before class. We can start catching up."

"I can't." He doesn't take my hands. I don't know if it's rejection or if he didn't see them wiggling. I push them down flat on my jeans. He says, "I didn't know why Stockley wanted to get here early, so I arranged to meet someone."

"Oh. Okay." I step back. "Who?"

"Someone from Jefferson. Nobody you know. It's for homework."

"Oh...you should have said something—"

"I was going to, but you were on the bleachers, and then you jumped right in about the van in the driveway...I'm pretty late so I can't walk you back; I have to run. I'll see you in Trig, okay?"

"Okay."

"Sorry," he says. I hear his footsteps jog away across the field.

Leaving me to struggle with what just happened. We had what sounded like a good conversation, as good as I realistically should have hoped for, but I still feel like I got slapped.

He changed his mind and said we could be friends—and it's perfectly fine for a friend not to hug me, or to run off to some other friend they had plans to meet. And he's still so...so *Scott* in every way. So why do I feel hollowed out and churning inside?

Did Scott say we could be friends just to stop these conversations, and me from showing up at his house and sending him notes to meet up when he has other plans...to stop me from being this crazy stalker like Marissa who can't let go of something that's never going to happen...

God, I think I'm going to throw up.

Chapter 25

Longest weekend ever. I survived through a combination of doing a ton of schoolwork and hanging out with Petey. Sheila actually played cards with us a few times, then she went out most of Saturday with Faith and Lila and Kennedy and returned insufferably cheerful. I'm really glad she had fun and was happier than I'd ever seen, but my own mood wasn't compatible with that kind of energy. I put on the best face I could.

Nothing from Scott. I don't know what I expected, but something. I finally texted him Sunday night about being my running guide. All he texted back was *Let's talk tomorrow.*

Which all seems miles from here, sitting with Sarah in the Junior Quad. She'd walked the line all weekend between asking about things and not nagging me, but now we've run out of material and we're sitting in silence waiting for patients. Which guarantees we won't get any.

I'm wrong. Again. I'm honestly getting sick of it.

"Hi." A girl sits across from us. "Do I need an appointment?"

I've heard her voice in class but don't know her. Jeffersonian. Confident. Loud. Usually people we don't know are either timid or overly loud to compensate for the inferior position of seeking help, so I'm already figuring she's the second type. We'll see.

"Drop-ins are welcome," Sarah says. "I haven't seen you around. I'm Sarah, this is Parker—"

"I know Parker—we have classes together. I'm Trish Oberlander."

"U.S. History?" I say, trying to recall. "And...?"

"English Lit. I hear you guys give out advice."

"We listen," Sarah says. "Advice only if you want some."

"For advice you *don't* want," I say, "that's my department."

That's good for a laugh all around. Maybe I can salvage the morning after all.

"So I have this friend—"

"Oh, um..." Sarah interrupts. "We don't do that. I mean, if we're really talking about you it just gets weird pretending we're talking about someone else—"

"It's definitely someone else."

"Then she should come talk to us. You can come too if she wants—"

"He's a he, and there's no way he's going to come talk to you about his problem."

"That's fine, but—"

"It's not like you're doing anything else," she says. "I'm not asking you to solve his problem. I want to talk about how *I* can help him."

Sarah doesn't reply and I wonder what her expression is. I say to her, "It's fine. I'd rather spend the next ten minutes talking about that than about why we can't. Go ahead, Trish."

"Okay, my friend Frank, he—"

"Frank?" I ask. "Is that a fake name?"

"Nope, his name's Frank, swear to God. You can't think you know everyone from Jefferson already?"

"No," Sarah says with her flat voice, still miffed I guess that we're even having this conversation.

"Frank was going with Bibi and then they broke

up. Now she's sniffing around again and I'm worried he's going to get back with her."

"What's wrong with that?" I ask. "If they want to?"

"That's the thing. Bibi broke up with him and treated him like shit the way it happened. It really wiped him out. But I guess she can't find anything better so now she's talking sweet and I don't want him to get hurt again. He says it's over but I don't know. He's really sensitive and I'm afraid he'll fall back into her trap again."

"Are you in love with him?" Sarah asks a bit sharply, not with her usual sympathy.

"We're just friends."

"That's not what I asked."

That's even more harsh for Sarah. Maybe she's also reacting to Trish's loud, raspy, softball team voice, except it's not like her to let this kind of thing show.

"I'm not in love with him, okay? Happy? It's possible to be good friends with a guy without wanting to have his baby. Or didn't you know that?"

"Totally," I say in my calming voice, marveling over this role reversal between Sarah and me. "What makes you think he can't go into it slowly this time, keeping his eyes open? To see if she can earn his trust again?"

"In a perfect world, sure, but this Bibi, I don't actually know her but she has a reputation for being a real bitch. You wouldn't believe the things I've heard she says. It's like she's willing to say anything and I can totally see her telling Frank exactly what he wants to hear. So there's trust and there's *blind* trust if you know what I mean, no offense."

I smile—it's all cool—though she is starting to wear me out, considering how little I had to start with.

"There's no halfway with Frank, there is no *slowly*. If he decides to get back with her, he'll jump all in."

I wait to let Sarah have a turn, but she doesn't take it. I say, "I don't think you'll like this but there's really nothing you can do. It's up to him."

"I figured you'd say something like that but what kind of friend would I be if I didn't try? I can't tell him what to do but maybe talking to Bibi, you know, if I warn her off, that could work. Maybe she'll back off and leave him alone if she knows she's not going to have an easy time, that I'll do whatever it takes to expose who she really is and what she's doing, to crush her."

"Crush her? How? Beat her up? Break a beer bottle over her head?"

"Maybe. If that's what it takes."

"Uh..." I'm not sure where to go next. Sarah and I have had plenty of weird ones, but this one's definitely Top Ten.

"I think we're done," Sarah says, using her we're-definitely-done voice.

"*No...*" I say. "Before we wrap things up I'd like to say for the record that going after somebody with a bottle is not just a bad idea, it's fucking insane, pardon my French. And it's not protecting your friend, it's more like you being in love with him and not admitting it."

"That's the point, *Parker*. Nobody's in love with anybody in this story. And that's how it's going to stay. Understand?"

"We get it," Sarah says.

"*I* don't get it. Is this real or bullshit? Is there really a Frank or are you screwing with us?"

Sarah puts her hand on my wrist.

"Oh, it's real, I promise you," Trish says, her voice closer. "His name's really—well, it's Francis—Frank's just a nickname—but it's his middle name—not many people know it."

My skin tightens down my neck and I finally see what Sarah must have figured out long ago, that Trish is talking about Scott Francis Kilpatrick. I know his middle name of course, it just seldom came up unless I was teasing him.

"Get it now, Bibi?"

"*I'm* Bibi?" My muscles clench, remembering the beer bottle. "That's a made-up name for me?"

"It's not a name...Oh, you mean like Bibi? No, it's B.B., like BB gun. They're initials. *Your* initials. The second *B* stands for Bitch. I'll let you figure out what the first *B* stands for, and it doesn't have the word *fold* in it."

She stands up suddenly and Sarah's hand twitches.

"You had your chance but it's over. Scotty doesn't want anything to do with you but he's too nice to just come out and tell you himself. That's not a problem for me, so here we are, me telling you to leave him the hell alone. And *now* we're done."

She stomps away.

"You okay?" Sarah asks.

Not okay. Not okay at all. Getting dizzy. I fumble in my bag for my phone. When I find it I hold it out because my hands are shaking and I want a fast answer.

"Text him for me. *Are you friends with Trish?* Just that."

"Aren't you going to see him in a few minutes anyway, in Trig?"

I wiggle the phone and try to keep my voice steady. "Please?"

She takes it. I hear the *swoosh* as the text goes out.

"I'm glad she wasn't drinking a beer," I say.

"Huh?"

"It's not a weapon I want to be on the receiving end of."

Keep the banter up. That's how to keep it together. Hang on, just see what Scott says. Maybe Trish is full of shit.

"Looks like I have a new nickname."

"Was she really calling you a...?"

"Yeah," I say. "Blind Bitch."

"Jesus."

"Bibi...B.B. You know, I think I like it—"

"No! You don't! And...well...even if you do, if anyone calls you that again, *I'll* start carrying a beer bottle!"

I try to smile but can't manage more than a wince. My denial barrier is stretching thinner by the second. Trish couldn't have said all those things without knowing Scott really well—

Bzzz.

"He says, *Yeah. She talk to you?*"

I don't know how to start breathing again without making noise, noise that would trigger a lot of other noises I don't want to make, not here in the Junior Quad...not again...

I put my forehead down on the rough wooden table.

"God, Parker...are you okay?"

Sarah puts her arm around my shoulders.

I swallow and clear my throat and somehow manage to get words out.

"Hug me later, okay? I...I can't...not now."

She pulls her arm away but takes my hand; I grab on tight.

Maybe I don't know Scott anymore...sending this stranger to tell me this...

Bzzz bzzz bzzz...

"He's calling."

"Turn it off."

It stops.

"I'm sorry, Parker."

"It's fine."

"Don't say that."

"It *is* fine. A week ago I didn't want to talk to him either. Now we're even."

Silence.

"What are you going to do?"

"Same things I always do."

"I mean, in ten minutes you're going to be sitting by him."

"Not that I'll be able to see."

Chapter 26

Despite feeling wretched I can't help being a little proud of myself. I'm dying inside but on the outside I'm putting on a pretty good show. I keep telling myself what I told Sarah ten minutes ago; I didn't want him or trust him until recently so I don't have far to backtrack. I'm confident our mutual silence will resume and we won't be making any scenes.

"Pop quiz," I say when a silence comes that I fear might lead to something serious. "Tell me the sine, cosine, tangent formulas."

"Okay," D.B. says. "Sine is opposite over hypotenuse, cosine is adjacent over hypotenuse, and tangent is opposite over adjacent."

"Hundred percent!" I say. "A-plus!"

"The hippies deserve some of the credit," he says.

"They deserve none!" I'm thinking bluster could get me through the day. "The victory is all yours. And you get a gold star for saying the word *hypotenuse* instead of *slanty side*."

"Hey, Parker." Scott plops down in his chair. "So Trish talked to you?"

Jesus, he sounds *excited*. What. The. Hell.

"What?" I say in my thousand icy daggers voice.

"Trish Oberlander. She—"

"I *know*. I was *there*. Why are you talking to me?"

"I...uh...okay..." His voice sets a record for speed plummeting. "I...I know it's not what you wanted to hear—"

"We don't need to talk about what you think anymore."

The icy daggers find their target because he doesn't say another word.

*

While we pack up after class, I'm not sure whether I want Scott to keep his mouth shut or try to say something else so I can shut him down again. Before I think about it too long he makes his choice.

"Parker, I know you're mad at me again," he says softly. "But can you at least tell me what you said?"

"To Trish? You want a reenactment? Why didn't

339

you just watch?"

"I just want to know if you're going to do it?"

"Do what?"

"Run with her."

My heart spasms in my chest, twice, and again, like it's trying to escape from my rib cage. My face suddenly burns hot enough to itch and I know it's turning red.

"Run...?" is all I can say before my throat completely clamps down.

"She's our fastest sprinter—I'm surprised if she didn't say that. She usually tells everyone who'll listen. I talked to her Saturday about being your guide and she said she wanted to find out about you first. I think she talked to Jason and some others, I don't know who. I thought when you texted me this morning it was because she asked you. She didn't?"

I can't speak. I shake my head but it's so fast it probably looks more like a seizure than an answer.

"Oh. Maybe she was getting to know you but didn't bring it up yet, or maybe she decided not to...Sorry, Parker, I...uh..." He exhales loudly. "Shit."

I can't breathe. I can't...fucking...breathe...

"We gotta go—get her stuff," Molly says quickly. She grabs me from behind by both shoulders and pushes me through the room and I let her, walking mostly without stumbling and trusting her to steer me right.

"Hey—"

"No, Scott, you stay. She'll be fine."

We're out the door, lurching down the hall, turning into the bathroom, and I barely manage to hold it together until the door closes.

*

I'm sitting on a toilet lid, Molly outside at the sinks. I haven't made a sound for at least five minutes, after twenty solid minutes of crying, and she doesn't ask if I'm okay. I'm grateful. This girl's a mind reader and after only a few weeks I hope she'll be my friend for life.

I finally leave the stall. "We'd better get to class."

"We'll catch the next one."

I hold out my hand. When she takes it I pull her in and hug her tightly.

"Thank you."

She squeezes.

"You didn't know what you were getting into with me. Any regrets?"

"Nope. Don't take that as a challenge, though."

"No promises!" I let her go. "What the fuck am I going to do now?"

"What do you want to do?"

"To get a braille tattoo on my arm that says *Don't jump to conclusions!* Just so I can remind myself ten times a day. God, I'm *such* an *idiot!*"

"Whatever it was you did, he'll forgive you."

"I know, but..."

"And he still loves you. I can tell every time I see him."

"Well, he doesn't. Trish told me this morning."

"Oh..." Molly laughs. "*Trish* told you. Is that what this is about?"

"You know her?"

"Trish the Oberlander? The overachiever, the overdoer, the overreactor, the over-everything? She said Scott doesn't love you? And you believe her?"

"She said Scott told her."

"What does your tattoo tell you?"

"Jesus, Molly, I'm not up for this right now."

"You and Trish have a lot in common; you throw

yourselves into everything a hundred and ten percent, leaping without looking. You'll either become great friends or mortal enemies."

"I'm nothing like her. I don't talk to anyone that way. Ever."

"What'd she say?"

"That she'd cut me with a beer bottle if I got back with Scott and broke his heart again."

"Hmmm. If some guy broke Sarah's heart and then came back holding flowers? What would you tell him?"

After a moment I say, "Molly, I don't think we can be friends anymore."

She laughs. "If that's how it's got to be. Are we done here?"

"Where's my stuff?"

"Oh...Stockley had it. He was following us..."

We walk to the door and Molly opens it.

"Hey, she okay?"

His voice comes from down near the floor—he must have been sitting in the hall. He stands and says, "Here's your...whatever it is. I didn't want to just leave it."

I put out my arms and I feel my bag brush against my right hand. I don't take it.

"She wants a hug, dummy," Molly says.

"Oh..." he says, but he doesn't.

"Put...the bag...down..." she says.

I hear rustling and then he hugs me gently. He's even taller than I guessed from where his voice comes from, and he's football-player bulky.

"Okay," Molly says. "If you ever hug someone breakable like Faith, that's how you should do it, but I think Parker can take more than that."

When I don't contradict this he squeezes and lifts me off the ground. I let out a small shriek and he sets me down again.

I say, "Thanks, Kent."

"Heh, nobody calls me Kent." But it sounds like he likes it.

Chapter 27

"You should at least eat your sandwich," Molly says.

"Yeah." But I don't. I'd sooner go out and lift a school bus than take a bite of turkey and Swiss and chew and chew and swallow and then do it again twenty more times.

"You want a soda? A...C-6?"

I shake my head. If she didn't see it, she'll ask again. She doesn't.

Sarah's still in the lunch line. I don't remember much about the past couple hours. I know I'm letting myself stay in this stupor, letting time pass, as if it will solve my problems, erase my stupidity. It's strange being aware of it, and how ridiculous it is, but still to keep doing it.

Sarah sits down with her tray.

"Shit," she says. "Be right back."

She starts to get up but Molly says, "Wait, let him come."

"No way! You—"

"It's okay," Molly says.

I guess it's too late to talk about it more because they stop, and then Scott says, "Parker, I heard what happened. Can we talk a minute?"

"She doesn't want to hear it," Sarah says. She's not using her Mama Bear voice; she's using a caught-in-the-middle-and-have-to-choose-sides voice and this breaks my heart even more. I haven't had the chance to tell her it wasn't his fault.

I stand. "I wasn't going to eat anyway."

"We'll watch your stuff," Molly says.

I hold out my hand and Scott's forearm pushes up against it.

Scott leads me outside and we walk for a minute, not in a straight line so I can't tell where we're going other than it's out on the grass.

"I'm really sorry. Trish shouldn't have said those things. You've got to believe me, I didn't put her up to it."

"I should have known better—I'm sorry I was a bitch in class."

"No, I get it. I'm really pissed at her and she knows it."

"But is it true? You want me to leave you alone?"

"I didn't say anything like that. I only talked to her about the running. I didn't even tell her we'd ever been together."

"Maybe she got it from Jason. I don't care. I just want to know if it's true."

"Of course not. I don't want you to stay away. We're friends."

"Just friends." My heart pounds because I didn't say it on purpose. It just popped out and I really wish it hadn't. It's honest, yes, but this isn't the moment I'd have chosen to go there again.

He laughs but it's forced. "Well, we've only just met, sort of."

I push my hands flat on my jeans. I'm afraid of what else might pop out if I open my mouth again.

He says, "It's just complicated, you know?"

I try to smile but it feels like a grimace. I don't know whether to back up or push forward.

"You can't fool me, Francis. I know what that really means."

"And what's that?" he asks in his smiling voice, his sad smiling voice.

"It means something's embarrassing or hard to confess, not that it's actually complicated."

"Ah, you're too smart for me."

I stop walking and turn to face him. "You don't get off that easy. Whatever it is, just tell me."

"What?"

"This doesn't have to be a long conversation. You used to love me, then I broke up with you, and sometime after that you stopped loving me...yeah? Or no?"

"Jesus, Parker...do *you* love *me*?"

"Yes."

I guess I'm pushing forward.

"Okay...did you love me a month ago?"

I frown.

"Be honest."

"Not exactly, but—"

"It just switched on again?" He snaps his fingers. "Like that?"

"No, but..." I don't know how to explain it.

"See?" he says. "It's *complicated.*"

I guess he's right. "You're too smart for me."

Silence.

"Please take me back." I hear how this sounds and add, "To the cafeteria."

"Okay. I really am sorry about Trish."

I just nod. We don't talk any more.

*

With all the work I did over the weekend it doesn't take Molly and me long to finish in the library. We did our trig homework in class so we don't have to wait for Kent. I head for the track and she goes back to her mom's classroom, but then I turn toward the street. I didn't lie, I was going to talk to Coach Underhill, but I can't seem to do it now. It's been a miserable day and I have nothing left. Aunt Celia's quiet ride home I could cope with, but everyone at the house, and Petey and his energy...just the thought of it all exhausts me.

I usually call for my ride later so no one's expecting it yet. I decide to walk home. I need the meditation, to calm this storm in my head. It's two miles and I haven't walked it for more than a year but I know the way.

After about a half hour I'm ready to call it a failure. I can't clear my mind. Scenes from the past few days play out, over and over, like songs stuck in my head. Even replaying the good scenes doesn't help—they either make the bad ones seem that much worse or they just make me feel pathetic again.

Is this self-pity? God, that would be rock bottom. But no, I don't want anyone feeling sorry for me, myself included. Part of why I'm walking out here is I don't want anyone to see me like this...except you can't hide from yourself, or at least I can't, me and my troll brain, always watching, always on alert. Maybe part of this wretched feeling is its vagueness. Maybe if I pin everything down and look at it honestly, I can sort it out, or at least see that it's not as overwhelming as it feels.

But it's the third time I've decided this and I'm lost in memories again...not just recent ones, but going back to Dad, and Scott before that...even Mom.

I'm never going to have a dad again, or a mom. Those relationships are gone forever. And my friends...it's just not the same. Vital members of my chosen extended family, but nothing can replace a soul mate of the kissing kind. Someone you feel *passion* for, and from.

That's what I lost in the eighth grade. It seemed a little ridiculous to believe you could find your soul mate in middle school anyway, but then last week I completely turned around and fell for it again like a little girl in a Cinderella costume.

Is that what happened? I found the one and screwed it up and now it's over for good? Whatever else may come later is just going to be settling?

I can't believe that. But just because lightning *can* strike twice in one place doesn't mean it will. Even if it does—in a year, or ten, or fifty—how's that supposed to fix this huge aching hole in my chest right now?

I'm not walking anymore and don't remember stopping. I'm slightly doubled over and breathing heavy, leaning way too hard on my cane and it's probably near the breaking point. It dawns on me that I've done something I've never done before; I've walked for blocks on autopilot without mapping in my head. I have no idea where I am.

All I needed to do was walk seventeen blocks, turn left, and walk nine more to get to Gunther Field. I usually zigzag, though: one block forward, one left, one forward, one left, till I've done nine left and then

I just walk eight straight forward. Have I done that four times? Five? Six? I've lost count. I also have a hazy memory that I haven't zigzagged every block. I'm lost.

I can't breathe. The pain in my chest is growing. How can an imaginary pain feel this real? I sink to one knee still leaning too hard on my cane. I don't hear cars or anyone walking nearby; there's no one to ask what street I'm on or what's ahead. I can't even call someone to ask them to come get me because I can't tell them where I am.

Calm down. This is not a big deal. You can knock on any door to ask their address and then call any number of people to come pick you up. Hell, your phone will give you walking directions from Current Location so you don't even need to know where you are. Now get up, take out your phone...

Just get up, get up before someone sees you like this. You don't want someone calling an ambulance or the cops or even just other people nearby and then you'd be surrounded by strangers. You're not in any real trouble. Don't be pathetic. Just get up. Get up! You're going to break your cane!

Oh, Jesus, don't cry. Don't cry. *Don't fucking cry!* Do it in your room if you really have to but not out here in the middle of God knows where. Just breathe and stand up and—

Shit! I *told* you you'd break your cane...

Chapter 28

Rules aren't just for other people. Some are for me. The most recent was the no-crying rule that Sarah talked me into revoking. I'm still not sure whether it was the right thing to do or just a big rationalization for not being able to make it stick.

Another rule is to have a spare cane. I used to have one but when my primary cane lasted so long and then only broke in a freak car-door accident, I switched to my spare and wasn't in a hurry to order another and never got around to it. This broken one is all I have now for at least a couple days even paying for rush delivery.

It didn't actually break. A middle section bent and my hand slipped. It jolted me and gave me a problem to solve. I sit on the sidewalk to explore the damage with my fingers. It bent maybe ten degrees but it's still usable. I need a new one, definitely, but this will work till it comes. I'll order two.

A car slows to a stop and an older woman asks if I need help. I give her my best smile and say no thanks but ask the address of the house I'm in front of. When she tells me I nod like it's a good answer and she drives away. I could walk home now but instead I call Sheila.

I tell her the truth, that I felt like walking home but bent my cane. I think she knows there's more to it but she just says she'll come get me. I find a tree by the sidewalk to lean against, fold up my cane, and put it in my bag—otherwise I know from experience it would work like a radio antenna, calling all do-gooders who think that if a blind person is standing still they must need help.

Aunt Celia's car pulls up. The music isn't on so I think my aunt came instead, but then the door bounces open and Sheila says, "What the fuck are you doing here?"

"Waiting for my prince to rescue me. Thank you, Prince Sheila."

"Okay, well, Prince Sheila's blocking traffic. You coming?"

Turns out there are parked cars all along the street. I pinball between two of them and get in and close the door. Sheila doesn't wait for me to put on my seat belt and she accelerates away.

"You want to go somewhere? Somewhere not home?"

"How'd you know?"

"You're out here for a reason. You know your way around this hick town...Where to?"

"Are we kissing cousins now? I know a good make-out spot."

"We are not, but on the slim chance I ever get a date here, it'd be good to know. How do I get there?"

"Take the next left."

She actually turns left.

"Now what?"

"Um, take the next three lefts. How the hell should I know? As much as I'd like to tell you where you can go, I'm a pretty shitty navigator."

"I figured you knew where we were, counting stop signs, knowing all the turns...You can tell when the car turns can't you?"

"Yeah, but not more than that. I wish I was that clever."

"I bet you could, you just don't bother. I wouldn't either if people always chauffeured me around."

"You see that big hill by the beach? You can see it from anywhere in town—"

"Yes, yes, I see it."

"There's a road that leads up to a vista point at the top—it's meant to be easy to find."

"Okay, just relax and let me do all the work."

"I will."

"Fine."

"Fine."

I lean against the headrest and smile. Not for long.

"Wait, what do you mean if you ever get a date here? You have a boyfriend."

"Had."

"Oh...when did...oh...shit, was it last week? Right before you came and picked me up?"

"See? You're plenty clever."

"God, I'm sorry. What happened?"

"We were chatting on Facebook and I found out he wasn't keen on a seventeen-hundred-and-forty-six-mile relationship anymore."

"Ouch."

"It was a bad couple of days, I admit...Now I don't even miss him."

"You weren't that into him?"

"I was, but part of how much I liked him was how much I thought he liked me. I don't want to be anyone's *convenience* girlfriend. Now I'm mostly mad at him for pretending he was serious, and myself for buying it, wasting all that time and energy."

"Do you talk to other friends from your old school much?"

"Mostly on Facebook. We don't call or text much anymore. They're all...busy with school and...whatever."

There's nothing I can say to that, nothing she hasn't obviously figured out already.

"I'm starting to think moving was a good thing. It told me who my real friends are. I don't like how the numbers are adding up, but I'd rather know where I really stand."

"Truth isn't happiness; it's just truth."

"Faith's right, you *are* a philosopher."

"She's never said that to me. Was it a compliment or an insult?"

"It's hard to tell with Faith."

"In that case, probably both."

The car stops and shuts off.

"You've got to be kidding me."

"What?"

"This is ridiculous. This is the make-out spot? Maybe for people in their sixties. There's even benches and a little gazebo. You sure this is it?"

"You know I'm blindfolded, right?"

"So take it off."

I snort.

"I know you're not really blind. It's just a scam for attention. It's a cry for help, really."

I smile. "I'm in too deep to stop now. Please don't tell anyone."

"Do you want me to treat you like you're blind?"

There's no joking in her voice. She's really asking.

"No. I get that from everyone else."

I want to put my head on Sheila's lap, like how Sarah did with me at her house. I don't, though. Feeling like I want to is enough.

"I'm sorry about the car last week. I was such a bitch—"

"Enough already! God, what's happened to you? I figured you didn't want to play cards with Petey all afternoon so I drove you up here but not to throw you a pity party! After a nice long summer of...of *thorns*, now it's all this mopey *I'm sorry, I'm sorry*. Is this because of Scott Kilpatrick?"

"Uh..."

"Faith told me. She said it wasn't a secret. Is it?"

"No."

"She thinks you've turned into this pile of mush because of your dad and that makes sense but I don't think that's all of it. She doesn't know what breakups are really like."

She pauses a moment and then switches from her lecturing voice to one that's conspiratorial. "Don't you think it's weird, how she's so popular but doesn't have a boyfriend? Usually being popular has as much to do with who you're with but she's not with anybody."

"That's just how amazing Faith is; she's popular all on her own, not because she's dating the head of the football team."

"The quarterback?"

"Whatever. And she dates, just no one more than a

few times. She has impossibly high standards."

"So do you."

"Yeah, well, not *impossibly* high. Someone did come along who meets them."

"Your problem is thinking no one else ever will."

I can't think of anything to say to this that doesn't qualify as woe-is-me.

She says, "I'm right, aren't I?"

"I haven't figured it all out yet. Maybe I never will."

Chapter 29

"I'm impressed you came for Office Hours," Sarah says. "Seeing how it's gone recently."

"I can't let 'em win. I have a reputation to maintain."

"You're going to get another chance in a minute. I just thought I'd give you a little boost of self-esteem first."

"What—"

"Parker." It's Trish. "Scotty wants me to say I'm sorry so I'm saying I'm sorry."

Wow, she is definitely *not* sorry. I open my bag and dig around. "Okay, hang on a sec..."

"What for?"

"I have a notebook...with a list of check boxes... Now I can check off the one that says 'Trish said the words *I'm sorry* to me, presumably for threatening me with a beer bottle.'"

"God, I did not."

"Actually, you did, but I've heard worse." I close my bag. "Never mind, I'll remember. I accept your apology. I'm guessing *Frank* is going to ask me about this later? If he does, rest assured, I'll tell him you said you were sorry."

"I guess you're not a complete idiot."

"The day may come."

"I'll run with you if you want to join the team."

I laugh. "Why the hell would I want to run with you?"

"I'm the fastest sprinter we have," she says, clearly not offended. "Including the guys. And no one else wants to. When you didn't show up yesterday Coach called us all together to talk about it."

"Wow," I say with my skeptical voice. "You were the *only one* willing to run with me?"

"Okay, a couple others raised their hands but they're slow as molasses. And I'm also closest to your height so we'll have the same stride length—those others would trip you up not even meaning to. No one else even likes sprinting. They're all on the team for longer distances but Coach makes some of them do it anyway to fill out the roster."

"At least I wouldn't have to worry about them steering me into a pole on purpose."

"Ha, you don't need my help for that. I saw you run for Coach and trip over your own feet. Not very impressive. I could run that fast if I didn't worry about keeping my face off the ground. I figured you'd say no but thought I'd offer anyway. See you around—"

"Hang on, I didn't say no."

"But you're going to," Sarah says.

"Why? She's the fastest next to me, she's willing, and I bet she'd be very glad to say in her college applications that she helped a blind girl achieve her dreams."

"*Definitely* not a complete idiot," Trish says in a smiling voice. It even sounds like it might be a real smile, not the shark kind, but I won't be dropping my guard anytime soon.

"You can't trust her."

"She wouldn't let me run into anything, especially with loads of people around watching all the time, right, Trish?"

"You're three for three. What do you say?"

It makes sense. A guide is just to stop me from

running into things and that kind of getting hurt doesn't frighten me. I don't need a saint to run with, just someone willing and able and most of all, fast.

"Parker?" Trish says.

"You can call me B.B." I extend my hand. "What it means can be our little secret."

She laughs and shakes my hand. "See you after school."

After she leaves, I say to Sarah, "Was that a laugh of grudging newfound respect or was she rolling her eyes because she really does think I'm an idiot?"

"Do you care?"

"Not even the tiniest bit. Just making conversation."

*

After school, Molly walks with me to the locker room and then splits off to head for the bleachers and read instead of hanging around in her mom's classroom. Our new plan is for her to do whatever for an hour while I'm at track, then we'll do homework, saving trig for last when Kent comes after football practice.

I pick up track clothes at the coaches' office and try everything on. The shorts and tank top are snugger than I like but that's fine. If I'm going to sprint in front of an audience I'd rather not have my clothes too loose and not secure.

"Parker, it's me," Trish says to my left. "I'm over here."

"Who? Where?" I turn my head all around like I'm looking for her voice.

"It's me. Trish. To your right, I mean left. Your left."

"Oh, good, thanks for telling me. It's not like I can recognize your voice or anything or tell where it's coming from."

"God, you're such a bitch. I really might call you B.B."

"The rumors are true. We can go faster if I take your arm. My cane's bent anyway. Unless you're worried people will think we're a couple."

"You wish."

We march out to the track, my free arm slightly forward to guard against her driving me up against any walls or poles. She doesn't but I'm not going to jump to any conclusions.

While we stretch, Coach Underhill talks about how we should take it slow and just get used to walking together, then jogging, and only going faster as it feels comfortable. I honestly thought we'd jump right in on moderate sprints and starting blocks. I'm glad he spoke first.

At Coach's suggestion Trish and I hold hands and walk around the track. I hear people talking and milling around, footsteps, and the clanking of various bits of equipment from people working on field events. There's water on the track midway up the far straightaway, deep enough to splash, which Trish says came from a busted sprinkler head. I flag this as potential bullshit and file it for later, but the rubberized track isn't slippery when wet so I'm not worried.

After one circuit we start to jog. I thought this coordinated running in step, arms cycling in unison, would be harder than it's turning out to be. The challenge is more in distinguishing between normal jostling versus her deliberately steering. After a few laps we start talking through it so I don't have to guess.

As much as I want to run a lot faster, I decide it's not going to happen today. This is just about the basics, getting to know each other's movements at a light jog. It's not long before things are working surprisingly well though my socks are soaking wet.

Scott joins us for a lap but it's awkward because Trish keeps interrupting with directional talk so we can't have a normal conversation. He finally says he'll leave us to it and peels off. The way it happens makes me think he regrets not being the one running with me. Maybe that's just wishful thinking.

After he goes, Trish says, "I swear to God if you hurt him again, you're on your own. You can run with Pokey Patricia."

"Did Jason tell you what happened? I mean all of it?"

"Yeah, all of it. I think it's bullshit. I mean, it was middle school. Big deal."

I don't reply. I wonder if she'd have thought that way when she was thirteen. Probably. I'm the paranoid one.

"Do you like him?" I ask.

"Everybody likes Scotty."

"You know what I mean."

"Oh, no, not like that."

"Are you sure?"

"What, because you like him everybody should?"

"No, I just think you'd have to like someone a lot to attack me the way you did."

"I stand up for people who don't stand up for themselves."

"Are you sure?"

"Are you a parrot? Scotty's great but I want more backbone in a guy. Someone I don't *need* to stand up for."

"He's got a spine, believe me."

"I guess we're figuring out why you want to have his baby and I don't."

I laugh. She doesn't.

"I'm serious, if you fuck with him at all, we're done."

I let Trish have the last word; I think it's what she wants. After another couple laps she needs to go— she's also a steeplechase runner and Coach Rivers calls a meeting that won't end soon. She turns me by the shoulders, says, "You're facing the lockers now," and trots away.

I pop in an earbud and call Molly.

"Hey," she says. "You know I'm just sitting right here in the bleachers? At the fifty-yard line? Watching you?"

"You know damn well I don't know where you are. Ready to go?"

"Done already?"

"For today. She's got other stuff."

"You know that puddle you kept running through?"

"Yeah." I laugh. "She was steering me into it, wasn't she?"

"No, she was steering you *away* from it—"

"Really?"

"It was so *she'd* run through the deepest part and splash you even more. She was doing all kinds of stuff to get you as wet as possible."

I laugh again.

"That doesn't bother you?"

"No," I say. "I hope it made her very happy."

"I guess everybody wins. We don't have much work to do, and Stockley's got a lot more football practice still. Let's just sit out in the sun awhile longer. I'll talk you in. Turn left some."

I do.

"More...okay, now you're facing me, but there's some guys between us so wait a—"

"I have a better idea. I have too much energy to sit."

I slide my phone back into the tight inside pocket of my shorts, freeing my hands. I turn away from Molly.

"If I walk now, will I be straight on the track?"

"Turn right...a little more...too much...there."

I start walking.

"Tell me *right* or *left* to keep me in the middle or to get around people or—they don't actually have the steeplechase set up, right? No hurdles or anything?"

"Nope, all clear, just people."

I walk around the track. After a couple laps we've refined our technique to Molly saying *in* or *out* to steer me toward the inner or outer lanes, since my right and left keeps changing and hers doesn't and it's confusing. She also says *straight* and *curve* when I switch between them and generally talks me through it since there's no reason for us to be quiet.

A couple of runners pass me. It seems the only people on the track are running, not standing or walking, so Molly doesn't have to steer me around anybody much; they have to steer around me.

"Straight," Molly says. "In...in...okay, that's good."

I start to jog.

"Whoa, Parker! In....*IN*...out...okay, good. Are you sure this—*curve*! *In*...*in*...in...out...in...in...almost there... okay, straight now. More out, *out*. Okay, good. Jesus, Parker...stop!"

I stop. "What's in front of me?"

"Nothing. It's just, this is crazy! I don't want you getting hurt."

"Me neither, that's why you're steering."

"It'd be safer if I didn't. Just because you want to run doesn't mean you can pull me into your crazy! I don't want to enable you into a fence."

"Then don't."

"Good, let's go—"

"No, I mean don't steer me into any fences." I start jogging again.

"Parker!"

I don't answer. After a dozen more silent steps I have to stop.

"Molly?"

"What are you doing?"

"What?"

"There are lots of things I want to do but can't. I live with it. Why's it different for you?"

"I can't see but I can run—all I need is directions. It's like...slow dancing, right? If you don't have a partner, people tell you to go find one, they don't say you can't dance. If you don't want to be my partner, that's cool—I know it's probably boring sitting there giving me directions—but don't tell me I can't run."

"Sorry, I...you just took me by surprise. It's weird to be more worried for you than you are."

"I told you I'm a mixed blessing."

"I just hope all this running...that you're running *toward* something, not away."

"Ha, well, even the wisest cannot tell."

"Is...is that from *Lord of the Rings*?"

"Truth is truth no matter where it comes from. I think I'm done anyway. Water's in my shoes and I want to change out of these wet socks. Walk me back to the locker room?"

"Okay, down in a sec. Are you going to make me steer you again tomorrow?"

"I can't make you do anything. Hopefully Trish will be with me all through practice tomorrow, but if she's not, then...I, Parker Grant, AKA Batshit Crazy, hereby absolve Molly Ray of all responsibility for any collision or other calamities that might result from running blind with only Molly on the phone to guide me. How's that?"

She hangs up.

I hear her voice a few feet away, coming closer.

"I think it's the best I'm going to get."

Chapter 30

The next few days are a blur of routine classes and lunches and homework and no one comes to Office Hours. I run at my usual time but I get up earlier and stretch in my room instead of at Gunther Field to listen for Scott and Jason's footsteps out front. Scott and I talk along with everyone else in Trig and at the track after school. Trish stays firmly in the conversations, though, like she's my chaperone, or more like Scott's chaperone.

After school Friday, Molly walks with me to the locker room even though I have a brand-new cane as of yesterday. Then she heads for the bleachers while I change. Trish finds me and we walk to the track. It's a warm day and I have a lot of energy.

We'd decided with Coach not to worry about starting blocks or even sprints for another couple weeks. For now we're just getting used to what he calls tethered running—we've graduated to holding separate ends of a short loop of shoelace instead of each other's hands. We technically don't need such a short line for jogging, but sprints will require perfect synchronization so we stay tight, side by side and in step. I'm getting a good feel for the oval now, though obviously I'll never be able to run it by myself—no amount of counting paces could get me to navigate the curves—but my body is learning the layout, and jogging with Trish is smoother every day.

Trish doesn't have steeplechase today or the thousand meters, her other distance, so it's just the two of us for as long as we want to push it. Which is bad news for her. I could run like this forever.

After about a dozen laps I say, "You ready to run?"

"We *are*..."

I laugh. "This is jogging!"

We've gone maybe three miles—I haven't really been keeping track—which is far longer than her distances but I figure at this pace she'd have plenty of juice left.

"I'm just the rudder," she says in a determined voice. "You're the motor."

I pick it up, slowly to maintain our rhythm. Once

we're out of the turn I push our pace until we hit the next curve. When we're out of it again, I push it some more.

Now *this* is running! Not my sprint speed but still a good solid run.

The next corner is rougher since the way we turn changes at different speeds and we're not used to going this fast—

"Annie!" Trish calls. "Annie, move!"

I keep going, trusting that Trish will stop us if we can't smoothly bend around people ahead or if they don't move out of our way.

We hit the straight again. I kick it up.

"Gary!" Trish yells. "On your left!"

I hear the squeal of a bullhorn turning on. Coach Underhill's voice blasts across the track. "Everyone clear lanes three and four! Don't make Oberlander do everything—she's got her hands full."

With me.

I hear some guy say "Holy shit" as we blow past him—maybe it's this Gary guy, I don't know—and Trish pulls me left into the curve.

I'm at the limit of Trish's pace in strides per second.

I know this because when I push a bit more we start to fall out of sync and I have to ease off a bit. It helps that she's always on my left, on the inside, to pull me with the tether into turns rather than push me, since this means her distance is slightly shorter than mine which compensates for my faster speed. We won't have to worry about turns when we start working on sprints later but running the oval will teach us how to stay together under harder conditions.

"More room!" Trish yells though it's more of a hoarse shout. There's no way she's going to let me outrun her even if it kills her.

I can tell she's trying to keep me in the lanes Coach cleared which is harder than just going around the oval. At the next curve I get out of sync again and stumble—not a big stumble—and I pull on the tether and she stays solid. I regain my balance and we're fine again.

More than fine.

I'm *running* on a *track*!

I'm *turning*! I've now run farther without stopping than I ever have.

"Parker!" Trish gasps. "We have...to stop..."

"What's wrong?"

She's slowing and I match her pace and ease it down. We stop.

"Woo-hooo, Parker!" Molly calls from the bleachers. A couple people clap a few times.

"Are you hurt?" Maybe she pulled something.

"No," she says, "I just...need...a break..."

When I hear she's okay, I hug her and lift her off the ground. She grabs on to keep from falling. I set her down again and whisper in her ear, "Thank you!"

"What for?"

How can I describe how fantastic this is? To be able to run this far without stopping every hundred yards to figure out where I am and reorient before starting up again.

"For running with me," I say. "Do you need to sit down?"

"No," she says. "I mean yeah...I mean...I have to go to the bathroom."

"Oh, sorry!" I laugh. "Go ahead. You know where I'll be."

"Back in...a minute. Well, maybe more...than a minute."

She heads away and I wrap our tether around my wrist. I pull out my phone, plug in my earbuds, and call Molly. My phone is tucked away again and secure before she answers.

"You ready?" I ask.

"Where's Trish going? I thought on Fridays she had nothing else to do."

"Potty break. But I don't want to cool down. Guide me?"

"God, really? I thought I was safe today."

"Why'd you think that?"

"Because I'm stupid. Except I'm not. I know it's not because you don't want to cool down. You're thinking about going faster than Trish can run. It's crazy."

"I wasn't thinking that...but...now I am."

"Great."

"How's the track look?"

"The runners are mostly in the inner couple lanes."

"I should be fine toward the outside? No equipment or anything?"

"It's all clear today."

"Ready?"

"You know you're wearing your scarf with stars on

it, right? You're going to see real stars if you run into a fence."

"You can tell me more than how to turn, you know. Tell me to slow down or stop if I get too close to anything."

"All right, then. Let's go crazy."

Molly tells me to pivot until I'm facing down the track. I intend to jog a full lap at this speed just to get in a groove with Molly talking me through it.

At the first curve I hear a voice I don't recognize say "What the hell is she doing?" as I jog past.

Halfway down the next straight I hear a couple more comments and I tune them out. I want to go faster but don't know if Molly can keep me on track. I accelerate slowly to find her top speed.

In the second curve I can't tune out the world anymore. Around me I hear pandemonium, people shouting at each other, but no one's telling me to stop. In my ear Molly's voice is steady and calm. "In... in...straight...out...Okay good..." I keep going...faster... and faster...

I hear the bullhorn whine again. "Grant! What..." Coach's voice goes fainter yet still amplified, like he turned away from the horn. "How the hell is she doing that?"

Faster. I lean into the next turn, connecting Molly's voice to my legs. "In...in...Okay...in...*out*...in...Okay...straight now..."

"Everybody off the track!" Coach shouts through his bullhorn. "Give her room!"

"If the track...is empty..." I shout to Molly, hoping my swinging microphone can pick up my voice, "...move me...to...the center...lanes..."

"You have tons of room now. Stay straight, you're drifting toward the middle now...Okay, now *out*...out...Good, you're good. Curve coming up..."

Now that I know the corridor is wide and clear, with me right in the middle, I can go even faster. When I come out of the turn, I open it up some more.

God this is fantastic! To run again without having to stop every ten seconds...Do people without broken parts know this feeling? Would I have ever felt something like this if I wasn't blind? To lose something, mourn it, and then suddenly get it back again?

The next turn is rocky—at this speed Molly has

trouble with me overcorrecting. I try to shift less when she directs me and let her use more urgency when I don't veer enough.

On the next straight I open it all the way. I'm flying!

People are shouting, whooping, and yelling, "Go, Parker!" Mostly from my left which is the center field but also on my right when I pass bleachers on the straight legs.

I come out of a turn and the shouting becomes a chant..."Par-ker! Par-KER! Par-KER!"

I hear it from the left and right and in my earbuds picked up by Molly's microphone...

"Out...Par-KER!...Ou—Par-KER!...*In*—Par-KER! PARKER! *IN IN STOP STOP*—"

My foot lands on something not track, not rubber, not turf—I'm off the track entirely and headed for the bleachers at top speed—

"*STOP STOP STOP!*" people yell but mostly it's Molly's voice rupturing my eardrums as I slam into someone and we go down hard...

...but the impact isn't as bad as it should have been. It wasn't a random collision—someone caught me and we fell and I landed on them. The heels of my hands and my knees scrape the ground, my head bounces off a sturdy chest, but it's mostly painless. We're lying flat and strong arms hold me tightly.

Scott's voice is a harsh whisper in my left ear.

"Are you out of your fucking mind?"

I kiss him hard on the cheek. "Yes!"

People help us up, which for me is more trouble than it's worth. I think I need to add a rule about letting blind people stand up on their own when they fall down.

"Are you hurt?" Coach is in front of me sounding half worried and two-thirds totally pissed off.

"Nothing broken." I check my scrapes. They feel meaty but dry so no blood yet.

"You are *never* doing that again!"

"I hope not!" I say, laughing.

"Not the crash! The running like a maniac with someone telling you where to go on a damn cell phone! They'd never allow that in competition, so it's pointless and downright stupid!"

And completely exhilarating!

"Hit the showers. You're done today."

"I'll take her," Scott says.

"Yeah, do that. Everyone else, show's over! Get back to it!"

Scott pulls my arm—I guess we're heading for the gym. Then I hear a lot of scuffling footsteps and someone breaks Rule Number Two and crashes into me with a bear hug.

Molly whisper-shouts in my ear, "You fucking lunatic! I'm so sorry, Parker!"

"*I'm* not sorry!" I let her go. "Same time tomorrow?"

"Hell no!" Scott says. "What the hell were you doing? Showing off to all your friends?"

"Of course not. Molly—"

"Not just Molly. Everybody."

"Everybody?"

"Sarah—"

"Sarah's not here—"

"Hey, Parker," Sarah says. "Nice run."

"Sarah, what are you—"

"And Faith," Scott interrupts. "And Kennedy and—"

"Faith?"

"Present," she says in her world-weary voice trying to cover her still-worried-heart-in-her-throat voice.

"And Lila," Scott continues. "And...and...?"

"Sheila Miller. Hi."

"Sheila? What are you guys doing here? Watching me? Why didn't you say something?"

"I told them they should come see you run," Molly says. "They showed up after we started, so I couldn't tell you then."

"What happened?" Sheila asks. "Why'd you miss that turn?"

"When everyone was yelling I couldn't hear Molly's directions anymore. I figured it out and was about to stop when I hit this guy." I wave toward Scott who's still marching me along with everyone following us like bees. "How did you manage to get in front of me?"

"He was running back and forth diagonally across the track," Sarah says.

"Huh?"

"It was obvious what was going to happen," Scott says. "If you lost it, it was going to be swinging wide on a turn in one of two places. It wasn't hard to run straight across between those corners to catch you if you ran off the track, which I knew you would, and you did."

I grin. "You're so smart."

I feel concrete under my shoes; we're almost to the gym.

"Who's smart?" It's Trish.

"Me, apparently," Scott says in his stern voice. "Just because I'm the only one here who knows better than to leave this one on her own. You have to keep an eye on her."

"What happened?" Trish asks. "Why the crowd?"

No one answers, not audibly anyway.

"God, Parker..." Trish says in her eye-rolling voice. "I was only gone five minutes. What could you have possibly done in five minutes?"

Chapter 31

I change back into my school clothes; it's easier to just shower at home and then put on PJs for the evening. Trish does the same and leaves first. I call Sheila and she's waiting in the parking lot listening to CDs in the car. She offers to come get me but I tell her it's fine, I'll cane over there in a few minutes.

As I leave the gym, Scott says, "Parker."

"Hey, you're still here? What are you up to this weekend?"

"What? I don't know. Look...you can't keep doing this."

"Doing what?"

"Throwing yourself off cliffs because you know I'm always there to catch you. If I hadn't tackled you...We were *ten feet* from the bleachers! You'd have broken bones this time. Or worse! It's...it's not fair."

"Fair?" I say, my anger waking up. But I'm torn. He

388

sounds mad yet I hear something more. He's afraid.

"You can't just assume I'll always be there to protect you. It's not my job."

"I didn't even know you were there. Just because you run by my house every morning doesn't mean I think you're shadowing me everywhere—God, you're not, are you?"

"Of course not—"

"Did you know I walked home from school this week and bent my cane and got stranded? You think I was mad you didn't rescue me?"

"I didn't know—"

"Of course you didn't. I just do what I do. It's got nothing to do with you. I don't know why it worries you so much. It's not like we're together."

"I still worry about you getting hurt."

"Well I don't know what you want from me. I'm grateful you caught me, definitely, yes, thank you, but you shouldn't feel any special obligations."

"But I do."

"Why?"

Silence.

"Because I'm blind?"

"Of course not."

"You sure? If some other random blind person came to school, you wouldn't run around and protect them too?"

"I wouldn't have to—how many blind people run around?"

I laugh but he doesn't. God, he's so...How am I ever going to get over him?

"I was wrong before," I say, feeling a calm I'm grateful for. "I did love you last month, and all the time before that. I just thought the Scott I loved turned out not to be real. I loved the Scott I thought you were and hated the Scott you turned out to be. Then I found out the Scott I hated was the one who wasn't real. You, the real Scott, I've never stopped loving you."

Wow, that came out a tangled mess. How can I say that more clearly?

My calm tells me not to.

Instead I say, "Things might be complicated now, and confusing, but we can sort it out. We're the two most honest people we know, right?"

"Right."

"So tell me one of two things. Say *yes, you love me, but...*Or say *no, you don't love me, but...*And we can go from there."

"It's not that simple."

"That's what the *buts* are for, to add complicated parts. You have to start somewhere."

"That's the problem. When your dad sent me away, I was ready to wait, but I thought it'd be a week or two, maybe a month. Then summer vacation came, and the months dragged on until finally a couple weeks into my freshman year, in a different school where we wouldn't bump into each other, it clicked. You weren't just mad at me, you were *gone*. Never coming back."

"I know...I'm sorry."

"I know you are, but just like you had this other Scott in your head that you built up as this guy who'd betray you, I got a Parker in my head who'd throw our entire history and friendship away in an instant, and...and just bail without even a word."

I start crying. On the inside anyway, tears soaking into my scarf. I struggle to keep my breathing steady. Not to hide; I just don't want him to stop talking.

"Do I love that Parker? I feel really bad that I hurt her, but for her to just disappear like that...And now you've decided the bad Scott in your head isn't real, so now he's gone and it's just back to the real me again...but..."

He doesn't want to say the rest. Neither do I.

"But that Parker in your head really is me." I can't stop my voice from quavering—I struggle to keep it from getting worse. "I did bail on you."

"Yeah."

"I...I..."

I was only thirteen!

Oh God, I will *not* say that. He deserves better. Better than me. And that's not self-pity, it's just a fact. A cold, ugly truth. You want the best for those you love.

I manage to hold back the sobs but he must know I'm crying. There's nothing I can say. I can't even say I'm sorry again and ask him to forgive me. I wouldn't want him to forgive anyone else who did this to him.

"So...it's complicated, yeah?"

I nod and try to stop my shoulders from shuddering.

I hear shuffling.

"But we're friends. Here, I have something for you. I made it at Marsh, right after it happened. To give you when you came back. Lately I started carrying it around, trying to sort things out, and...here, put out your hand."

Something light and metallic touches my palm, with a pin. A button.

I don't trust my voice enough to ask what it says, but then I feel bumps on the front; it's braille. Like he pounded them into the thin metal with a tiny nail.

Even before I read what it says, I stop breathing. Of all the buttons on my vest, none of them are in braille. I stuck braille labels on the backs so I can tell what they say, but this button is in braille on the front, like the first button for me instead of everyone else.

I run my fingers across it:

> *seeing*
> *is not*
> *believing*

I break.

I sob and cry, not hysterical or afraid, just profoundly sad, like the world is ending and I can't do anything about it. He takes me in his arms and I bury my face in his neck.

It takes a few minutes to get it all out. Once he tries to stroke my hair but my scarf makes this awkward, so he just holds me. You can read a lot into a hug if you pay attention and there's nothing guarded about how he's holding me. He doesn't fidget, like he could do this forever. I could too. But I have to let him go. I finally do.

My voice comes back. "You can't trust me because I didn't trust you. It was the biggest mistake I've ever made. I won't make it again. That's a promise."

"Oh, well," he says with his sad smiling voice. "You say that *now*..."

"I mean it. I can live with you not wanting to be with me, but I can't live with you never trusting me again. I want to prove it to you...I just don't know how."

"It wouldn't be trust if you had to prove it."

"No, that's how faith works," I say, my heart pounding hard in my chest and throat over what just popped into my head. "Trust...trust needs proof."

I take a step back.

"What is it?" he asks.

"Are we alone? I mean completely alone? I want to show you something...something I've never shown anyone and I don't want anyone else to see."

"No one's around but I don't want you to do anything you don't want—"

"I *want* to. But are you sure no one can see us? Are you *positive*?"

"There's no one else here, I promise, but I—"

"Shhh," I say.

I slowly reach up with both hands, and with one smooth movement, I pull off my scarf.

"Parker..."

I wipe the tears from my face and lower my arms.

I open my eyes. My dead, empty, useless eyes.

I strain to listen for any hint of how Scott's reacting. I don't hear a thing, not even breathing. I think he's holding his breath. I know I am. I feel like I might never breathe again.

This is the thing I *absolutely* hate most about being blind.

"They're blue-green," he whispers. "Like the sea."

He's using his boyfriend voice. I breathe in deeply to take it all inside of me.

"I know they used to be."

"They still are. They're beautiful."

I snort. "Yeah right."

"I've never lied to you."

I can hear him breathing again.

"I thought you'd have more scars."

"Not on the outside."

"Well, they're beautiful. Your eyes, I mean."

I smile. "They're my mother's. Father's nose, mother's eyes."

"I wish I could have met her."

"Me too...she would have liked you."

Silence.

Well, except for the pounding in my chest, my ears, and in the air all around us.

"So..." I say. "Which way are they pointing?"

He laughs so I get to laugh too.

"Does it matter?" he asks.

"No, I'm just curious. What are they looking at?"

"Well, which one?"

"Jesus, Scott!" I swat his arm, happy to score a direct hit on his bicep.

"They're not looking at anything. It doesn't matter.

Seeing isn't believing."

"That's right." I smile and hold out the button to him.

"It's yours."

"Find a good spot."

I concentrate on his hands fumbling just under my collarbone. When he's done, I tie my Starry Night back over my eyes. I do it slowly, to put off what I know I need to say next...

"I have no right to ask for anything, but I really need a favor."

"What?"

"If we're not going to be together, I need you to stop being so nice to me."

"Huh? We're friends—"

"Running three miles to pass my house every morning? Running back and forth across the track today? If you had a girlfriend, first she'd think it was sweet that you're watching out for the blind girl, then she'd start resenting it. There are things you only do for your girlfriend. If I'm not, you need to stop."

"But I—"

"This is really hard to ask, because I like it, I like it

all more than anything...but I can't take it if you say we can't be together yet sometimes act like we are. If we're going to be just friends, I need you to stop acting like we're more. Those special things you do feel good at first..." I put my hand on my chest. "Then it just hurts."

Silence.

I want to fill this silence with more talk but I force myself not to. It's his turn.

"I'm not saying we can't ever be together," he finally says. "I just know it can't be right this minute."

Even this much makes me dizzy. *Swoony.*

"Well, think about it." I try to use my matter-of-fact voice and I'm relieved it comes out that way. "In the meantime, please, just stand there and eat popcorn and watch my disasters like everyone else. I might get bruised or break a bone or two, but I'll live."

He chuckles. "Nothing's easy with you."

I smile. "Some things never change."

"How long do I get? To think about it, I mean?"

"As long as you stay back far enough, take all the time you want." I gesture vaguely. "You don't see a bunch of guys waiting in line, do you?"

He chuckles again. "There should be."

"See, you can stop that shit right now." I dig my new cane out of my bag and unfold it. "Compliments and flirting's on the wrong side of the line. I've got to go. Sheila's probably wondering where I am."

"I'll walk you over—"

"No, you stay here."

"C'mon, I walk lots of friends to their cars. That's not special treatment."

"I need a bigger buffer, okay?" My voice catches, tripping over these words. "So I don't get excited every time you come close hoping you're about to cross over. That's the favor, that's what I need. Don't come close unless it's on purpose. I can't take it otherwise. Please?"

God, don't start crying again...

"Okay. No special treatment unless it means something. I promise."

"Thank you. I have to go."

I held it together pretty well I think—turning jovial at the end, light, witty, strong—but I need to walk away now. Not to be dramatic but because my voice is going to crack again and I feel like I'm dying inside.

I know if he decides to never be more than friends I'll survive it and be okay again, but that's later...much, much later. Right now my eyes are leaking into my scarf again and my chest is caving in.

"I'll see you later," he calls after me.

I wave my free hand over my head.

"Not if I see you first."

Chapter 32

I wake up Saturday morning before my alarm and tap the speech button. Stephen Hawking says it's five-thirty-five AM.

I think about how when I first lost my sight some kids asked me how I knew when I woke up in the morning if I couldn't open my eyes and see anything. I should have realized then just how steep a hill I had to climb.

I crank open the window and feel the cool morning air outside, much the same as it's been the past few weeks but a bit crisper.

I put on my running clothes including my hachimaki. I usually save it for Sunday with Petey but this morning I definitely feel like Divine Wind.

I stretch in my room like I have been lately but I don't hear any footsteps outside. I finish and tap my alarm clock. Five-fifty-three. I wait until six and hear nothing. Scott's sticking to our new deal. I'm on my own.

I walk to my door and remember my Star Chart is still there. I unpin it, fold it a few times, and push it into my trash can. I retrieve the plastic prescription bottle of gold stars from the dresser and toss it in the trash, too.

You know it's just because I don't want to remember you that way anymore. Every night I pulled gold stars out of that stupid bottle it never occurred to me how morbid that was. I thought it was part of remembering but it was slow poison, like if I kept water to drink on my nightstand in the wine bottle Mom polished off that night. It's amazing how people can be so blind to what's good for them and what isn't, what's truth and what's not, or the difference between secrets and things just not yet known.

Oh, and Rule Number Infinity, the one about no second chances I added after I broke up with Scott? Got rid of it. The first rule I've ever taken off the list. There shouldn't be an infinite number of rules anyway. Don't know what the hell I was thinking.

Now the troll in my brain is making me worry the sidewalk isn't clear. Which is stupid since I didn't think anyone was checking it the past three months and didn't worry about it, even after that near miss at the Reiches'. But now that I know Scott was checking up on me all that time, the thought that he didn't this morning...Damn it, Dad, why do we have to live with trolls in our brains? If you ever figure it out, let me know...subconsciously or something. Or in a dream...

...because I can't keep talking to you like this. I thought it was remembering but it's about not letting go. I need to talk to people who can hear me, and answer, and laugh when I make them happy and bark when I'm an idiot. I keep trying to do everything on my own but I learn so much better with other people, and—irony alert—most of what I think of as my independence I really learned from you. Even though you left way too soon, you taught me enough for a lifetime.

And I'm not afraid anymore of what might have happened that night. No matter what it was, it wouldn't change the sixteen years of goodness that came before it one bit, and especially not the nine years of darkness you helped me through. There's so much good to remember and be grateful for, Dad, and I am. I'll always love you for it.

I pause at the bottom of the stairs. I haven't had a

dream about Dad in a couple weeks. It's not how I'd prefer him to visit but it's definitely welcome. My silent monologues are over but I hope to see him again soon.

Outside, I lock the door and slip the key into my sock. I'm still worried about the route...

No, I'm not going to start being afraid now. I told Scott I would own my safety, so I need to stop being an idiot or at least try. If there's a van parked across the sidewalk up ahead, I need to be smarter and deal with it myself.

I jog holding my left arm outstretched, elbow slightly bent, so if it hits something it'll fold safely and I'll have enough warning to turn my shoulder in and protect the side of my head with my right forearm. Just for the sidewalk part; I won't run like this once I get to the field. It's pretty awkward, and it'll take getting used to, but it's smarter. Or at least it's less batshit crazy.

I stop at the intersection. The only sound is a couple of birds so I jog across the street, my left arm still out on the minuscule chance someone parked in the crosswalk since yesterday and didn't get towed. That and to get more practice doing it.

I reach the chain link fence, turn right, walk fourteen steps to the gap, turn left, and pass through without touching either side, like always.

Click.

I freeze.

From the far side of the field, I hear the soundtrack to *Grease*.

This time it isn't endlessly looping while he waits with his phone a few blocks away. I heard it start just now.

I grin. I try to stop, but then I stop trying to stop because why shouldn't I smile? I remember what else he did the last time he met me here, and while that might be too much to hope for this soon, at the very least, with Scott here now, Gunther Field has never been safer.

The question is, do I run like always or should I just walk over and play it cool?

God, who *is* that person? I silence the troll in my brain and start jogging...running...sprinting...

Just how fast *can* I run? I mean *really*?

Time to find out.

Acknowledgments

Thanks to Jennifer Weltz, my agent at JVNLA, for being amazing, calm, patient, and for never letting me get away with *anything*. To Nicola Barr, UK co-agent extraordinaire, and to Tara Hart for walking me through the myriad details.

Thanks to Pam Gruber, my editor at LBYR, for immediately understanding Parker and helping me tell her story better. To Copy Chief Barbara Bakowski, Production Editor Annie McDonnell, Copyeditor Ashley Mason, and Proofreader JoAnna Kremer, for helping improve the telling while protecting Parker's voice. To Liz Casel for her excellent book design. To Alvina Ling, Farrin Jacobs, Shawn Foster, Victoria Stapleton, Kristin Dulaney, and Leslie Shumate, for their praise and encouragement during this exciting process; and to internal champions Megan Tingley, Andrew Smith, Dave Epstein, and the rest of the stars

I've yet to hear about at LBYR who chose to believe in Parker Grant. And to my brilliant partners in the UK at HarperCollins, Ruth Alltimes and Lauren Buckland, for sending her out to the rest of the English-speaking world.

Thanks to Saralyn Borboa, Literary Committee Chair for the National Braille Association, for kind and thorough advice, with consultants Bonifacio Lucio, Jo Elizabeth Pinto, and Marilyn Breedlove. For those interested, employed here is simulated Unified English Braille (UEB). Scott communicates to Parker with uncontracted grade 1 braille, which uses one cell per letter, but all other instances here are contracted grade 2 braille, which shortcuts certain whole words and common letter combinations. Working out what they mean requires some effort, looking up contractions and formatting conventions, or consulting a transcriber. Have fun!

Thanks to Jon Horsley, for showing me by example the value of crafting moments along with plot and character; to Andrew Trapani, for introducing me to the perfect agent; and to Suzanne Pertsch, for opening the door to a new way of thinking that led to where I prosper today.

Thanks to Frederick Hampton, for being my Sarah Gunderson (and for letting me be his, depending on the day) since we were thirteen. If I ranked everything in my life that has contributed directly to my growth as a writer, you're top of the list.

Thanks to Susan, for boundless love, support, and encouragement; to Shannon (hi Sunshine!) and Rachel (my go-to insider), for showing me what the world should become; to Jake (my personal hero) and James (not Petey...well...maybe a little...), for making me believe it will come one day soon; and to Mom, who always believed, and to you, Dad, for too many reasons to list reaching back to my earliest memories.

And thanks to all of you who've read Parker's story. I'm immensely grateful for the time you've chosen to spend with her.

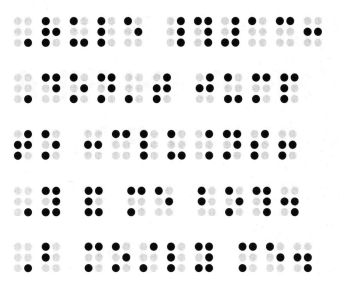

G